Shadow Warriors

CHRIS BOSTIC

First printing, May 2019

Copyright © 2019, Chris Bostic

All rights reserved.

ISBN-13: 978-1097162390

Cover Design by Chris Bostic

All characters and events in this book are fictitious products of the author's imagination and are not to be construed as real.

CHRIS BOSTIC

DEDICATION

To everyone who wastes no time
picking up my new releases.
You guys are the reason
I keep living the
writer life.

CHAPTER 1

I blew on my hands, but it did little to loosen up my frozen fingers. Even flexing my knuckles didn't help. If anything, I was surprised my bones didn't creak like a rusty door hinge, or seize up tighter than an old truck engine.

"What's up, Zach?" John whispered. "Little chilly, isn't it?"

"This sucks."

"Better get used to it, bud. It's not getting any warmer."

I admired the thick beard on Katelyn's brother, and scratched at my own stubble. Although I hadn't shaved in weeks, my dark hairs amounted to little more than fuzz—and spotty at best.

Unlike John, I wasn't technically an adult, yet everything about life on the mountain made me feel that way. The rifle on my lap and shoot to kill orders played oversized parts in that.

The rocky terrain made for a poor recliner. Worse yet, the early morning chill cut right through my jeans. It felt like sitting on a block of ice, but not numbing enough to hide the discomfort.

I kept hidden from prying eyes by scrunching up under the yellowing leaves of a mountain holly bush. Behind my position, a canopy of towering trees higher on the slope helped to complete the seclusion.

About fifty yards below, an even larger mass of vegetation blocked an asphalt road. Seeing how the trees had been purposely dropped over the road to block it several months before, their leaves had long since curled and fallen. Soon the rest of the forest would match the dirt brown appearance of death.

"We're gonna need coveralls soon," I said, and blew out a steamy breath.

"True story," John agreed. "I thought about throwing them on, but it didn't seem so bad last night."

"I didn't stay up that late." I scratched my head. "I guess that's kinda weird. I shouldn't be tired. It seems like all we do is sit out here or sit back there."

"It's good exercise," John replied. "To think people used to pay to go to the gym. We get to hike five miles a day for free."

"Yeah, free." I balled myself up inside my coat to conserve heat, and turned my thoughts to the way things should have been. "There used to be a lot more freedom, eh?"

"Yep, and no more gyms. One day society wasn't healthy enough, and we needed to spend more time outside. Next thing you know, they're dropping bombs on our neighbors for being out in the streets."

"Well not exactly just out in the streets," I said with a chuckle. "We might've burned down a building or two."

"Exercising our rights," John shot back. "That's the kind of exercising I like."

That brought a smile to my face. "Our parents do, that's for sure."

"And you don't?"

"I mean, uhm…I dunno. I totally get how what's going on is insane. Nothing's the way it used to be. I just don't like the idea of sitting here, holding this gun, maybe having to use it."

"Look on the bright side," John encouraged. "The roadblocks have been quiet for a long time. I'd say so far so good."

My head bobbed, though my mind wasn't in full agreement. I knew firsthand the Feds had shown little interest in clearing out the obstructions farther back inside the park. Nevertheless, I couldn't help feeling concerned. "I wish. I'd say too quiet.

With all the activity in the air, it seems like something big is coming."

"Maybe…" John swallowed. "I guess you probably know there's been talk about that."

"Yeah, I'm not totally clueless," I replied, though it seemed like my folks still tried to keep me in the dark as much as possible.

John retrained his eyes on the roadblock. His head turned to the side like a curious dog. I tensed immediately, straining my ears to attempt to hear anything other than the whisper of wind slowly stirring as the sun threatened to rise.

My companion turned to me and easily noticed the concern in my eyes.

"Don't worry. That was nothing…nothing at all. I guess that's one good thing about the cold. The birds take longer to wake up."

"I guess so."

"Anyway, just be glad you've got company."

I agreed with that statement. Still, I had to ask, "What's that all about anyway? Earlier this summer you guys were going out alone. Should we be worried about the soldiers coming?"

John shrugged. "It's the weather, I reckon. A person's probably more likely to fall asleep on duty when it's cold."

"All I can do is shiver."

"Whatever it takes to keep you awake," John said with a laugh. "That's another reason to love the winter…and dress light."

"Forget that. I want a snow suit."

"That's coming soon enough."

My eyes turned to the lightening sky. The grayness of early morning still hung heavily over the mountain like a blanket, though not as wet and wispy as the usual haze that gave the Great Smoky Mountains their name.

A turkey gobble carried to us through the stillness of the frosty morning.

"That's my cue." John stood up and slung his rifle over his right shoulder. He reached behind me to retrieve a bow and a quiver of arrows.

"I didn't know turkeys gobbled in the fall."

"Sure they do. It's just for different reasons." John hung the bow over his other shoulder. "In the fall they just gobble to talk. In the spring they want to get it on with the ladies. Kinda like you and my sister."

"Whoa, what?"

"You don't think I see you strutting around?"

"I do not strut."

"No, not really." John dropped to a knee. "But we should talk about that whole situation sometime."

"Uh oh." I had been waiting for that moment ever since I'd started watch duty with John a couple of weeks earlier. I swallowed exaggeratedly, and couldn't meet the eyes of Katelyn's big brother. Her much bigger brother, who made my thinner frame look scrawny in comparison.

"I'm just messing with you." John clapped me on the back so hard he nearly pushed me off my seat. "You're a good kid. But don't you dare break her heart."

I had no intention of doing that. Katelyn was the best thing that had ever happened to me. One smile from her made the drudgery of our primitive camp life seem like a picnic. The only thing she couldn't do was completely erase the fear whenever a bomb blast echoed across the expanse of the park.

"I won't," I said softly.

"Good. I'd hate to have to hurt you."

"I'll bet you could."

"Anyway, I'm gonna go put the hurt on a turkey now. We could use a good meal."

Despite the threat of physical violence, I wasn't ready for John to leave. I hadn't taken a watch alone, and felt an odd sense of foreboding about that one. Before he could step away, I asked, "How does fall hunting work? Do you still call them in like the springtime?"

"Yes and no. The best way is to find a flock all bunched up together. You can't get close enough to pop one with an arrow, so you run at 'em all crazy like and bust 'em up. It's perfect when they scatter to the winds."

"Really? What good does that do?"

"You sit quiet, right where they bugged out. Give it a few minutes and then start calling. They'll think they're getting the band back together, and try to regroup to the sound of your call. They get close and blammo! Winner winner turkey dinner."

"Huh. Sounds easy enough."

"You wish. It's more of a challenge than it sounds."

"So's guard duty," I suggested. "Maybe it's super boring, but we're essentially sitting out here waiting to be attacked."

"I suppose, but don't worry. You're gonna be fine, and I'm gonna be back here in no time."

"I know." I hoped I sounded braver than I felt. Being confident wasn't always my strong suit, and I still couldn't quite overcome it. The less I had time to think about something, the easier it was for me to do it. Even better, if I had company—especially if that company was a pony-tailed, round-cheeked, brown-eyed beauty who turned my heart to mush.

"Okay, good talk," John said. "I'll be back."

He wheeled and stalked down the slope behind me. His camouflage blended in perfectly with our surroundings. In seconds, he'd vanished through the brush in the direction of the turkey gobble.

"Great," I muttered under my breath. "Just don't worry. In with the bad, out with the good."

I pulled my coat tighter and hunched my head down into my shoulders. Looking like a vulture perched on a rock, I stared numbly toward the roadblock. My eyelids grew heavy. So heavy. I shook my head and sucked in another frigid breath.

Somewhere below me, a turkey gobbled again, and I wished John good luck. A hot turkey dinner would be a big improvement over the tasteless canned vegetables and powdered MREs I'd eaten for the past couple weeks. Ever since the explosions seemed to have ramped up across the park, the adults had been more concerned about shooting at game. Squirrels were almost too small for a bow kill, and the deer had proved elusive, though I was sure John wouldn't have trouble bagging one someday soon. Until then, all I could think about was the gnawing hunger in my belly, and the cold pressing down on me like a weight.

"In with the bad, out with the good," I repeated, and blinked my tired eyes open again. "Think of somewhere warm. Think of something positive."

Unfortunately, my active imagination had other ideas. Another turkey gobble turned to a visual of a great hunter surprising a flock of turkeys. But rather than John breaking up the party, I saw images of cruise missiles sailing into the middle of our hideout, right through the mouth of the cave. Blackened survivors scattered like rats from a billowing cloud of smoke.

I sat upright with a jolt only to realize it had all been a dream.

"Jeez, keep it together." I hugged myself tightly, and blinked my crusty eyes toward the roadblock. I decided that if I sat out there much longer my eyes would freeze shut.

"Holy crap it's cold," I moaned a second later. What I wouldn't give to be back with Katelyn, sharing a blanket and maybe a cup of something warm. Soup, tea, even coffee. The adults loved that black tar, and I was coming around to their side on that one. At least it might keep me awake.

From down the slope behind me, the bushes rustled. I watched for any sign of movement, but the world grew still again.

I assumed it wasn't the turkeys busting up already. The ones I'd seen would take off flying when they were scared. They'd bash their giant wings into tree branches in a frantic escape. It seemed certain they'd break a wing. But somehow they got under control, and after a few more flaps glided off to relative safety. Only for John to call them back and pick one off.

More images of being hunted raced through my head. Our flock of rebels were the turkeys, scattering when a government helicopter appeared overhead.

"Don't sleep," I told myself, trying to stop the nightmares. But, even awake, I couldn't turn the filmstrip off. I'd seen too much violence already.

And so the bushwhackers in my drama ran from the chopper. The younger kids scattered to the winds, leaving me and Katelyn to chase after them. I instantly went to my sister first for help. No matter the situation, Maddie was brilliant at calming them down.

After that initial burst of adrenaline, my rebels were back under some semblance of control and hiding out in the vast forest. In real life, I told myself that we wouldn't be the turkeys. We wouldn't get tricked into going back. If things went south like the way the adults had been hinting about, then we couldn't make that mistake. We'd run again, and not look back. Supplies would be replaced, but not our lives.

"I hope we don't have to do that again," I muttered under my breath, thinking about having to take another trip back into town to gather replacement supplies. Our group's biggest adventure into town had been early in the mission, and we'd nearly lost Katelyn's mother in the process—along with several other people, myself included.

Recently, the adults had been sneaking in much smaller parties to gather specific items and try to get a better handle of what was going on in the real world. The only problem happened to be that Gatlinburg was a desolate tourist town in a country with no more tourists, so news was incredibly hard to come by.

Movement on the road far beyond the fallen trees caught my attention. I pushed aside any lingering thoughts to focus. Between tree trunks and dying leaves, a dark blur zipped along the edge of the pavement.

It's really moving, I thought, and squinted to try to get a better look. At the same time, my hands involuntarily wrapped around the hunting rifle on my lap.

"Probably a turkey," I whispered. "John's busted them up."

The shape looked bigger as it weaved along the roadside, drawing ever closer. But it remained little more than a blob at that distance, and without a clear line of sight. I leaned to the side to try to catch a glimpse between the trees.

I wondered if it might be a bear instead, and cursed my misfortune at letting John run off with the binoculars. I cursed myself again a moment later when I realized I could use the optics on my rifle.

Shouldering the weapon, I trained the scope on the road. The field of vision was small. Too small. I lowered the weapon long enough to reduce the magnification to its lowest setting before glancing again. It took me a while to first find the road, and then scanned along it.

The bear turned out to be a bearded man in a camouflage jacket. He moved stealthily in the brush along the roadside.

"Huh. What's John doing here?" I whispered, and felt around to find my elbow a place to rest to steady the scope.

Doubts immediately crept into my mind. John wasn't supposed to be moving. The guy didn't have a bow or a rifle slung over his shoulder.

My heart rate ramped up to a fever pitch, and I forgot all about being cold. I strained my eyes to make out more than the man's profile, but he was still too far away. And now the rifle shook in my trembling hands.

Jamming the weapon against my shoulder to stabilize it, I twisted the magnification higher. The movement was enough for me to lose the man. I jerked the scope in a frantic rush to relocate him.

I chided myself to calm down. It didn't work immediately. My heart thrummed like a woodpecker against my ribcage, rattling throughout my body. Eventually, I steadied the scope.

I swept slowly to my left. A man's face filled the eyepiece—and only his huge face with eyes seemingly as big as saucers. I lowered the gun. Rather than finding the bearded creeper, a clean-shaven man had somehow closed to only twenty yards away.

CHAPTER 2

"Hold it right there!" I shouted as confidently as I could muster.

The man clutched his chest and stumbled backwards. "Whoa! Whoa! Don't shoot!"

"Don't move," I said, slowly rising to my feet and hoping I wouldn't pass out from the sudden rush of blood to my head.

"I didn't see you there," the man said between ragged breaths. "Don't shoot."

"I won't if you keep your hands up. No sudden movements."

"Yeah, yeah."

There was no way I was going to step any closer. I had to know more before I would feel comfortable taking the gun off the man. I lowered my voice, and said, "Tell me what you're doing here…and where the other guy is at?"

"What other guy?"

"The dude with the beard. Following behind you."

"There's no one with me." The stranger appeared genuinely surprised.

For a second, I wondered again if it could've been John. It seemed unlikely.

"Sit down and be quiet." I gestured with the gun toward a rock a good twenty feet in front of my spot. "You had somebody following you."

"Did not."

"I said be quiet."

My eyes shot back and forth between the roadblock below and the man cowering before me. He wasn't much older than John, maybe thirty at the most. A green stocking cap covered hair that looked to be no longer than my pitiful beard stubble. Most importantly, his jacket was definitely not camouflage. It was the typical canvas brown chore coat of every farmer I had ever seen.

At least the guy wasn't in military fatigues or some kind of police uniform, I decided. But I still didn't know what to make of the stranger. It was entirely possible he was from a different camp. According to my mother, I knew there had to be thirty or more other small groups of rebels spread out across the park. However, two concerns nagged.

First, my group hadn't seen anyone in this area of the park. In all our watches, no one had ever tried to get around the roadblock, even on foot. Second, and more concerning, there were rampant rumors of traitors in our midst. The untraceable two-way radios that kept the separate camps in contact had all talked about infiltrators slipping into the camps to get their coordinates back to the Feds. And thus, the uptick in aerial bombardments.

My mother had hammered in one precious piece of information more than any other: No one could be trusted.

Seeing no further movement down by the road, I focused back in on the man in front of me. All the male rebels I knew were bearded. No self-respecting prepper would waste time or supplies on shaving, though it wasn't out of the question. Sometimes my growing beard itched, and it could be torturous enough to make me want to shave.

"What camp you from?" I barked, breaking the long silence.

"Uhm..." The man swallowed, and looked at the rifle pointing squarely at his chest. "You mind putting that thing down."

"Yes, I do."

"The way you're shaking, you know that could go off."

I ignored my bruised ego, and gripped the rifle tighter. I shook it emphatically. "Don't you worry. Now answer the question."

"What was it?"

"Don't play stupid."

The man didn't answer. I stole a quick look at the road, and still found no trace of the camouflaged man. Though I really wanted John to hurry back, I wasn't about to yell for him. He'd know what to do. And if he didn't, he had a two-way radio with him that we could use to call back to camp. That was what we were supposed to do if the Feds launched a major offensive on the roadblock.

Rather than allow the stranger anywhere near camp without having answers, I turned back to him and decided to go with threats. I wasn't about to do any actual violence, though I hoped the prisoner didn't realize that.

"I can tie you up and leave you out here."

"You and what army? You put that weapon down and you won't be so tough."

"Maybe not, but I'm the one in charge right now. So I'd suggest you start talking before my partner gets back. He's not nearly as, uhm, polite."

"Partner, huh? I figured you might be a bit young to be out on your own."

The man had a way of hitting me in my weak spots. I could only work on one of my two big flaws: age and apprehension. Both would take time, so I went with firming up the latter.

"Not so young that I can't leave you for dead, so you'd better start talking. I'm not just gonna turn you loose."

Nor was I going to let the man come close enough to rush me. As much as I didn't want to pull the trigger, not even to scare him with a warning shot, I found my hand creeping toward it as the man shifted from a seating position to a crouch.

"I understand. Here's the deal." He leaned forward conspiratorially, which looked odd given the separation. "I need to talk to your leaders. There's something big they're gonna want to know."

"You some kind of agent?"

"What would you know about that?"

"Plenty," I said, remembering back to all the visits my father had received for posting pro-liberty, anti-government writing on a variety of different websites and blogs. His freedom-loving rants had the long, oppressive arm of the law parked in our front yard on and off for the last year until the big collapse.

"Anyway," the man continued, "I need to share some intel with your superiors. It's, uhm, classified."

"You're not going anywhere until I hear something I can believe."

The man's hard eyes stared at my newfound resolve, and his expression softened. "Fine. Here's the deal. I'm Noel, and I'm looking to share information in exchange for a place to stay."

"Thanks. I'm Zach, but that doesn't mean we're gonna shake hands and be best buds from here on out." I kept the rifle pointed in the general direction of the man, and wouldn't lay it aside until John returned. Until then, I had to deal with the fact that I was stuck alone with the new guy.

The man nodded at the lowered gun, and offered a thin smile. "Understood, Zach."

"So, Noel," I repeated his name sarcastically. "You're sure you weren't followed?"

"I think you've been seeing things. I promise you I wasn't followed."

"Well we can't exactly give you a safe place to stay if you're being tracked. You'll have to be searched for wires and GPS trackers and all that."

"Ten-four. Have your people meet me out here, unless you want to do it yourself."

Not really, I thought, but I had a feeling that John wouldn't have any such qualms.

Seeing how it looked like we might be waiting a while and the guy seemed forthcoming enough, I decided it was time to cut him a little slack. I reached in my pocket and offered him some food.

"I only have a couple granola bars, but you're welcome to one."

"Thanks." He rose to his feet, and I quickly tightened my grip on the rifle.

"Just stay there." I tossed him the packet. "Sorry, but I'm not taking any chances…at least not until you can explain a little more about what you're doing out here."

A deep voice rose from behind me. "I'd like to know the same thing."

I wheeled around to John standing there. He'd climbed the slope behind me as quietly as a cat, and apparently caught a fair amount of our conversation. Tossing a turkey and his bow and arrows to the side, John stepped next to me.

"Spill it about who you are and what you're doing here, or you're not going anywhere."

The man tilted his head. "And you are?"

"Asking the questions," John replied sharply.

With a smirk, the man nodded. "Alright, tough guy. I'm Noel, and I'm here to share some intel with your leaders. And I've got a feeling you might be one of them."

"Close enough. You can call me John." He squinted at the man, seemingly examining him from head to toe. "Spill it."

"There's something major in the works. I'm sure you've noticed the way the attacks have increased, and it's about to get a whole lot worse."

"We've noticed," John said. "That's why you're not getting anywhere near the others until you've been checked out."

"If you treat all the other camps this way, how do you even get along? Maybe the Feds have nothing to worry about after all."

"But you're not from another camp, are you?" John said. "We can easily find out."

I nodded along at the ping pong match. At the same time, I continued to scan the road for the other person, if there had been one. As much as I was sure there had been someone else, I couldn't shake the suspicion that my mind had played tricks on me again.

When I focused back in on the conversation, I noticed that John had taken an edgier tone again.

"What's with those boots?" John pointed to Noel's feet. "Those are government issue."

"So is everyone else's gear. It's military surplus. Like a bunch of preppers wouldn't know all about that."

"Take off your cap."

"C'mon, man," Noel protested. "It's cold out here."

"Just do it."

The man obliged. The buzzed hair on Noel's temples changed over at the crown of his head to a slightly longer cut.

"Military issue haircut," John said. "Take off your jacket."

"Yes, I have a tattoo also. You got me." He stood and saluted. "Noel Ridings, Sergeant First Class, Fort Benning, Georgia."

"That's name and rank. How about serial number?"

"I forgot. I've been out of the service for a while."

"How does that happen?" I interjected. I looked to John. "I thought they were conscripting more soldiers to the cause, not letting them go."

"Good question." John turned to Noel. "You care to answer that?"

He looked to his boots and shrugged. "Well, what can I say? I'm a deserter."

CHAPTER 3

"Why didn't you say that right away?" I asked.

"I'm not exactly proud of it." Noel shrugged again. "And now you know why I need somewhere to stay."

"Get up," John said. He seemed to me like he still wasn't that trusting. Nobody liked a deserter, but I couldn't really blame the guy. With the way the government had perverted law and order into oppression and murder, I was happy to learn there was someone who was willing to stand up to that. Or at least run away.

For the longest time, I had thought my parents were simply running away. My mom, a devoted prepper, had us ready to bug out of our suburban Knoxville home before the first bombs had fallen. To my dismay, it had seemed as if we were set on a life in hiding. Sometimes it still did.

I knew my dad had bigger ideas. Always the one to speak out, the former banker had witnessed the beginning of the end firsthand, and had railed against the skyrocketing national debt, limits on personal freedom, travel bans and so on. I didn't necessarily understand the issues much better than when we had been living back home, but I had more time to listen as we sat around the boring cave. I didn't have a room to hide in when my dad went off on another tangent about banking regulations, debt defaults, and everything else that derailed the economy. I just knew things were bad, and all the preppers turned rebels were going to actually do something about it.

"Let's head back," John said, interrupting my thoughts.

Katelyn's brother stooped over to pick up the bow, and then grabbed a good-sized turkey by its legs.

"Nice bird," I said.

"It won't feed us all, but it'll be nice to get a little fresh meat."

"How big is your camp?" Noel interrupted.

He walked closer to us. I didn't raise the rifle that time. Not sure how much information we should be sharing, I deferred the answer to John.

"Big enough. Let's get going." John turned to me. "Wait here a second while I go use the radio."

I nodded. "He'll just tell 'em we've got company," I said when Noel's eyes met mine.

He pulled his stocking cap back over his head. "Makes sense."

John was back a moment later. He knelt over to stuff the turkey into a backpack. It was not a simple task given the size of the bird. Throwing the swollen pack over his shoulders, he turned to us.

"Spread out…in a line." He pointed to Noel. "I want you in the middle. Zach, right behind him. Keep me covered."

We took off down the slope in the direction John had gone to ambush the turkeys. I kept my mouth pinched shut when we didn't follow the usual path back to the cave. Instead, John led us off farther to the west down to a wooded valley.

A narrow stream, one of thousands in the park, ran alongside us. John kept beside the rocks lining the stream bank, and eventually turned to the right to follow the falling water uphill from the narrow valley.

No one spoke. Though I had become accustomed to climbing steep mountain trails, my breathing was soon labored.

The sun popped over a distant hillside, and bathed us in an early morning glow. My breath no longer spewed forth with the cold condensation of winter morning.

It was a typical, glorious autumn day. Cool mornings and warm days prevailed, only to repeat all over again until the dreaded snows would come and taint the air as bitter as day old coffee.

I relished the fall. With the humidity slowly dropping and the blazing heat gone, I was comfortable during the daylight hours like no other time. The morning chill wasn't enjoyable when I was sitting on the hard ground watching a roadblock that never showed any sign of activity—at least until that day.

The coolness of that fall morning made the long, steep hike from camp to the roadblock almost pleasant. For me, not sweating was pleasant enough.

I'd gotten markedly better at estimating distance. I figured we'd covered at least a mile, which should have put us almost halfway back to the camp. Although I didn't know exactly where we were at, I knew John had been skirting around the mountain range that harbored our secluded camp.

Midway up the hill, John stopped abruptly. He motioned for us to gather around him.

"You can take a little break. Have a drink."

He offered his water bottle to Noel, who gratefully accepted. After a big swig, he handed it back to John with a tight smile.

"Thanks, man. Best drink I've had in days."

John looked at him curiously, but didn't question the statement. Instead, he replied, "No problem. Hang out here for a second."

John gestured at me with his head to direct me off to the side out of earshot.

"What's up?" I asked.

"Just being careful. No reason to show him the quick way back."

"Good call. Speaking of careful, you heard that I saw someone else down by the road before this guy, right?" I whispered.

"Yeah. Guess I got a bit sidetracked."

"I kept looking for the guy, but he never showed himself."

"Me, too. That's kinda why I really took my time questioning this guy. I didn't want to leave until the coast was clear."

I noticed that John continued to look around the woods, even though we were so deep into the timber that we couldn't see a hundred yards in any direction. Truth be told, I had been watching too. I'd been trained by the best to remain attentive at all times; however, my penchant for letting the daydreams take over was something I still needed to work on.

"Weird thing was," I said, "the guy had a camo jacket. A beard. Kinda looked like you."

"It wasn't me, bud. I didn't go anywhere near the road."

"I figured." I exhaled out the frustration at not knowing. "Great…I mean, unless I was imagining things."

I instantly regretted admitting my failings, but John didn't follow up on it. Instead, he said, "We'll keep our eyes open. Could be another camp has been trailing this guy. There's something fishy about him."

"Agreed. I wonder if we're doing the right thing bringing him back."

"I'm already on that. Like I was saying, we're not going back to camp the normal way."

"Yeah, of course," I agreed. "I wasn't going to say anything."

"I didn't think you would." John leaned in closer. "Here's the deal. Your dad's gonna meet up with us at Rainbow Falls. We'll do a full debrief and check him over for trackers before he gets anywhere near the cave."

"Just my dad?" I asked before realizing how desperate that made me sound. But it had literally been a couple weeks since I'd had a moment of alone time with Katelyn outside the cave.

"Yeah. I didn't think we needed both of your parents for this too." John narrowed his eyes, and a sly grin broke over his face. "Oh, I get it. You're wantin' to take my sister to the falls, aren't ya?"

"No. That's totally not-"

John waved off the lame explanation. "Look, bud, it's pretty cool over there, but I'd take a woman to Bridal Falls if I really wanted to show her a good time."

"Dude, you're sick. That's your sister."

"Hey, I'm not the one trying to cozy up to her. I'm just trying to help you out." John tapped me on the arm. "I like you, man. Besides, I haven't forgotten what it's like to have a crush."

I took offense at the last word. There was no doubt my initial feelings for Katelyn had been borderline obsessive, but not in a bad way. Months later, I felt as strongly as before, if not more so. And that shouldn't have qualified as a crush any longer.

Before I could object, John dropped a bombshell.

"You know I think it's only fair…if you get to hang all over my sister, then you should set me up with yours."

"What?"

"Dude, I'm joking. Seriously."

"Good, 'cause you're like twice her age."

"I'm not that old," John said. "I'm twenty-five."

"And she's barely fourteen. Good God, that's sick."

John seemed legitimately offended. He grabbed at his heart before patting me on the shoulder. "That hurts. I said I was joking. I mean seriously…lighten up."

I took a step back and recognized the honesty in John's voice, but it didn't make it any less creepy. In fact, John had to take things one step further and keep blathering on about Katelyn.

"I get that we're all kinda crowded into the cave," he said. "Ever since the attacks have started up again, my folks have been really overprotective. You two could use a trip to the falls."

"Shouldn't we go?" I asked, shooting a look over at Noel. He'd taken the opportunity to sit down, and had pulled off his boots to massage his tired feet. I thought the man's footwear looked pretty good for someone who'd supposedly hiked a long way to get there.

I wanted to share that thought with John, but my would-be brother-in-law was still going on about Katelyn. So I walked away from John to hopefully put an end to the awkward conversation.

Noel looked up at me. "We ready?"

"More than." I motioned for him to get up. "Let's go."

Noel pulled his boots back on over thick wool socks. They looked to be in as good of a condition as the boots, which made me more jealous than suspicious. I had been able to borrow several pairs since my first campsite had been destroyed, but I'd never found the perfect pair for hiking. Something thick to cushion but wicking for moisture was ideal, and most of my socks were wearing out quickly after five mile hikes day after day.

I would really need thick socks when the weather turned, I thought, as a cool breeze slipped through the trees like a harbinger of winter to come. Fortunately, we were well into mid-morning, and the sun rapidly climbed higher. The rays slipped through gaps in the canopy to paint the forest floor in spectacular reds and yellows of freshly fallen maple and poplar leaves.

My mood always brightened when the sun came overhead, especially when the accompanying light didn't bring heat to the magnitude of a sweat bath. I blinked as the leaves rustled again in a gentle breeze, temporarily exposing me to a direct shot from the sun.

A dark shadow crossed my eyes. I blinked again to remove the bright white still painted over my retinas. My vision slowly cleared to reveal a buzzard-like object circling high above the treetops.

When the object passed over an opening in the canopy, my improving mood turned as sour as old milk. The bulbous nose and swept wings of a different kind of predator were plainly outlined in that clear sky.

"Drone!" I yelled.

CHAPTER 4

"Get down!" John shouted, but I hadn't needed him to tell me that. John flopped next to the trunk of a giant tree, and instantly zeroed his gaze on Noel.

"Are they tracking you?" he asked sharply.

"No way, man." Noel seemed equally nervous as his eyes turned to the sky. I kept my own on the stranger, partly because I felt like the drone could spot raised eyeballs easier than my camouflage hat and jacket. For all I knew, maybe it could.

"Just keep still," John chided from a couple trees away. "We're gonna be fine."

"You believe that?" I asked, knowing that the drones had been far more menacing in recent weeks than earlier. The lack of an answer unnerved me even more. "John?"

"Nothing we can do about it now but wait."

"And be ready to run if the Hellfires come raining down," Noel added.

"Like we'd survive a missile attack," John muttered under his breath, but unfortunately loud enough that I heard him.

Drones scared me far more than helicopters. They might not have carried as much firepower, but they had a way of appearing like phantoms—whisper quiet and lethal.

"Don't say that." I choked down a wad of stress in the back of my throat that felt bigger and hairier than a tennis ball. I snuck a quick drink and looked to John for a word of encouragement. He was too busy shooting Noel his iciest stare. Any colder and Noel would've frozen in place for real.

"It's not following me. See?" Noel pointed to the sky, making me cringe at the sudden movement.

I finally raised my eyes skyward, and noticed the drone had expanded from a narrow circle out to a wide area. I watched with relief as the noiseless aircraft seemed to effortlessly glide off to the south and eventually out of sight altogether.

"Thank goodness," I announced with a sigh.

John stood and adjusted the heavy, bulging pack on his back. "Let's make tracks, fellas."

"Good," I said, but crept over toward John rather than head up the rocky stream. "What was that all about? I mean I've seen plenty of drones before, but the timing was a bit, uhm, suspicious."

"Totally." John subtly nodded his head toward Noel. "Good thing we're not going back to camp yet. Keep your eyes on the sky."

I wasn't done watching the woods all around us either. I could only hope I didn't trip on my way up the hillside with my eyes constantly flitting between the two different directions.

As the stream thinned out in the higher elevation, John took the opportunity to guide us out into the water rather than battle the brush along the edge.

Giant boulders and fallen logs provided a clean path, but reminded me of another place altogether. When I wasn't checking the sky, I imagined I was some kind of dashing explorer climbing the eroded stone steps of a Mayan jungle pyramid. Complete with snakes and whistling birds, I made the climb with my rifle slung over a shoulder. It always helped to have my hands free in case I needed to catch myself. The wet rocks were slicker than snot.

Besides spending time with Katelyn, climbing the cool mountain streams was my all-time favorite activity, though my mom often said it was sleeping late. I certainly didn't mind lying under the blankets as long as possible, but the hard stone floor of the cave usually had me up plenty early—at least I thought so.

My mother was the earliest riser I'd ever known, which always made for entertaining arguments back home. Ever since my brother, Austin, had moved to the basement, I seemed to take all the heat for sleeping in. Never mind that Maddie rarely left her room for pretty much the entire day. Now that her room was a cave about the size of the school cafeteria that we shared with forty other people, she still never left it for anything other than field trips and bathroom breaks with the youngsters.

I couldn't blame her for that. As the aerial attacks had ramped up, outside travel had been mostly restricted to checking on the roadblocks, followed by hunting or fishing trips. With drones, jets, and helicopters occasionally passing overhead, there was no reason to risk being too exposed. The cave had to stay hidden.

The thought made me wonder again about the logic of bringing Noel back to the hideout. I had a feeling my dad wouldn't allow it, which in turn made me wonder what would happen to the stranger.

Noel hadn't complained a bit, or shown much aggression beyond a couple smart-alecky comments early on. He'd followed what few orders John had given with perfect attention, and kept any questions to himself. If anything, he seemed rather accepting about being kept in the dark. I wasn't so sure I could relate. When my family had bugged out of town before the bombs fell, my parents had tried to keep the truth from me and my sister about what was really going on. It hadn't taken me long to realize it was no family summer vacation, and I'd soon gotten the real answers—whether I'd wanted them or not.

"We're almost there," John announced, but I couldn't make out the telltale sounds of the plummeting water of Rainbow Falls.

I wasn't sure how John knew exactly where we were at. Granted, he'd been out to explore a lot more. An experienced hunter and nimble climber, it only made sense that John had the most physically demanding job of all the rebels in my camp. Still, the forest looked the same there as pretty much anywhere else. Stopping to give it a better listen, I heard nothing but chirping birds and stream water tumbling around the rocks under my feet as it raced downhill.

"You sure?" I asked.

"Yeah." John pointed ahead through the great leafy tunnel. "Not much farther to Rainbow."

"If you say so."

"I just did." John shot back a grin. "Quit being lazy and get on up here. You can see it for yourself."

"I can't see a thing," I said, bristling at John's words. "And I'm not lazy." Though I said it, I didn't make any actual movement to resume climbing the boulder staircase.

"I'm just joking. You can't see it yet." John waved for me to catch up. "But hurry on up here."

"I will," I replied, but remained planted.

John went on ahead several more paces, and worked his way over a fallen tree before turning back to check on me. "You coming, loverboy?" John's hands went to his hips. "Better quit your daydreaming."

"Busted," Noel said, trying to pile on when it wasn't his place. "You got told."

"Nobody asked your opinion," I snapped.

"It is true, though," John said, choosing sides with the stranger to my dismay.

"What the heck?" I said, but quickly realized how whiny I sounded. "Why you riding my ass? I haven't done anything."

"You can say that again. Nothing." John sat down as if to prove the point that I was trailing so far behind that he had time to rest.

Noel burst out laughing and sat on the fallen tree next to his new best buddy.

I snorted with disgust. "That's crap. You jokers twist everything I say."

"Just giving you a taste of your own medicine. You always think you're so clever." John stretched his hands out and slapped them back down on his lap. "Revenge is sweet. If your sister could see this-"

"Whoa, get off my sister."

Noel laughed even louder, which made my face turn redder than canned tomatoes—not completely from embarrassment. No one was allowed to pick on Maddie but me. As far as I was concerned, even my brother Austin wasn't allowed to get too cruel.

"Just go!" I hollered. "Let's finish this. I'm ready to be rid of you both."

The two of them watched as I found my legs and charged up the hill. I leapt from one boulder to another, easily managing to keep my feet dry as I scaled the towering steps. "I'll show you daydreaming," I mumbled under my breath.

Before I caught all the way up, John took off again with Noel following behind. I knew it was my job to be watching our new companion along with the sky, but I didn't feel quite as bad now that John had sided with Noel over me. Still, I rushed to keep up. I couldn't quite catch them, and soon grew winded.

While I wouldn't give them the satisfaction of seeing me quit, I let my mind wander as I reverted to climbing and dreaming like John had accused.

The sun beat down through a little opening in the trees, adding sparkles to the crystal clear stream. The water looked like liquid joy as it spilled playfully over small stones, and rushed past the bigger boulders with pure delight. After stealing a quick glance at the clear, drone-less sky, I slipped back into full daydream mode.

It was impossible not to. Some of my best memories involved Katelyn, streambeds, and soaking wet clothes. The way they clung to her figure in just the right way, and how she'd laughed and shrieked when we'd doused each other. I resolved right then that we were sneaking out of camp later that night, no matter the repercussions from our parents.

I shook my head to clear the memories and focused back in on my companions. Somehow I'd almost closed the gap, and quickly resorted back to cautious mode. Given my latest transgression, I was overeager to do a better job—arguably to the point of hyperawareness of everything in the sky and the woods all around us.

As a result, I felt cross-eyed by the time we made it close to the waterfall, and was relieved when John held up a hand to stop us short.

The sound of pounding water masked any other sound from the surrounding forest, which did nothing to take the edge off my nerves. But I was exhausted enough from the climb that any trembling was far more related to tired limbs than fear. If anything, I was past the point of dread.

Although hardly possible, I should've been paying more attention. As we closed on the sound of pounding water, I initially missed the lone figure stepping out of the woods. A rifle was leveled at the three of us before I could get mine off my shoulder.

Worse yet, the person holding the weapon wasn't my dad.

CHAPTER 5

"Hold it!" the man shouted.

I skidded on a wet rock and dropped to one knee. The cold stream water knifed through my jeans.

"No sudden movements," the man added, but seemed to chuckle as I hopped up to get my soaked pant leg out of the creek.

I scowled and examined the man through squinty eyes. He wore a camouflage jacket that made him look like pretty much every other prepper hiding out in the park. He also sported a full, light brown beard. It seemed more neatly trimmed than most of the other mountain men.

"You were at the roadblock," I said before I could cover my mouth.

The man nodded. "Where you boys going?"

"Rainbow," John replied, looking not at all concerned. He stepped forward and extended a hand. "And you are?"

"Spotted Owl."

A load lifted off my chest. To an outsider, it would've seemed bizarre the way the dynamic instantly changed, but I had indeed relaxed at the use of a code name. I knew from my mother that all the preppers on the forums had used screen names to keep things anonymous, yet built a strong alliance of likeminded people.

"I'm with Spotted Fawn," John said, referencing his mother's screen name. He laughed. "I guess that almost makes us like family or something."

"Ha, yeah. The Spotted family." The man turned to me. "You?"

"Sunning Bear." I grimaced at my mother's less than tough sounding name. If I'd had an account, I thought I'd have gone with something grizzlier, or at least less sunny—especially given the situation. Then again, I wasn't sure that being named after a baby deer was particularly terrifying either, and I decided that women had no business naming themselves in a war.

"Outstanding!" Spotted Owl exclaimed. "Couple sons of the real heroes of the rebellion here."

I was taken aback by the praise. Though I had learned that my mother had built up a nice network of fellow preppers, I hadn't quite realized the extent of her reach. Beyond Katelyn's parents and a few others, I hadn't seen much leadership out of her besides the risky raid on Gatlinburg way back when the world first fell apart.

"So who's this?" Spotted Owl pointed with his head toward Noel. With pleasantries out of the way, all our guns were safely slung over our shoulders again.

"Don't you know?" I asked. "You were following him."

"I was hoping you'd figured that out by now." Spotted Owl looked from me to John and apparently realized we weren't entirely sure if Noel could be trusted. "Seems risky to bring him wherever you're bringing him without vetting him."

"Well, he says he's a deserter from the Army," I offered.

"I'm standing right here," Noel interjected. "I can speak for myself."

"Then you better do it, boy," Spotted Owl suggested.

I though it odd that our potential new ally acted like we were all kids, especially seeing how he couldn't have been a day over thirty. Even so, that made him significantly older than me. Just not that much older than Noel.

With no detailed answer forthcoming from Noel, Spotted Owl jumped right in to interrogate him.

"What unit you in?"

"Third Infantry, Fort Benning, Georgia."

Spotted Owl's eyes narrowed. "That's not the way I remember it. The Third is at Fort Stewart, Georgia."

"They still are."

"You said you were in the Third." Spotted Owl looked to John and me. "That's what you guys heard, right?"

Our nodding heads provided the answer.

"So..." Spotted Owl seemed to tense up. "Care to explain?"

"I was Third Brigade, Third Infantry. We're a supporting unit to the Airborne Corps...at Fort Benning."

I traded a confused look with John. Turning to us, Spotted Owl admitted, "Could be. It's a big base."

"It sure is." Noel agreed. "We, I mean they, can project power all over the globe, and with a standing force well over a hundred thousand."

Spotted Owl chuckled at the rehearsed line. "Well, kid, there's not much need for that global influence anymore, is there? At least not when there are so many problems right here at home."

"Plenty of that, sir," Noel replied. "And I don't want any part of responding to that. I signed on for foreign adventure."

"Good for you." Spotted Owl softened his expression further. "Now if we could just convince about a hundred thousand of your comrades in arms."

"Right on," John agreed. He pulled Spotted Owl aside. "We're close to meeting up with some others from our group. You want to hang around?"

"You bet. I actually came looking for you. Spotted Fawn invited me over for a little powwow."

"Cool. That was convenient," John replied, though I had to wonder if it wasn't a little too convenient. Nevertheless, I felt far better about Spotted Owl than Noel, though the deserter had gained some standing in my opinion.

John waved for the group to gather up. "Follow me and we'll finish this little hike."

He led us up toward the waterfall. The volume grew to the point where I thought for sure it had to be on a magnitude far greater than the falls where I'd first met Katelyn out in the woods months earlier. Though I occasionally liked to pick on her about letting Jonas, one of the kids she had been babysitting, fall over the side of the waterfall, I tried not to rub it in too often. After all, everything had turned out fine, even for Jonas. But I resolved to pick on her even less in the future now that John had pointed out my smart-alecky ways.

We closed on the waterfall, getting to the point where we could feel the cool spray on our exposed faces, but I still couldn't see the falls. Or my dad.

John showed no signs of caution. He hopped up on a big boulder, and skirted around a pool of deep water.

"Watch your step here!" he shouted over the roar, and disappeared around a corner.

I brought up the rear, also edging around what looked like a little pond tucked into the depths of the forest. Waves rippled across the surface as the sound of falling water splashing into the far end of the pool drowned out practically everything else.

Turning the corner around a clump of bushes and towering trees, I finally caught sight of the waterfall. From atop a giant ledge of stone, a weak stream plunged about thirty feet into the standing water.

I stopped, surprised to see that it was no more ferocious than where I'd rescued Katelyn and Jonas, though about twice as high. The other falls had pounded onto a field of rocks below, while this pond looked like one of those old movie scenes with showering water splashing into a tranquil pool. Only this time, a man stood at the top of the falls.

It was my dad, who was oddly out in the open. Of course, he'd been expecting us. Perhaps for a while. Still, he should've known better than to do something so risky.

Then again, Dad had sometimes seemed a little less cautious and more inquisitive than the hardcore preppers. I supposed being a banker could do that. My father and Katelyn's had worked at the same corporate office in Knoxville before the crash, though the place had been so large that they apparently hadn't know each other very well before the collapse. It didn't help that my dad had been fired months before given his penchant for sharp criticism of the new regime.

My banker father wasn't nearly as big of a prepper as my mother, and his fondness for wearing dress pants and ties, even while unemployed, seemed curious at best. But Dad knew what he was doing in the woods—at least most of the time. His apparent lack of concern about being exposed to the hostile sky was troubling.

John hurried off to the right, ducking under some limbs to find a narrow path to the top of the falls. We followed in single file, and soon found ourselves on a ledge of slippery rock that was bigger than my old living room. I ran on ahead.

"Hey, boy. Great view, isn't it?" Dad said as I came into sight.

"Not bad. You saw the drone, right?" I said.

"I haven't seen any, at least not today," he said with a shrug. "Lousy things are everywhere."

"Yeah, they are." I waved him away from the edge of the falls. We all gathered up under the shade of some big trees by a rock bluff that ringed the wide open ledge. Dad hung out at the fringe of the shadows where the sun spilled over his shoulders.

"Another beautiful morning. That sun'll warm you right up." He took a moment to look us over, and turned to John. "I thought you found one stranger?"

"We picked up another along the way," he replied.

A raised eyebrow followed, which crinkled the balding top of my dad's head enough to send a sunshine glare into my eyes.

Before John could explain, Spotted Owl stepped forward and extended a meaty hand. "Nice to meet you. Spotted Fawn or Sunning Bear?"

"Neither," my dad replied.

"Oh." Spotted Owl looked at John. "I thought-"

"No worries. This fella here is very much related to Sunning Bear."

"She's back at camp," Dad explained. "She's working on plans for-"

John raised a hand to cut him off. "Whoa. Save it for later. Let's deal with the problem at hand." He pointed to Noel and said, "And what should we do with this guy?"

"Let's hear his story."

My dad waved John and Noel over for a private conversation, leaving me standing next to Spotted Owl. Not knowing what to say, and never having been much of a talker, I gazed at the edge of the cliff where the falls loudly spilled into the pond below.

"Thought this might be bigger," I finally said when the pause got too awkward.

"What's that?" Spotted Owl asked.

I realized I needed to speak up. I debated keeping quiet, but decided it might be more rude than prudent. With Spotted Owl looking at me, I said, "Just talking about the falls. It's not very impressive."

"It hasn't rained much all year. It'd be a lot more water if we'd had normal rainfall this summer."

"Huh. Makes sense. All the falls seem kinda wimpy."

"You've seen others?" Spotted Owl asked, which caused me to go back into quiet mode. Not sure what I should share with the stranger, I settled for a quick bob of the head.

We stayed back in the shadows. With a sidelong glance, I watched as my dad gave Noel the type of enhanced pat down that would have made an airport security guard proud. Then he launched into a seemingly spirited interrogation of Noel—or so I hoped.

Dad hadn't been the tougher of my two parents. Education was his big push. He'd put a strong emphasis on my performance at school, both academically and behavior-wise. But Mom had dispensed most of the discipline around my house for any other infractions.

I was happy to see the mild-mannered accountant taking his job vetting Noel seriously. He was much more expressive than usual as he alternated between hands on hips and arms wrapped in front of his chest.

Growing tired of the waiting, I leaned back against the rock bluff and debated sitting down. Assuming it wouldn't take that long, and not wanting to show any more weakness in front of Spotted Owl, I remained standing on my aching feet.

I wasn't made for wearing boots, I decided. Tennis shoes had always been my number one choice, though not sturdy enough for the cross country hiking. Or waterproof.

Glancing at the clear sky, I stepped out far enough outside the tree cover to soak up the sunshine beating down on the rocks. Dad was right. I needed to enjoy it while I could.

Of course, it didn't last. Over the rumble of the waterfall, I picked up on the sound of a constant, deeper growl. As the noise grew closer, a whop-whop-whop sound built in the tiny amphitheater that was the grotto.

"Helicopter!" Spotted Owl yelled.

I ran back under cover, crouching in the shadows. Five pairs of eyes glued themselves to the sky, and we were soon rewarded with the sighting of a dark green helicopter cruising in the distance.

The aircraft was long and bulky, unlike the short hard angles of the typical attack helicopters. There were no pylons under stubby wings holding a litany of rocket pods, but it was just as fearsome.

I cowered in the shadows, tucking my head to my chest as the chopper glided past. The sliding doors on both sides were open, with a man sitting in each opening behind a Gatling gun.

A pair of smaller helicopters trailed behind it, each with bulbous glass windows around the cockpit. Sitting inside with feet dangling down onto the metal legs, two soldiers were on each side wearing helmets and body armor.

As they flew past with a roar, John shouted, "Those aren't Apaches!"

"Blackhawk and little birds," Spotted Owl answered. "They're carrying troops for an insertion."

CHAPTER 6

I sprinted toward John. "Which way are they headed?"

"To the east," he said calmly.

"Don't we need to warn the others?" I shouted. I wasn't positive, but I thought our cave near Grotto Falls was almost due east of Rainbow, and that put the others in mortal danger.

"Your dad's on it," he replied, and motioned toward my father.

Dad held the walkie-talkie to his ear. He lowered it to thumb the button, and said, "Ten-four. We're inbound." He waved to the others. "Let's move out."

I didn't need to be told twice. I forgot all about keeping watch over Noel, and took off right behind my dad, eager to get back to our cave as quickly as we could.

"Everything alright at camp?" I asked him.

"Sure. Why wouldn't it be?"

I could only shake my head at that response. For someone so concerned and cautious when it came to financial matters, he could be clueless or undisturbed about other things. Despite the fact my stomach ached with anticipation, I didn't press the questions with him. While he seemed to be in a fine mood, it hadn't translated into a boatload of conversation. Even on a good day, he wasn't the most talkative guy around. I supposed I took after him in that respect—and possibly little else.

When I finally remembered that I should've been helping watch our prisoner, I slowed to talk to John. Pointing a thumb at my own chest to indicate Noel behind us, I whispered, "Should we be worried about him?"

"I think we've got bigger fish to fry." He adjusted the load on his back. "Or turkey. Either way, bud, I wouldn't worry about it."

"Why not?" I instantly thought of the helicopters. "You think those guys are assaulting the camp, don't you?"

"I'd be running if I did. Wouldn't you?"

I nodded sheepishly. "Would we be able to hear the gunshots?"

"Maybe." He scratched at his beard. "Probably. Besides, your dad warned 'em. They could've cleared out already."

I breathed a giant sigh, but didn't feel completely relieved. Sound travelled funny in the hills, especially the explosions. What sounded like a bomb from one ridgeline over was sometimes more like three or four miles. I could never tell the difference.

"I'd say those troops are dropping in to clear out a roadblock. Or doing a trial run." John looked to the sky before focusing in on me. "It's just not worth worrying about, bud."

"Like drones and now choppers? And not just any choppers. These have soldiers that were definitely ready to bail out, maybe on our camp." I swallowed exaggeratedly. "I'm gonna worry about it. We haven't seen that before."

"It was just a matter of time. You had to know that."

"Of course I did. It's just…I dunno. I can't not worry. That's what I do."

"That'll take years off your life," John said with a grin.

"So will the soldiers."

"True that. You got me there."

I clammed up and focused on putting one foot in front of the other. We hiked an old trail for a little ways before plunging off into the depths of the forest again. The tree canopy was taller than a cathedral's ceiling, choking out much of the underbrush. So we made good time crossing the final mile over to the cave.

My dad, not always the quietest one in the woods, had stepped on at least a half dozen fallen branches before we made it halfway there. Every time one had cracked under his boots, my heart had stopped—along with my feet.

Another crack split the quiet. It turned to a booming rumble that rolled from the hill off to our left.

"Hold up," John called forward to my dad.

We ground to a halt, and gathered up waiting for another blast that never came. I looked to John questioningly. At long distances, gunshots and explosions almost sounded the same, though the bomb blasts tended to have a bit more of a thunderous rumble. I hadn't been able to tell that time. A sixteen-year-old wasn't supposed to know those kinds of things, I supposed.

"Rifle shot," John explained, understanding the question before it had to be asked. "Pretty far."

"Not from camp?" I asked.

"No. Definitely not."

I wanted to believe it so badly when I asked, "So the birds put down somewhere else?"

"Maybe," John admitted. "Or it could be hunters."

"Not ours."

"Well, no. They would know better than that." John tapped the bow on his shoulder. "That's why we use the primitive methods now."

I was inclined to agree with that, but wasn't done with the questions. "So say it was the soldiers…"

Spotted Owl stepped in to answer that one. "It was closer to town. Probably back by the roadblock, I'd guess…but sound travels funny in the hills."

I nodded. I knew the way the mountains jutted to the sky in ridgelines like the ribs of emaciated rebels, only more broken and random. Like the way our little group could end up if the food supply ran out and the soldiers pressed the attack.

Between those crooked ribs, streams curled like serpents. They raced down hillsides to the finger-like, scattered, small valleys that eventually came together into the river. The Pigeon River ran alongside the narrow canyon town of Gatlinburg, but the city was no longer the jewel of the Smoky Mountains. The place had been devastated, with burned out souvenir shops, restaurants, and hotels sitting as decimated as the rest of the nation's economy. Hopefully worse, I thought, seeing how it would take years and a small fortune to bring the town halfway back to its former glory. The country would take decades longer, if ever.

Before I could dwell on those dark thoughts, I noticed the first recognizable landmark in our long, out of the way hike. Rock jutted up at a severe angle from two sides, meeting in a point about ten feet taller than the trail. It highlighted how the mountain range had been formed by shifting crust of the Earth eons before. Behind the pointed rocks, fern-like bushes opened into a narrow, rock-lined path leading up a slope. It was the back way into camp, which was only to be used in case of emergency. I thought two strangers and the flight of soldiers probably qualified.

Thankfully, there was no sound of a struggle from up above.

Regardless, I rushed up the trail, eager to get back to the relative safety of the rock enclosure. Dad kept pace with me. We made it to the top of the rocky steps to a flat, tree-covered plateau at the base of a massive bluff and paused. After taking a quick look at the sky and finding it to my satisfaction, I raced across an open area and into a field of round boulders that could've made a mammoth-sized snowman replica, if stacked and painted white.

Weaving through the boulder field, I raced for the entrance. Somewhere back in the shade of the cave, I knew there would be eyes watching my approach. Though I could see no one in the concealed position, I tossed a wave in their general direction anyway and pressed on. Seconds later, the blazing light of noonday sun turned into the black of the cave.

Situated under the ledge, a big room spread out before me. Except for the low ceiling that provided a touch of claustrophobia, the expansive room could've been a dank, darker replica of my school cafeteria. Cots took the place of tables; however, there were several tables fashioned from crates and plastic tubs ringing the room.

It took a while for my eyes to adjust to the shadows. Rather than rush inside, I stood backlit against the opening. It felt as if I had to crouch to avoid scraping my head on the roof of solid rock. Of course, it wasn't any lower than the basement of my house back in the suburbs, and just about as cold. I assumed my older brother Austin felt perfectly at home there, other than the lack of video games and screeching anarchy metal music.

A shape rushed toward me, and I squinted into the blackness in time to see the prettiest girl from Henry Clay High School inches away. Katelyn launched herself toward me, nearly knocking me back out of the entrance.

"Wow, what a greeting," I said as she wrapped her arms around my waist.

"Where have you been? I was worried about you."

"You didn't hear?" I asked, wondering why she was simply missing me rather than on high alert about the helicopter soldiers. "You know, about the helicopters?"

"I heard 'em." Her eyebrows pinched together as she studied my face like a painting. I hoped more like an outdoorsy print than some kind of angular modern art masterpiece. "Nobody said anything but stay inside…but you look, I dunno…worried."

"I was." I had grown less worried about hiding my feelings around Katelyn, and volunteered, "It scared the crap out of me, you know, to think they might be coming your way."

"They didn't sound that close. What's up?"

"It wasn't the usual choppers. These had soldiers all geared up, hanging out the sides like they were ready to jump or rappel down or something."

"Oh, dang. That's serious." Katelyn released me, and shot a look across the cave toward the back corner.

Gathered around a table made of plastic tubs, I saw my mom talking to Katelyn's. Both of them looked like safari guides in their matching khaki outfits. The only thing missing was a wide-brimmed hat.

"Huh. They really don't tell you anything."

"That's what I've been trying to say." She spun around to face me, but ended up looking past my shoulder. "And who the heck's with you?"

"You didn't hear about that either."

"No," Katelyn huffed. "And I'm getting sick of it too. This babying crap has gotta stop." She stepped away from me, her eyes shooting daggers across the cave at her mother.

"Easy, babe," I said, and immediately regretted it. I grabbed her wrist to spin her back around to try to calm her down, and came face to face with the prettiest brown eyes—only they'd turned as dark as her mood.

"Don't tell me to calm down," she snapped.

"I know better than that." I could relate. No one liked being told what to do. I hated it when my parents did it. The whole group was no big fan of our corrupt government trying to boss us around either. So I tried to soften the blow. "Look, I get that you're pissed. We went through the same deal when this all started, when our folks wouldn't tell us anything. They were always like I'll tell you later, or not now, or…you know. At least mine were."

"Mine too. And now it's back the way it used to be. A couple camps get hit, and they think they have to lock me in my bedroom." She huffed. "As if I actually had one of those."

"Yeah, it sucks. If it wasn't for the extra patrols, I'd never get out of this place."

"That doesn't make it any easier."

"No, but ...I mean you can't blame them for being worried."

"Everyone's worried, Zach. It doesn't do me any good to be stuck in here." She looked back at the adults, and added, "I'm having it out with them now."

"You might want to wait a second," I said. "They need to talk to the new guys."

"And who are they?"

"The camo guy is from another camp. He goes by Spotted Owl."

"Of course," Katelyn said. "That won't be at all confusing."

"Look on the bright side. I guess that makes him your, uhm...uncle?"

"Very funny, Sunny Boy."

"I try. And that's *Sunning* Boy to you," I shot back at her play on my mom's code name.

"More like Sunning Cub...and she still treats you like a baby too."

I failed at hiding a grin. "I like it when you're sassy."

"I try," she parroted, and slipped her hand into mine. I squeezed it, and brought it to my lips. Her dark eyes finally lightened after a soft kiss on the back of her hand—or maybe I was just hoping.

Nevertheless, she wasn't fully calmed down. "So who's the dude in the brown coat?"

"That one's a little trickier."

I paused uncomfortably, causing Katelyn to ask, "How so?"

"He says he's a deserter from the Army. I stopped him at the roadblock."

Her eyes widened. "You did?"

"Well, yeah," I replied, getting a little swagger going to mask any lingering concerns. "Your brother took off to get a turkey, and this guy comes up on me while he was gone."

"Came up on you, did he?" Her subtle, dimpled grin warmed me more quickly than any bonfire. "Like he surprised you. Like you were sleeping on watch."

"Hey, I wouldn't do that."

"Right. This from the guy who doesn't get out of bed until noon."

"You been talking to my mother again? Maybe you do need to get out of here more often." She opened her mouth to object, but my thoughts shifted gears quicker. "Oh, babe! I've gotta tell you something."

She mashed a finger over my mouth. "Shh, they're gonna hear you."

"Good call, 'cause this is serious."

"What?" She raised up on her tiptoes, bringing her ear level with my mouth. "This sounds good. Tell me."

"We're sneaking out tonight," I whispered. Her brow furrowed again. Before she could object, I told her the rest of the plan. "I found this awesome creek today. You remember when we used to gather water?"

"How could I forget?" she purred, obviously recalling the times we'd done a little more than filling a few pails of clean water. "It's been at least a couple weeks since I've gotten to go that far."

I knew she meant leaving the cave, but I couldn't resist a little flirting when she was standing there looking so good in tight jeans and a sweater. "We can go as far as you like."

"Hush," she said, her rounded cheeks blushing. "You know-"

"I'm kidding, babe. Well, sorta."

"So tonight, a creek. Sounds cold, but I'll bet you've got a way to warm me up."

I wrapped my arm around her waist and pulled her close. "There's something else I want to show you. There's this awesome waterfall-"

"Waterfall? Why you gotta be a jerk?" She harrumphed and turned her back on me. "You're always picking on me."

"I didn't mean it that way." I reached for her and tried to coax her into turning around. "C'mon, babe. I was just thinking it was time, you know, for us to get outta here for a while."

"Yeah, we've been over that," she deadpanned. "I wouldn't count on it now that we have visitors. Mom will be all freaked out that you even brought them here."

"We can still slip away. Not for long." I flashed a quick grin. "What could be more romantic?"

"Not a waterfall. Like I'd really want to be reminded of Jonas unconscious on the rocks, or my leg twisted up like a pretzel."

"You can't blame yourself for Jonas. Besides, it wasn't that bad," I said. "But alright, we'll forget the falls. There's still a pretty sweet stream out there. Not too far." I raised an eyebrow in a failed seductive look. "Full moon tonight."

"Mom's not gonna let us leave."

"Probably not. That's why I mentioned sneaking out."

"With strangers, and soldiers on helicopters, and all that…"

I shook my head. "Yeah, I get it. Thanks for killing my joy."

"It's not that I don't want to go." She squeezed my hand. "I'd be happy going to get water."

"I heard that. So let's work on that plan instead."

"Deal." She leaned in to nuzzle her head against my shoulder, but only for a second. "Now tell me more about those strangers."

"The clean-shaven guy in the brown jacket, that's Noel. He said something about big plans that he needed to tell our leaders about."

"What kind of big plans?"

"He wouldn't say. It was real vague. Something about how he needed to talk to the adults, but I'm not sure that I trust him."

"Trust no one, right?"

"Exactly." I looked across the cave and found both sets of our parents gathered around the new arrivals. Noel seemed shrunken back a little as the others trained a withering fire of questions and sharp glances in his direction.

"I'm not really sure about that guy. Drone flights and the helicopters all came outta nowhere as soon as he showed up," I said, but the look on Katelyn's face made me immediately change my tune. I didn't want her to worry. "Anyway, I'm sure that's all a coincidence. I really kinda wonder if he was just saying that because he needed a place to stay, like he was trying to trade something."

"That's how this whole thing works," Katelyn said. "We get along with the others by trading supplies, information."

"Yeah, the barter system. Dad says that's the way the new republic is going to have to rise until things get all sorted out. Kinda like twenty-first century people living a pioneer's life."

"Can't say that I'm a big fan of all that." Katelyn pulled on my hand to slowly lead me over to the adults. "Anyway, I'd like to hear more of what this guy has to say."

"Judging by the scowl on your mom, you might not want to know."

"She's always like that."

"Not this bad."

Right on cue, Katelyn's mom took off running for the front of the cave. She locked eyes with Katelyn. "Did you see your father? We need to stop him." She kept running, and over her shoulder called, "Find John too. Hurry!"

"Okay, yeah," Katelyn whispered to me. "That's a total freak out. Definitely bad news."

CHAPTER 7

"John was right with us," I told Katelyn, though she seemed to have no interest in finding her brother.

"I hadn't even noticed my pops had left too." She shrugged. "I thought they were all together a second ago."

"He has a way of blending into a crowd," I blurted. Fortunately, she took no offense at my unintentional jab at her relatively boring father. It's not like mine was any more exciting. Apparently it was just something about accountants, at least according to our mothers.

Before I could change the subject, Katelyn took off toward the back of the cave. I followed behind. My mom and dad were the only ones left gathered around the table of plastic tubs. Noel and Spotted Owl sat on collapsible camp chairs behind them. A small solar-powered lantern lit up a well-worn map spread out on the makeshift tabletop.

"This looks serious." I nodded my head toward Noel. "So I guess he told you guys the big secret or whatever."

"Yeah, you could say that," my mom said.

She stepped around the tubs to give me a quick embrace. I held up a hand to try to stop her, but she was her usual unrelenting self.

"I'm so proud of my big boy," she gushed.

"Jeez, Ma. Stop." I pulled out of her grip, and jumped behind Katelyn as a blocker for my overprotective mother. "You're so embarrassing."

"I'm just proud. Leave it to my boy to bring home the first prisoner. That's great work."

"Prisoner?" I said, and quickly turned to Noel. He watched us, but remained quiet back in the shadows.

The deserter certainly didn't look like he was being treated like a captive, but I knew my mother had a way of overemphasizing my accomplishments. My dad had never been one to cheerlead or praise me at my peewee soccer games and tee-ball, but my mother's voice could be heard from three fields over. Thus, my athletic career ended at a very early age.

"You know what I mean," she replied. "You subdued him and brought him in."

"I guess I sorta did do that," I agreed, "but the whole subdued thing might be a bit of a stretch."

Katelyn poked me in the side, and I flinched so hard I nearly fell to the ground.

"That's my hero," she beamed, obviously more playful than serious.

I shot her an icy stare that quickly turned into a chuckle as she came after my fleshy sides with the dreaded tickle fingers.

"Stop it," I pleaded, failing at being manly as I playfully slapped her hands away.

A narrow-eyed stare from my mother put an end to any joking around. I fell in next to Katelyn and zipped my lips.

"Busted." She snickered, and I bumped her with my shoulder to quiet her down.

"So, Mom…" I paused for a second to erase the untimely grin. "What's up with Mrs. Jennings?"

My mom looked to Katelyn. "Your dad went up the mountain a minute to, uhm…get a signal."

"What for?" I asked. "And what about John?"

"Sort of a change of plans, so John was gonna go run after him and bring him back."

"Alright, I'm confused." I looked from Katelyn back at my mom. "So, Sunning Bear…you gonna explain this, or do we have to stay in the dark?" I waved an arm around the cave. "Pun intended."

"Good one," Noel said out of the blue, reminding me that he was actually close enough to hear us when I raised my voice.

As I stared at Noel and Spotted Owl wondering how the two played into this, Katelyn continued with the interrogation for me. "So, uhm…would you please tell us what's up?"

"Your dad was going to raise the other camps, hon. We've kinda got something big to discuss."

"What's wrong with right here?" I asked. "You guys never needed to climb the mountain before."

"You need kind of a direct line of sight to use the walkies," she explained, albeit cryptically.

I frowned. It took me a moment, but I figured out what she meant. "And you need to talk to the camps on the other side of the mountain." I gestured with my hand toward the back of the cave which, through the depth of the mountain, was in an easterly direction. "You mean the camps behind us…in North Carolina." I paused when I realized what that meant. "And that's rare. Very rare."

Sunning Bear nodded.

"So what's going on?" Katelyn asked. All trace of hilarity had long since disappeared from her soft voice.

My mother looked to my dad. "Harold, what do you think?"

"It's your call, but I'd tell them," he said before I could jump in and plead my case.

"Fine."

I didn't like the way my mom's eyes shifted to the roof of the cave. Before she spoke, she ushered me and Katelyn off to the side away from the new arrivals. In a hushed voice, she said, "If we can verify what these guys are telling us, there's been a bit of a change in plans."

Katelyn's voiced dripped with kindness as she said, "You mentioned that."

"We have plans?" I wisecracked. Even when my mom narrowed her eyes at me, I didn't let up. "I thought we were just hanging out eating powdered eggs and pretty much trying to stay alive."

"Very funny, mister."

"I'm just saying that it's not like we're doing much. After the big trip into town, it's like we've been sitting around here hiding out." I looked over at my dad. The low light wasn't kind to him. I was suddenly struck by the way he seemed to have aged a dozen years over the last four months. "What happened to Dad's rebellion, or whatever it is?"

"We've made a few other trips to town. We've been making contacts with the other groups. It takes time to build up a trust level."

"Apparently a lot of time."

My mom didn't disagree. Instead, she said, "I'd say things are about to get a whole lot more interesting from here on out."

"Ma, please. Enough with not answering the question." I brought out Dad's favorite line, and added, "It's like you're a politician or something."

"Fine. Here's the deal. It's sort of a weird coincidence that both these guys show up on the exact same day, each with a little piece of a story. When we put the two together, especially along with everything else, I get the feeling that we're going to stay plenty busy the next few days."

Katelyn shook my hand, and I looked down to realize I'd tightened my grip unknowingly. "Sorry, babe," I mouthed, and watched with regret as she slipped her hand from mine and massaged her fingers.

Taking a deep breath, I turned back to my mother. "Just spill it. Please stop being so cryptic."

"I'm getting to it, kiddo."

Before she could, Katelyn's mom came hurrying back toward us with her dad and brother in tow. John seemed less happy to follow, seeing how he shared a lot of the leadership qualities of his mother.

"I didn't quite…get there in time." She was so winded that she needed to stop to catch her breath in the middle. "But it worked out okay. We have corroboration."

"Really?" Sunning Bear replied. "I guess I mean to say I thought it would check out. Spotted Owl seems legit."

"Yeah, we got three others to say pretty much the exact same thing," Katelyn's dad said. "It's definitely time to make a move."

"Then it's settled," my mom said. "Ready or not, we convene the War Council tonight."

Saliva caught in the back of my throat, and I choked myself trying to swallow it down. The adults shot me annoyed looks, but I was more worried about breathing than creating a disturbance. Katelyn patted me gently on the back until the wracking coughs ended, and I sucked in a deep breath of dank cave air. It was yet another thing I disliked about our dungeon-like home.

"Did she just say what I think she said?" Katelyn whispered.

I grabbed for her hand, but made a conscious effort to not squeeze it to death like a python. "Yeah, and this can't be good." I paused to reconsider. "Well, you know what I mean."

"I think so." She offered me a sad smile.

When I finally focused back in on the adults' conversation, I heard my dad saying, "The best defense is a good offense. You keep coming after them. You keep the ball in the red zone, and hammer away until you wear 'em out. Control the clock. Uhm…and whatever else the announcer guys are always saying."

"Oh, Harold," my mom said. "You don't have to pretend like you watch sports. Nobody out here cares about that stuff."

"Ouch," I whispered under my breath. The way she could cut my dad down in front of the others was an art form. But he never took it badly. Instead, he usually let the comments roll right off him—unless the antagonist held contrary opinions on treasury bills, interest rates, or the freedoms guaranteed by the Constitution. The Constitution that had basically been suspended by the new regime, as he often explained, in the name of law and order. Only the law was corrupt and order enforced by a police force so oppressive that ordinary citizens feared for their lives—just like me and my family.

Though I had practically begged for action, the idea of some kind of offensive set me on edge. I knew the risks of going into town to face the soldiers. We'd nearly lost Katelyn's mom in our earlier foray into Gatlinburg, as well as several others.

As I focused back in on the adults, I heard Spotted Owl saying, "Harold is right, Sunning Bear. We need a preemptive strike."

I'd always wondered why my dad hadn't been worthy of a code name. I supposed it had something to do with the prepper forums that my mom frequented. For all I knew, she actually administered several of them.

To my detriment, Dad had always been slightly less concerned about anonymity, which led to him losing his job and the federal agents showing up to raid our house and threaten him with imprisonment.

I had also always wondered why they hadn't locked my father away. They'd taken him in to their offices a few times, but he'd always come back home a few hours later. Apparently, he was a master at hiding his most inflammatory work under aliases, and encrypting all the files on his computers. So there was never anything damaging enough to pin on him.

In person, he was a soft-spoken, humble bookkeeper, who probably didn't trigger enough alarm bells to make them want to rough him up. Lucky for him, he'd never put up a fight. That might have ended horribly.

Then I realized what we were about to do. It was one thing to hide in the woods—and become a hero like I had today, I thought with pretend pride. Going on some kind of mission sounded dangerous, especially given how it had something to do with the strangers.

But I wouldn't be left behind again. Our parents had gone into Gatlinburg without us, so Katelyn and I had luckily followed them and arrived in time to save the day. I wasn't about to wait behind with the little kids again.

A newfound confidence stirred in my chest. Tugging Katelyn forward, we stood side by side with the adults. As soon as I heard what we were up against, I wished I was back on babysitting duty.

CHAPTER 8

"Cherokee?" Katelyn's shoulders were hunched so far over I thought she resembled my grandmother. "We're seriously going to North Carolina. That was a shocker."

I steered her over toward her pallet, and let her sink onto the air mattress. Settling in next to her, I wrapped her thin, cartoony sleeping bag around her shoulders and chuckled. Princesses and ponies were totally out of place in the war camp. Unicorns would've almost been fitting seeing how it felt like an extreme fairy tale land.

"This is bad, Zach," she said, and leaned her shoulder against mine.

I wanted to encourage her, but couldn't lie. Finally, I settled on, "At least we'll be prepared this time."

"For what?" came a high-pitched voice from behind us.

I spun around to find my baby sister, Maddie. Granted she was only two years younger, but I'd always thought of her as a little girl. Perhaps because she often acted the part, or she had until recently.

Camp life had been good on her. She wasn't wearing heavy layers of makeup anymore, especially the dark eye shadow. Her black hair was still shiny, though more of a raven tone than the unnatural purple. Like our father, she'd aged about ten years as well. Unlike him, it suited her nicely.

"What's up, guys?" she asked, settling next to me on the air mattress. Thankfully, she was still rail thin; otherwise I might've been concerned that she'd pop it. Then Katelyn would've really been hating life.

"Not much, sis."

"Yeah, right." She leaned across me to look at my hunched over girlfriend. "Are you crying?"

"No, Mad." Her sad eyes had no trace of tears. That didn't surprise me. She was as drama-free as any girl I'd ever met, and not one to turn on the tears in any situation, even if they were deserved. "It's just that things kinda got real for a second."

"Sounds like every day to me." Maddie switched sides to go wrap an arm around her.

"I'm not one of your kids," Katelyn told her sharply. "I don't need watching over."

Maddie's dark eyes pinched to slits, but she didn't let go. Apparently realizing what she had done, Katelyn twisted to give her a hug. "I'm sorry, Mads. That was really nice of you."

"I'm here for you," she said, which seemed preposterous to me given how she was better suited to babysitting kindergartners than hanging out with people closer to her own age.

Katelyn disagreed with my assessment. "Thanks. You're the best."

"No problem." Maddie patted her on the back while I sat there feeling useless.

"Your whole family is so great," Katelyn said, straightening up. "If we had to be stuck here with anybody, I'm glad it was with you guys."

"Except for maybe Austin," I said.

"That's true," Maddie agreed. "Where is our brother?"

"I dunno. I thought he'd be all up in the planning. He loves the idea of a good fight."

"Fight?" Maddie asked, and I cringed. I hadn't planned on telling my sister about the mission, but I'd really screwed that up. Then again, I thought she had every right to know.

I kept quiet, reverting back to my initial concern that maybe she wouldn't handle it so well. There was no sense getting her worked up. But the more I thought about it, the more I saw how I was treating her exactly the way our parents treated me, and I hated being talked to like a child. Still, I could easily rationalize it. Maddie was younger, more fragile, and far better suited to watching kids than fighting a war.

By the time I was done playing a mental tennis match over whether I should spill the details, Katelyn had already launched into the whole story.

"Are you serious?" Maddie asked. "We're going to North Carolina?"

"You're not," I interrupted.

"I didn't think I was." Maddie focused back in on Katelyn. Her voice barely rose about a whisper as she asked Katelyn, "How long will you be gone?"

"I don't think I'm going either."

"Cool. We can hang out while all the adults are gone."

"You're okay with this?" I asked, shocked once again at my sister. She'd come a long way from the sniveling kid stuck in the back seat of our Jeep while our parents raced us into the mountains ahead of the coming storm.

"I know my place," Maddie said. "I'm more use here." She looked me in the eyes, and a crooked smile appeared. "You think I don't worry, but I'm terrified. It just doesn't help for the kids to know that."

"Wow, Sis. That's…uhm-"

"That's what I do. Speaking of which, I need to get the afternoon activities going. You leave these monsters alone too long, and the Feds will be able to hear us from a mile away."

I noticed the background hum of younger voices had grown while we'd talked to Maddie. Feet scuffed on the cave floor as the grade school kids rushed around, playing tag and hide-and-seek around people's gear. The first time one of them knocked something over, the parents would flip out.

Maddie hopped up off the mattress and scurried away to round up the kids.

"Huh. She took that well," Katelyn said.

"Surprisingly. That was kinda the way I expected Austin to react...well with a little more swagger and big talk."

"Yeah, he'll want to take on the whole army himself."

"He thinks he's some kind of super spy secret agent or something." I couldn't resist taking a shot at my older brother even though he wasn't there to hear it. "But I'm the first one to bring back a prisoner. How cool is that?"

"You're my hero." Katelyn slugged me on the shoulder. "Just don't get too brave when you take off for Cherokee."

"No danger of that." I shrugged. "You know I don't want you getting hurt, but I kinda wish you were going too. I can't believe your folks would make you stay here."

"Maybe they'll change their mind." She looked across the cave at the adults, who remained deep in conversation. "I'll talk to 'em again when they don't look so busy."

"Are you..." I let the question fizzle out. No one liked to be asked if they were sure of their decisions. She didn't need me pushing her, and so I changed the subject, just not to anything more cheerful. "Anyway, can you believe this is happening? I guess I knew we'd have to go on the offensive in a big way sometime, but who knew it'd be against the whole army? I thought we'd just do more raids on towns and have some rallies or something. I never planned on taking on a base. Like a well-protected base crawling with soldiers."

"I don't like it any more than you do, but it sounds like we don't have a choice."

"Not really. I was kinda doubting when Noel said the Feds are staging to make a big raid on the park, but then to have Spotted Owl pretty much say the same thing."

"And then my folks on the radio," Katelyn added.

"Yeah, it's serious alright." I thought about what it meant for troops to be massing outside Cherokee, and had to almost chuckle at the ridiculous thought that came to mind.

"What's so funny?"

"There's a Visitor Center by Cherokee, and these thugs are pretty much sitting right there, probably right by the welcome sign. It's like come on in and visit the park, soldiers. Have a nice look around."

Katelyn didn't laugh. Instead, she asked, "You've been over to Cherokee before?"

"Oh, yeah. A few times, back before all this. There's some buildings at the Visitor Center area, which is a lot like the Sugarlands one by Gatlinburg. The town of Cherokee's a lot smaller, but there's the same kind of restaurants and shops. Just not as many, or as many hotels."

"Sounds like a repeat of the Gatlinburg raid," Katelyn said.

"Sort of. Only we need to bust up the soldiers' camp, not steal supplies from the town."

Understandably, Katelyn grew quiet.

The sun had already crested overhead, and began dropping down behind the mountain we sheltered under, plunging the cave rapidly into an early darkness. Adding in how the changing of seasons was giving us fewer minutes of sunlight every day, the more I felt trapped. People had talked about winter bringing on depression, and I was finally beginning to understand what they'd meant.

"So much for sneaking out tonight," she whispered.

"We could go now," I said hopefully. "Go, uhm, gather some water before this big war council thing."

"You'd like that." She smiled, and lay back on the mattress. "I would too, but…"

I nodded. Under my breath, I cursed my bad luck again.

Still sitting next to her, I watched as Katelyn tucked her arms behind her head and stared back at me.

As badly as I wanted to stretch out next to her, I knew that could get me in more trouble than the enemy. Our old-fashioned parents would come unglued at the two of us lying together, especially in front of all the children.

Neither of our parents had shown any objection to the two of us being a couple, but mostly in the platonic sense. Like a school dance, we had to keep at least a short distance between ourselves no matter how deeply I felt for her. We'd grown so close in the last several months, but sitting next to each other was as far as we were supposed to go—particularly in public.

My mom's voice called out from across the cave. "Zach! Come here."

I didn't move for a moment, not wanting to leave Katelyn alone.

"You better go before she starts yelling again," she suggested.

"What's new about that?" My mom had always been a yeller. Back in my house, whether I was up in my room or across from her on the other couch, she always had her volume set too high. When she wasn't looking, Dad would pick up the television remote and pretend to hit the mute button. He had been incredibly lucky that she'd never seen it.

"Zach!"

"Guess I better go. She's only gonna get louder."

"Holy crap. She gets louder than that?"

"Yeah, it's not pretty." I patted Katelyn on the leg, and resisted the urge to lean over and kiss her. "I'll be back."

"I'll be napping," she said with a wink. "But come back anyway. If I don't get to go, there's no way you're leaving without saying goodbye."

Little did she know how our plans would change.

CHAPTER 9

"We'll meet some of the other folks from my camp tonight," Spotted Owl told the assembled group. "You might remember some of them from the forums. There's Wood Duck, Box Turtle, Golden Eagle, and Field Mouse."

"Field Mouse?" my dad said. "That name doesn't exactly inspire confidence."

"That's exactly what we need. Small, quick, and able to sneak into tight places. I'd say she's the perfect one for the job."

"She?" my mom noted. "I like that."

"So like I've said, we've verified most of Noel's claims." Spotted Owl gestured with his head toward the deserter in the corner. Noel watched with interest, but kept his lips pinched in a thin line. "Mouse has already been into Cherokee a couple times, and there's definitely been more activity. Before the night is over, she'll know if they really are stockpiling temporary bridges and massing troops by the city."

"Still seems like a huge waste of manpower to me," Katelyn's mom said. "There have to be bigger targets than a bunch of scattered groups hiding out in a giant park."

"They're there," Noel said. "They need to get the highway back open."

"That makes sense," Spotted Owl replied to Spotted Fawn. "When we closed that road, it's put them in a bind. They've literally gotta drive hours out of the way to get around the park." He pointed to the map. "The road from Cherokee to

Gatlinburg is the only way through, when it was open. It was only a matter of time before they made a serious effort to clear out the roadblocks."

"And they'll do it with overwhelming force," my mom added. "I wouldn't want to try to fix all those bridges and push out the downed timber without a whole army. It would be too easy for us to pick off a few little groups of soldiers at a time."

"So they moved the troops out of Fort Bragg," Noel said. "My unit was coming up to join them. They've got temporary bridges, probably a whole mechanized battalion."

Although I had an idea what he meant, I asked, "Mechanized?"

"Armored Personnel Carriers or Infantry Fighting Vehicles…whatever you want to call 'em," Spotted Owl told me, then turned back to the group. "So we need to stop them before they get started. Mouse will get us the intel. I'll gather the troops, and we'll move out tomorrow." He looked around the assembled group with grim anticipation. "Any objections?"

"We're onboard," my mom said. "You, Spotted Fawn?"

Katelyn's mom nodded firmly. "Yep. We don't have a choice."

Mom looked at me. "We'll still need to watch the roadblocks in case they try to insert troops by chopper. We'll need to leave people behind to watch them while the rest of us head out."

"Wait…you want me to do that?" I deduced. I shouldn't have been surprised that they would leave me behind, though I'd obviously assumed they would need the help in the big fight.

"And Katelyn," Spotted Fawn added, which didn't surprise me about them wanting to leave her behind. It was more the part that I could be with her unsupervised. The last time they'd allowed that, we were practically strangers, at least in their eyes.

For a second, I liked the idea of staying with Katelyn, but my attitude quickly darkened. I shouldn't have minded a cushy, but semi-important, job; however, their suggestion turned to anger.

"You know that didn't work out so great when you left us last time." I looked to my mother with pleading eyes. "You said that wouldn't happen again."

"Someone needs to watch the roads. You want Maddie to do it?"

I couldn't stifle a laugh. "Yeah, right. Be serious."

"Austin's not doing it either," my mom said before I could ask.

"What about the Olsens?" I asked. "They're pretty useless."

"Zachary!" Mom shot a glance across the cave, but the stern look faded as soon as she locked eyes on Katelyn's former neighbors. Softly, she said, "You have a point there. Those two really haven't been pulling their weight."

Spotted Fawn didn't stick up for them. "I've been thinking that too. Glad someone else saw that." She leaned across the table, focusing on my mom. "But can we trust them to actually watch the roads? They'll probably be sleeping out there."

"No worse than Zach," John said with a grin.

"Hey!"

"I'm just kiddin', bud."

"Good, 'cause I'm the first one to bring back a captive. Remember?"

"Oh, jeez." My mom buried her face in her hands." "I'm gonna regret saying that."

Dad agreed. "Yeah, you know he's gonna milk that for all it's worth."

"Like going on this trip," Spotted Owl said. He focused his dark eyes on me as if sizing me up. I straightened to my full height and stared back with equal intensity. "And I'd say we could use him." He looked to Spotted Fawn. "We're gonna need every able body we can muster, including your daughter."

Until that moment, I wasn't sure if a person could feel proud and sick to their stomach at the same time.

"Go grab your gear," Spotted Owl told the group. "After supper we're heading off to my camp."

I nodded numbly and tried not to think about what I'd just volunteered for. Both of us, in a sense. I knew life would've been so much easier back on the roadblock. Perfectly boring, most likely, and with Katelyn by my side. We could've had our quiet time together without even having to sneak away.

I walked over to Katelyn to break the news, and mumbled under my breath, "I'm an idiot."

"Maybe," she said with a smile. "Why this time?"

"Getting volunteered to take on the whole army. That's about as dumb as it gets."

"You never back down from a fight," Katelyn told me as we walked toward my bunk. "That's why I don't argue with you. You always have to win."

"That's not true."

"Well, I do like to argue too. You got me there. But you most definitely don't like to lose."

"I'll give you that." I blew out a frustrated breath. "But now I've got you coming along with us. You should go back and tell 'em you want to stay here."

"I get to go with you?" she said, sounding excited at the prospect.

"Yeah. I'm sorry. I shouldn't have said anything."

"Wow, it's just…I didn't expect that. Not at all." Her eyes brightened. "I'm sick of staying here."

"You could go watch a roadblock. It's way safer."

"No way. I'm coming with you."

I didn't give up on trying to convince her to stay behind. "They're gonna have the Olsens watch the road. You should do that. Those two are worthless."

"You're not arguing, are you?" A sly grin crept across her face.

I mirrored the look, and stifled a laugh. "I guess so…which means you're staying, 'cause I always get to win."

"Does not," she shot back.

"How do you figure that?"

"I only said you like to win, not that you always win." Before I could object, she added, "And you already got your win today. Thanks to you, we're taking on the whole army."

CHAPTER 10

"Let's move out," Spotted Owl commanded with a wave.

To my surprise, my mom had seemingly ceded control of the group to the burly, steady-handed rebel from a camp over on the other side of the state line. Into the fading light, we rolled out in single file with Spotted Owl taking the lead. My mom was right behind him. Spotted Fawn followed her. The two dads and Noel were right behind them.

I brought up the rear with Katelyn, with Austin in front of me. He was already grumbling about being stuck in the back, and also a fair amount about the hike. Austin would've made the perfect helicopter insertion trooper. He was all about getting to the fight, but not the actual work involved in getting there.

"Someone has to watch the rear," I told my older brother. "You want to take over?"

"I belong up front with the doers, not back here with the slackers." He harrumphed. "So much for being the leading edge of the spear. I got the shaft."

"I heard you liked it," Katelyn wisecracked, causing me to laugh uproariously.

Dad whirled around. "Keep it down back there."

Austin was too busy working on a retort, and failing. "Shut your face, stick boy," he finally said with a growl.

"I didn't say it," I protested.

"Hey. That's not cool." Katelyn nudged me. "Way to stick up for me."

"He won't hit you," I replied.

"You afraid of him?" she whispered once Austin had turned around to face the front.

Austin grumbled something again. I opened my mouth and had to pinch it back shut as Dad laid into the both of us, threatening to leave us behind if we couldn't get along. I assumed our father should've known that was practically impossible, but I was more concerned why he had snapped at us. That was unusual. Discipline was Mom's job, which implied he was edgier, and perhaps more worried about the mission than I'd expected.

"Keep complaining and you can go keep Pops company," I whispered to him once our father's chastising was over. "Wouldn't want you to be stuck back here with the hero."

Katelyn sighed, no doubt having already grown tired of the bragging. Austin wasn't smart enough to keep quiet.

"Oh, whatever," he hollered, and was promptly moved up front closer to our mother.

"Ha, it worked," I whispered to Katelyn.

"Are you about done with that hero business?"

"Oh, yeah. I was totally joking." My voice grew even softer. "If you'd been there, you'd know there was nothing heroic about what happened."

"Whatever happened, it's worked out for the best." She ducked under a mass of dense vegetation as the trail narrowed up into an indistinguishable path. As she handed the branch back to me, she couldn't help but notice my frown. "Not that this whole going to war thing is some kind of picnic. But I guess it was something we really needed to know."

"That's true."

I took a moment to check through the thick canopy at the blackening sky. The last few minutes of dusk remained before we would be pushed into darkness. Fortunately, the sky remained clear. The moon had hit full bloom a couple days before, and would provide enough light to make it through the forest. Or so I hoped.

We slipped off the side of a mountain into a narrow valley. It was wooded as densely as what we'd hiked so far. Possibly more so. After another twenty paces, the tiny footpath dwindled away until there wasn't a trace of a game trail, much less any hint of civilization.

"Glad he knows where he's going," I whispered.

Having looked at the map before we left, I knew we were headed down to the main road, then skirting along a highway a good six miles before we took off toward a rocky-topped spine named Thomas Ridge.

Six miles in daylight should've only taken maybe two hours. Three at the most on a hot, uphill climb. It seemed to me like we'd hiked half the night before we made it to the highway.

We struck off along the road, staying on the gravel shoulder so we could scatter into the woods at a moment's notice. Muted chatter from the adults didn't travel all the way back to my position at the end of the line. All I could hear was the crunching of gravel under our boots, which wasn't any quieter than the crinkling of dried leaves that had plagued my ears for the whole first part of our hike.

"Sucks that we blew all these bridges," Austin grumbled as we stopped short of the first of several stream crossings. A thirty foot expanse at least fifteen feet deep cut through the roadway like a miniature chasm. There was no getting straight down into the creek without ropes for rappelling.

"And now they're coming back to fix them," Spotted Owl said. "But we kept them outta here a long time. I'd say job well done."

"Whatever," Austin said, not one to be contradicted. Apparently, that trait ran deep within our family.

"We never went this far east," my mom said as we huddled underneath the shadowy tree canopy that had to be taller than the roof of our two-story house back in the suburbs. "How many more miles until Cherokee?"

"A long ways. If we were gonna keep goin' on to town, there's at least ten more miles to go, and a whole lotta roadblocks. No worries, though." Spotted Owl flashed a thumbs up. "We've got pretty good teamwork for a bunch of strangers."

"That's true," Spotted Fawn agreed. "We've worked well together, if always camped apart."

"Until now. Y'all get to spend the night at my place for a little Carolina hospitality. But that comes later." Spotted Owl motioned off to the side of the highway. "We can slide off the road here, and cut through the woods to get around the bridge. The stream narrows about forty yards up that way."

"Up the hill," I muttered under my breath.

We slid down the road slope into the woods, and found a rocky ditch at the bottom of the viney, brambly slope. Spotted Owl led us immediately back up, hopping around protruding boulders as he climbed as steadily as a mountain goat. I figured the big man could've easily scaled down the canyon where the bridge had been, and assumed he only took us this way because he didn't trust our climbing skills. And that was fine with me. I didn't trust my climbing abilities on slick, vertical slopes either.

The sound of gurgling water materialized into a steep stream moments later. Water poured down the rocky staircase, generated a spray much like a small waterfall.

I considering sharing my thoughts with Katelyn, but ended up keeping them to myself. Having been touchy about Jonas before, I had a feeling she might take it the wrong way.

To my surprise, Katelyn sidled up next to me and said, "I could fall again…maybe fake an injury here." Her brown eyes twinkled in the moonlight as she pointed up the hill. "Maybe have a little quiet time over there, by that little falls."

"Oh, man. Wouldn't that be great?" I whispered, but my mom interrupted the moment.

"Keep up, kids. You guys have been dragging."

That didn't sit well with me. "What? Says you."

"That's right," Mom chided. "You're being lazy."

My face got hotter than a firecracker, but it was a totally different reason from the moment before. "Dude, that's bull-"

Katelyn mashed a hand over my mouth to keep me from saying something I might regret.

"We're coming," she replied. After a warning glance, she uncovered my big mouth to grab me by the hand. "C'mon, slacker."

"Okay, great. Use Austin's nickname," I shot back, but quickly bit back on the anger. "That's real funny, Katie."

"Ooh, the nickname. You must be pissed."

"Not at you." I struggled at putting my thoughts into words. I wasn't sure if I was more upset about missing out on the alone time, or being labeled a slacker when we'd been doing perfectly fine keeping up. If anyone was a problem child, I was sure it had to be Austin.

The way I figured it, Mom was probably just worried about the job ahead. That thought only served to make me more concerned about what we were getting into.

"C'mon, babe." As if she was reading my mind, Katelyn added, "I was just kidding about stopping."

"I know, and that's what makes it worse."

"Then fine. I won't try to lighten the mood."

"Nah, you're welcome to try. I'm just a bit, uhm, edgy."

"A bit, huh?" She picked out a path across the stream, and tugged me toward it. "Follow me, hero."

"Whatever." I debated pushing her into the water; playfully, of course. In addition to hearing both sets of our parents freak out, I decided against it when I wiped the back of my free hand across my forehead. The mist from the waterfall had settled in like cold dew. The stream water would be icy at best. There was no way I would do that to her. Had it still been summertime, it was almost a given—especially if we had been alone.

"You daydreaming?" Katelyn asked, catching me with a goofy grin.

"Maybe."

She urged me along, erasing the look from my face. We hustled down the slope and caught up to the others at the edge of the road only to have my mother turn around and give me another annoyed glance.

I bit down on my lower lip to stifle a retort, and took Katelyn's hand. She slowed ever so slightly so I could come up alongside her on the gravel.

"Why they gotta pick on me when Austin's always the one complaining?"

"Who's complaining now?" she replied, but softened the jab with a squeeze of the hand.

"Yeah, yeah."

"I know what you mean. It's like you always say…he's the favorite."

"But I have no idea why."

"First born son," she suggested. "Look at John. My parents let him do everything."

"He's the only son," I replied, "and like ten years older than you."

"More like eight." She kicked at a loose rock on the shoulder sending it off into the woods with a leafy crash. "Oops."

"They're gonna blame me," I said right as my mother turned around to scowl at me again.

"At least they know you're here," Katelyn said after my mom had spun back around. "The middle child is supposed to be the forgotten one."

"And then there's Maddie." I picked up the pace to a brisk walk along the side of the road.

"Don't you dare say anything bad about her."

"Oh, really?" I tugged on her arm like a slingshot, and cut ahead of her. "I almost forgot you guys were best buds."

"So? I like her." Katelyn was frowning as she caught up to walk next to me. "Besides, I'm the one stuck in camp all day. I have to have someone to talk to when you're not around."

"Anyone but my sister would be nice."

"She's not so bad, Zach."

"I know. I'm just kidding." I watched my brother moping along behind my parents and grunted. "I like her way better than Austin."

"I know. Anyway…we should change the subject," Katelyn suggested.

The sound of pounding of gravel, the aching in my feet, and heavy thoughts about the unknown future were all I could come up with. Apparently, it was the same for Katelyn. We both remained quiet as we worked our way up the entire length of a big hill.

I was sucking wind by the time I made it to the top, and couldn't have been happier to see Spotted Owl stop to rest. He hopped off the shoulder into a shallow roadside ditch. Putting my hands behind my head, I tried to reinflate my aching lungs like a runner. The cool air burned as I inhaled gulps.

Katelyn unzipped her jacket and threw it over her shoulder. It hung on her backpack like a cape, and I chuckled at the superhero image.

"What's so funny?" she asked. "I'm sweating over here."

"Me, too. It's just…" I didn't want to go the hero route again and make her think I was actually getting a big head about the whole prisoner thing, and ended up whispering, "Supergirl."

"Say what?"

"You look like Supergirl." When she frowned at me, I added, "The cape. Your jacket looks like a cape."

"Does Supergirl even have a cape?"

I didn't answer right away. Comic books hadn't really been my thing. I wasn't even sure there was an actual Supergirl, and I was plenty sure Katelyn was way too young to bear any resemblance to Wonder Woman.

"I dunno," I finally said, but Katelyn had long since moved on.

She'd edged over by the adults, listening between her mother and father like she was standing at a crack in a doorway. I slipped up behind her and caught the last little bit.

"Choppers are out again," Spotted Owl was saying. "They didn't get an ID on 'em, so base is saying we might need to sit tight a while."

"Here?" my dad asked, twisting around to scan the sky like a Doppler radar.

"We should be able to see 'em coming," my mom answered. "We can see a long way from up here."

"True story," Spotted Owl agreed. "I'm good with hanging out until we either get the all clear or figure out if they're Apaches."

Unfortunately for us, there was no such thing as an all clear. From the valley below, the roar of engines turned to the telltale whopping sound of helicopters.

CHAPTER 11

"Get in the woods!" Spotted Owl hollered, though most of the group was already off the shoulder.

"Austin!" Mom howled. "Get back here."

It came as no surprise to me that my brother had stepped out to the middle of the road.

"I don't see it yet," he shouted back. "It might not even come this way."

"There's more than one," Spotted Owl. "Get down here now."

"C'mon, pal," Dad said, hopping back to the gravel. He reached an arm out to pull him off the road if he had to.

Austin huffed, but eventually listened. He slunk to the roadside, but in no great hurry. He kept looking over his shoulder as the roaring built up.

I crouched under a bush close to Katelyn. I was no less interested than Austin, but kept more concealed with eyes peeled to the sky. My only view was straight ahead the way we had been hiking, and it was soon filled with a whirring sound that rivaled a hurricane.

Metal gleamed in the moonlight as the first one appeared over the horizon. I swore the pilot was face to face with me, though obviously a long distance separated us. Still, I instantly buried my head in my hands as the forest came alive.

It took a moment for me to hear Spotted Owl screaming, "Spread out! Fast!"

Before we'd left camp, Spotted Owl and Noel had discussed the possibility that the government might start employing attack helicopters in night operations. Unlike the Blackhawks and little birds that were made for inserting troops, the Apaches were thought to have been equipped with thermal imaging. That would overcome any advantage our group had moving around after dark. The only defense was to scatter like rats and hope we blended in with the deer and the bears and whatever else might be big enough to throw off a heat signature.

Or find somewhere safe to hide.

I looked up and stared at the first helicopter hovering closer on the horizon. Pylons stuck out on short, stubby wings, each loaded with rocket pods. Bullets from the nose-mounted Gatling gun were bound to tear through the woods any second.

As badly as I wanted to grab Katelyn's hand, it was more important that we separated.

"Meet back here when they're gone!" I yelled, and pointed for her to take off downhill. "Run!"

She nodded sharply and spun. I lingered a second as I watched her scamper down the hill the way we had come. Then I took off, veering slightly to her left to stay separated.

The slope was steep enough that I couldn't run at full speed. The darkness didn't help either. Brambles rose up from nowhere to trip me. Branches slashed at my face. My jacket helped deflect the worst.

In the low light, I couldn't see the smaller branches in my way until I'd already run through them, so I raised an arm in front of my face and plowed forward like a battering ram.

The helicopter growled behind me, gaining in elevation as it crested the hill and tilted to where it could scan down the slope.

I didn't look back anymore, trying to concentrate on nothing but running as fast as I could. One wrong move would send me tumbling all the way to the bottom, but I wasn't going to complain about having to climb that steep slope again as long as I got away. All that mattered was running, as much as I hated that particular activity.

With my forearm doing a better job of shielding my face, I ran even faster. The rifle slung over my shoulder snagged a branch, pulling me back. I shrugged the vegetation loose and picked up the pace.

I kept my eyes trained on the ground, and risked not seeing far enough ahead to steer around the bigger obstacles. Even so, I tripped when a vine wrapped around my boot. I careened to the side, knocking into a smaller tree in the process.

With a *brrrrr* sound, the Gatling gun on the lead chopper opened up at the same time. I fell to the ground as bullets tore through the trees all around me. Never had I been more thankful to have been tripped. I rolled to the side as cut branches fell from the sky. But I couldn't move. The fall had forced all the air from my lungs. I was too exhausted to suck in a much needed breath.

The helicopter came almost directly overhead. My rifle had flung uselessly off to the side in the fall. I didn't give a second thought to retrieving it.

The trees all around me lashed in the breeze. Saplings bent over and bushes thrashed. Dried leaves dropped like rain as the rotor-powered wind pulled them loose. By the time the first chopper floated off farther downhill, it appeared like I was a kid again hiding in a pile of leaves.

I played dead. The swirling dust aggravated my eyes but I dared not move to rub them. Already overtaken, I figured a motionless heat signature splayed out on the forest floor might be enough to convince the other pilot that I was down.

I couldn't help but flinch when the second chopper appeared, heading back toward me. A whooshing sound erupted from right over my head.

"Holy crap," I whispered as I peeked up to see the twin fiery trails of rockets streak toward the top of the mountain. A sharp white flash and explosions quickly followed.

I resisted the urge to pull my arms and legs up underneath myself. I tried to fight off the shudders that wracked my body. It was worse than falling in a frozen pond.

I struggled to suck in a breath as visions came to me. Katelyn blown apart. My parents leaking blood into the soil. Worse images continued as the helicopter loosed another volley of rockets onto the hill above me.

Finally, the second helicopter glided off farther down the slope toward the valley, but I felt no ease. It had seemed easier for the choppers to rocket the hillside when facing uphill, and I braced myself for another volley.

Seconds stretched to minutes. The two helicopters hovered side by side well below my position on the hill. I dared not move, not even when I heard the impact of bullets rip into the hillside, ricocheting off rocks.

"Please let everyone be okay," I whispered, and repeated similar words over and over until the whirring of the helicopter rotors finally changed pitch and began to drift away.

Even though I was sure they'd left, I stayed motionless for several minutes. The forest didn't come alive around me the way it would have during the daylight hours. The birds and bigger animals had all quieted for the night, and the early frost had taken care of most of the bugs. That left nothing but the still night to keep me on edge.

I wanted to call out for the others, but held my tongue. I couldn't explain why, except that I wasn't feeling anything other than numb. In fact, it took a great effort to finally sit up again.

A deep breath would've helped, but I continued having trouble forcing more than little sips of air into my aching chest.

I finally gathered up my rifle, and sat still for a moment longer, scanning the woods in every direction. Nothing moved. No one made a sound. And then I heard the whimper.

From up above me, my mom wailed, "Harold!"

"Crap, not Mom," I uttered, terrified that she had been shot or rocketed.

I scrambled to my feet ready to run when she cried out again. "Someone help!"

CHAPTER 12

I rushed up the hill, heading toward the sound of my mom's voice. She continued to call for help, several times before I was sure I was headed in the right direction. Though I knew I had been sprinting downhill before, I couldn't believe I'd made it that much farther than the others.

"Ma!" I yelled back when I thought I was getting close. She didn't reply, but an unexpected sulfur smell verified that it couldn't be much farther. The stench led me into a pit of cratered earth. Splintered trees leaned to the side. Several smoldered.

"Mom? Where are you?"

"Over here! Hurry!"

I squinted through the blackness. Zeroing in on the sound of her voice, I adjusted course to the right to skirt around the blast zone.

"Where's Dad?"

"With me."

And he hadn't replied for himself, I realized. My stomach turned to concrete, and I nearly tripped on a stump as my thoughts went to a place much darker than the rocket-scarred forest.

I righted myself and finally closed the distance. My mother sat on the ground, hunched over like an old woman. As I slid in next to her, she spun around and dug inside her backpack.

"You need to keep pressure on that," she ordered, fully immersed into nurse mode. Or at least that's the way I anticipated her days had been back when she'd worked in the emergency room. "He's losing too much blood."

I stared at my father's face long enough to see his eyes were closed. One cheek was completed covered in dirt or soot. The other side looked deathly gray.

"Now, Zach," Mom chided as she continued rummaging through the pack.

"Yeah," I mumbled and went to work.

Dad's jacket had been pulled wide open. His button-up shirt had been slit from top to bottom with a knife. The tan fabric had been soaked black with blood that continued to pour from his right side.

In a shell-shocked daze, I mumbled, "Oh my God."

"The rag, Zach!" Mom said anxiously. "Keep pressure on the rag."

"The stocking cap?" I asked, having seen nothing that resembled a scrap of fabric.

"Yeah, it's all I had." She wheeled around. "Here, use this."

She handed me a pair of cotton work gloves, followed by a gauze pad and tape.

"What the heck?" I said as I pressed what had become a sponge of a hat against my dad's abdomen.

"The rag's soaked. Put that gauze pad on there, then the gloves over that while I wrap him tight."

I nodded numbly. In a smooth movement, I tossed the dripping cap aside and shoved the gauze pad against the wound. Even in the low light, during the quick transfer, I could plainly see a jagged slit from the lower part of the ribs all the way to the top of his hip bone.

The pad soaked through almost immediately. I pinched the skin together, and mashed the gloves on top to try to put some pressure on the gash.

"Roll him," my mom commanded, somehow calm when panic was bubbling around us like spilled blood.

I swallowed down the bile building in the back of my throat and tried my hardest not to vomit. I didn't think I had a weak stomach, but watching my dad lose what seemed like gallons of blood was enough for me to feel light-headed. I could only imagine how he felt—if he was even feeling.

"Dammit. It's not working." Mom abruptly jumped up, making me flinch, and yelled, "Anyone! We need help!"

Someone answered, but far off. Mom continued yelling as she rummaged back through the backpack a second time. "Someone's got clotting agent," she muttered, and whirled around again.

She looked like a crazed gopher as she flung the leaves aside and jammed her hands into the rocky soil under our knees.

"We need to pack it in mud," she said frantically. "We've gotta try something." She jumped up to yell again. "Over here, dammit! Someone! Anyone!"

By that point, I was paralyzed with fear. I kept my hands pressed on the gloves, which had already soaked through underneath the tape. Rather than stare at the blood seeping into the ground, like the tears dripping from my face, I watched my father's mouth.

Dad's lips were parted slightly, but not moving. Looking to his chest, I noticed that it didn't seem to rise or fall. Perhaps a little, but no big breaths seemed to be going in and out the way they should.

"Ma," I said tentatively. Tears streamed from my eyes, and I wiped them on the back of my jacket sleeve. "He's not breathing."

"Are you sure?" She dropped a handful of dirt next to her husband's side and scooted in next to me.

"I don't know."

"It's okay, hon," she said, though clearly it wasn't. She turned her head to the side and put her ear right over her husband's mouth.

Bushes rustled all around them. A pair of shadows appeared, rising up out of the darkness. "We're here," Austin said.

"Now they show up." Mom cursed, and yelled, "Quiet! I can't hear."

She held up a hand, freezing the new arrivals in place, and leaned back over to listen.

"We need chest compressions. Now!" she told me. "Go!"

"I-I..." I stammered, and froze up like a block of ice.

Mom moved in to take over.

"No. I got this," I said. I locked my hands together over Dad's chest and shoved over and over. "Check his pulse."

Mom put her fingers along the side her husband's throat. As I pushed away like a mindless machine on Dad's chest, I noticed her slide over to grab his forearm. Two fingers pressed into the fleshy part of his wrist below the hand.

She shook her head, but I wasn't about to quit. Sweat poured off my temples as I kept going with chest compressions, over and over again. I couldn't lose him. Not my dad.

Mom grabbed my arm. I kept going, pushing many more times until I thought his chest would cave in. Eventually, I was too weak to continue. The fact that I couldn't go on was almost more painful than anything else.

"He's gone," Mom said, sitting back. A solitary tear shone in the moonlight as it slid down her cheek. "He lost too much blood."

"Bro, it's over," Austin said from right behind me.

I whirled around ready to bite his head off, but the anger sat like an obstruction in my throat. "It...It...It can't be..."

"Damn, this sucks." Austin choked back a tear. It was the first time I'd ever seen that happen. "It's not supposed to..." He cursed loudly and creatively, surprising even our mother with some of his unique combinations.

I felt a tiny bit better watching him vent, though I lost it again when my eyes drifted to our mother. She had her back against a tree, face buried in her hands. The way her shoulders shook, I knew she was sobbing without having to actually hear her, and that tore me apart.

Austin paced back toward me and spread his arms wide. I fell into them, and was surprised to find his jacket dripping wet. I pulled back and quickly verified it wasn't more blood.

"Thanks, Austin," I whispered.

"It's me and you, little bro," he replied softly. He gestured to the side with his head. "Mom needs us."

I wasn't ready to hear that, nor was I prepared to see my older brother acting both responsibly and compassionate. I could only nod and say, "True that."

A couple deep breaths steadied me, at least as much as possible given the gravity of the situation. I slowly stepped away from Austin and locked eyes with Spotted Owl. He'd come back with Austin, though there hadn't been anything he could've done to save my dad. And he apparently hadn't wanted to interrupt my family's grieving either.

I pinched my lips together and nodded at Spotted Owl. The big man lowered his head respectfully.

"Where do we go from here?" I whispered to myself. "How do we go on?"

My mom was a broken shell, still hugging her knees to her chest and sobbing. Austin was no leader, and Maddie would be absolutely devastated whenever she heard the news. That alone made me want to continue on with the mission to delay the inevitable. Still, I didn't see how I could muster the strength to go on, emotionally or physically.

Then again, if it turned out to be a suicide mission, no one would have to break the news to Maddie. Rather selfishly, I knew it wouldn't have to be me in that situation. The thought initially relieved me only to make me feel ten times worse seconds later.

I looked to the sky. Rage built up within me. I couldn't fathom how my own government turned the death machines on us. How they'd taken my father. And for what? For hiding out in the park? For hiking off to do whatever we were about to do?

Granted, that might have been illegal, but the government had fired the first shot. The first thousands of shots, all across the country. Through their shooting down of rioters to bombing crowds, I had never directly fought back. And what had that gotten me? Fatherless.

I kicked a fallen branch on the forest floor. It clattered against a tree and broke in half, just like my heart. I stooped to pick it up. I ran my hands over the decayed, scorched wood. With a quick twist of the wrist, I snapped it again. And again. I broke it into tiny little pieces, one satisfying crack at a time.

Tossing the scraps aside, I stared back at the star-filled sky once more. The lingering sulfur smell burned with every heavy inhale.

I assumed our attackers were long gone, though I knew better than to think we could afford to let our guard down any longer. And we still had people to round up. The wallowing in self-pity would have to wait until later.

I started back to the others to retrieve my rifle and arrange a search party when I heard Katelyn calling.

"Zach!" she shouted from close by. "Where are you?"

"Here." My eyes scanned the woods, but I could see little farther than the nearest trees. "This way," I repeated over and over until her shadow grew into the soft features of my one true love.

I ran to her, and wrapped her in a hug. I pulled back and looked her over from head to toe. "You're okay."

"I'm fine, silly." She hugged me again. "And you too…" Her voice trailed away.

"Thank God." Tears built in the corners of my eyes, but I fought them away. My nose ran, and I sniffled that up too, not wanting to appear weak.

"Jeez, you missed me, huh? I like knowing that," she said playfully, before growing more somber. "I was a little worried I wouldn't find you back, but at least we knew where to meet up."

I hugged her so tightly she could barely breathe. "I don't know what I'd have done if I'd lost you too."

"Too?" She pulled her head back to meet my eyes. "Oh, God. What happened, Zach?"

"My pops." I choked on the last word and hung my head.

"What? We'll find him."

"He's not lost. He's…" I couldn't say it.

She didn't make me. "Holy crap." She laid her head back on my shoulder. "I'm so sorry, babe."

"It's okay," I said weakly, when everyone knew that was only what people said.

"Not really. Take me there."

I let her go, and slumped down on a fallen log. I kept my head buried in my hands. Katelyn sat next to me and wrapped an arm around my shoulders.

"I'm not sure I want to go back," I said. When I realized I looked too much like my mother, I sat up a little straighter to look at Katelyn. "I just…I dunno. I'm numb."

"You should be." She stood and offered me a hand. "Come on. They need you."

"Whether I'm ready or not."

She nodded. "Pretty much. We can't stay here."

"I know. Believe me, I know. But what about Dad?"

That was a question Katelyn couldn't answer. We saved it for later, after we'd gone back up the hill to where my mother stood talking in low tones to Spotted Owl. Katelyn's parents had joined them, and they rushed over to hug their daughter while I looked on.

I would never have another pat on the back from my dad. Never get a hug, or have to listen to another diatribe about financial markets or the government crackdown. All had been lost before we'd accomplished a single useful thing in that rotten park.

"I'm so sorry, Zach," Katelyn's mom said, and pulled me into the hug.

"Thank you," I mumbled. I shook hands with Katelyn's apologetic looking dad, and then slowly walked over to my brother. The grieving had to stop. It was time for action.

"Who's missing?" I asked. Looking over the group, I finally noticed John standing back in the shadows keeping to himself.

"Noel," Austin replied, holding out my rifle for me. "I think that's it."

"That's convenient." I slung it over my shoulder, and gripped the butt of the weapon tightly. The anger coursed through me all the way to my fingertips wrapped around the cold, wooden stock.

Austin didn't reply. Instead, he shivered as a gentle breeze stirred through the trees.

"Why are you wet anyway?" I asked. "You're soaked."

"Couldn't find anywhere to hide. I ran up on a little creek, and figured I could use the water to mask my heat." He gritted teeth as if reliving the moment. "Wish I could get some back. It was frickin' cold enough."

"No doubt. Clever though."

"What did you do?"

"Played dead." It pained me to say those words. I shook it off and threw my arms out to the side to play act. "I was like that crime scene tape with arms and legs all flailed out."

Austin laughed under his breath. "Not a bad idea."

We stood there together uncomfortably. I noticed out of the corner of my eye that my dad's face and upper torso had been covered over with his jacket. After seeing that, I couldn't look in that direction any longer.

Turning back to Austin, I said, "What do we do about Dad? We can't just leave him."

"I don't know. We'd better ask the adults."

Unfortunately, that started a whole new battle.

CHAPTER 13

"We need to make tracks," Spotted Owl insisted. "I don't mean to be insensitive, but we've been here too long. Those choppers could come back any time."

I knew he was right, but couldn't bear to think about leaving my father behind. That motivated me to point at Austin and say, "We can carry him."

"No, boys." Mom gave us a pained smile. "I wish we could, but that's the emotion talking. Your father would want you to do the smart thing."

"And leave him here? Hell no," Austin objected. "The animals will tear him apart."

Though it was true, I wished Austin hadn't said that. Our mother's face blanched, but she quickly composed herself.

"We don't have shovels," Katelyn's dad said, unhelpfully. "We could come back…"

"He won't be here when we get back," Austin said, again making me cringe at the thought.

Spotted Owl tried to diffuse the situation, saying, "Now Austin-"

"He's right," Mom said, apparently coming around to our side. "That's my husband he's talking about, so y'all best shut up and let me decide."

Katelyn's mother nodded approvingly and went to stand by her friend.

"Thank you," Mom whispered to her, and looked at Austin and me. "He can't come with us, and we can't leave him."

"I know," Austin said. He suddenly perked up. "There's a stream close. Lots of rocks. We could at least bury him."

"I don't know how prudent-"

Mom cut off Spotted Owl with a sharp look. "I'll decide if it's a waste of time or not." She continued glaring at him. "That's what you were going to say, wasn't it?"

He nodded, and took a step back.

"That settles it. I've decided." She pointed toward her husband without looking at him. "Grab him and lead on, Austin."

I went with my brother to help, thought I wasn't sure I could do much. I could barely handle getting close to my father's lifeless form. I kneeled beside him, almost wondering if he wouldn't sit up, as if the jacket draped over his face was shielding him like his daily newspaper. Back home, he'd lower that paper every day after school, give me a quick greeting, and turn right back to the financial pages. The visual was too much to bear.

"Let me help, bud," John said, having slinked up next to me. It was the first words he'd spoken, but all I needed to hear from him. I blinked away the tears as John patted me on the back.

"We've got him," Katelyn's dad said as he crouched on the other side of me. Spotted Owl was right next to him ready to help out.

I wasn't happy about that, but relented. At least Spotted Owl was willing to put his concerns aside.

Though fighting off despair was my overriding concern, I found myself checking the sky often. The night had grown deathly quiet to the point that I thought I could've been able to hear more helicopters coming from miles away. Still, I remained too rattled to want to dawdle, and appreciated the extra help.

I let the two older men and John take my dad's upper body while Austin and I each took a leg. At least that way I didn't have to feel the cold blood that had soaked through my father's clothes. It dripped onto dead leaves with little smacks as we raised him to walk.

"It's up ahead," Austin said. "Not far at all." As we got underway, he provided directions like the professional backseat driver he had always been. "Little more to the left. About another twenty yards."

My dad was a big man. Standing over six feet tall, he easily topped two hundred pounds. As a result, we five pallbearers struggled, though no one dared make a sound. The noise of shuffling feet and labored breathing was eventually drowned out by the sound of gurgling water. I flinched thinking about the sick, mushy sounds that had come from my father's damaged abdomen and was never more relieved to smell the fresh stream water. Soon after, I saw the ripples flashing in the moonlight.

"Are we seriously doing this?" I whispered to Austin as we placed our father beside the creek.

"I...I think he'd...he'd like it here."

I stood back for a second, and stretched out my back as I looked up the hillside at the water pouring over the rocks. Waterworks of my own threatened to burst loose, and I choked out, "Me, too."

"I know he would," John agreed.

"Let's do this," Austin said. He shooed the other men away and reached out for Mom's arm.

"I wish Maddie was here," she whispered.

"Could you imagine?" Austin said, causing our mom to lift her head sharply.

"Austin."

"It's true, Ma," I agreed with my brother's sentiments. I didn't want her to have to see our dad that way. "Better to bring her back when this is done."

"Then we'll do it," she said. "She deserves to know where he's buried."

She stood back for a second, sucked in a deep breath, and came forward to kneel beside her husband. I backed away. She stayed with him for a minute or more, then slowly rose and walked over to us. Tears streamed down her face, turning me to mush.

"Let the others do this," she said. "But say your goodbyes."

I nodded slowly. Austin waved for me to go first. I followed orders and crouched next to my dad. I couldn't stand to see the jacket over his face, much less speak to it. Instead, I closed my eyes and finally offered a short, internalized prayer, though the words were hard to find. Praying didn't come easy for me, and my head was a jumble of thoughts.

Rather than drag it out too long, I simply whispered a quick goodbye. I touched my father's cold, muddy hand and walked away to collapse into my mother's arms. Katelyn stood close to me, and we welcomed her into the hug.

When Austin was done, Spotted Owl insisted that he would take care of everything. Mom guided us back toward the road as the others stayed behind to bury my dad.

The sound of stones chinking as they knocked together was almost more than I could bear. Each sound was like stone nails being driven into a coffin—and into my own shattered heart.

Fortunately, we got far enough away that the sounds faded. All that was left was the shuffling of feet through leaves, and sniffles from everyone.

We reached the edge of the road, and remained huddled there quietly. Finally, Katelyn's family and Spotted Owl caught up. No one seemed to want to make eye contact with my family other than John. Even his tight-lipped, bobbing head didn't linger on us for long.

"Should we stick to the road?" Austin asked, breaking the silence. He sounded clearly skeptical. I agreed with those sentiments, if a little too late to do any good.

"Maybe not, but it won't matter much," Spotted Owl explained. "At the top of the next hill, we're taking off cross country anyway. Down the Thomas Divide Trail, along the top of ridge."

"Without Noel?" I asked, wondering if the others had forgotten about him.

"We called, we've checked around…we can't wait any longer," Spotted Owl suggested as we gathered up along the edge of the highway. He looked to the adults. "Agreed?"

It made me wonder once again whether Noel was a traitor. Whether he had set us up, and brought all the pain down on me. Before I could vocalize those thoughts, Mom concurred with Spotted Owl, followed by agreement from Katelyn's family.

"We've got all we need to know from him," Spotted Owl said. "So let's move out and put this, uhm, unfortunate event behind us."

I felt inclined to argue, or worse. No one deserved to talk that way about my father's death. I simmered to a boil inside, but was composed enough to realize that fighting among ourselves would do no one any good.

"Maybe he's right," I muttered as we trudged off.

"What's that?" Katelyn asked. Even her gentle voice was too syrupy to my ears.

"Nothing."

"I heard what he said. That was rude."

"I don't want to talk about it," I growled, and instantly regretted it. Her frown couldn't quite ugly up her features, but it pained me all the same to see it. "Sorry. I didn't mean to snap at you."

"It's okay, babe."

"Not really. I shouldn't take it out on you."

"Better me than someone else." She squeezed my hand. "I'm here for you."

"I know, but I'll deal with it."

She nodded and pinched her lips closed. I knew she might've been disappointed in me; hopefully not hurt. Mostly, I needed time to process the evening. I could make it up to her later, I hoped. Just in case, I whispered, "Just give me a little time. Okay?"

"I'll be here."

"That's all I need to know."

No one spoke for quite a while. We quickly moved up the hill, keeping even closer to the edge of the woods. Sorrow and high alert was a strange mixture. I found myself constantly wanting to look back over my shoulder. Not always for enemies, but sometimes to remember all I was leaving behind.

We crested the hill, and I wanted to run back to the last one. I couldn't go on that way, only thinking of helicopters swooping in and my world crumbling apart.

The emotions sapped my strength faster than the hiking. My feet moved robotically while my insides burned. The gasps of air I sucked in were heavy and cold.

Somewhere past midnight, I became as lifeless as a zombie. I only wished I was as brainless.

"This way," Spotted Owl was saying when Katelyn tapped me on my shoulder to get my attention. "We go down the Divide Trail here, then turn off toward Newton Bald."

"You made camp on a bald knob?" Austin said. "That's stupid."

Lucky for everyone, Spotted Owl ignored the insult. "It's not *on* the knob. We're in a cave around behind it, well off the trail."

I ignored the rest of the conversation. I remained stuck in the past, and that sparked my memory. Remembering that nothing but bad luck had come from taking the first prisoner, I randomly asked, "Does Noel know where your camp is at?"

"I didn't tell him," Spotted Owl replied. "Why? We don't really need him anymore."

"That's not what I was thinking…" The adults all focused on me. I swallowed, and firmed up my resolve. "I just mean that all the bad stuff happened when he was around. The drone and then choppers with the soldiers. The attack. Did we even have a reason to trust him?"

I was glad that no one thought to mention that I was the one who captured the guy in the first place. I hadn't meant to call out John, and quickly traded a glance with him to make sure I hadn't spoken out of turn.

John shrugged, but offered no disagreement about Noel. No one could have known.

Nevertheless, a quick discussion sparked about whether Noel was trustworthy, which wasn't ideal for me to hear seeing how my father had a part in deciding to bring him back to our camp—not that I thought he had made the wrong decision, or really had much of a choice.

The end result was that it didn't matter. Better yet, no one specifically remembered telling him where Spotted Owl's camp was located, though he had obviously been looking over the maps with the other adults in the back of the cave. At the very least, he knew it was somewhere relatively close to Cherokee.

"As big as this park is, that means nothing," Spotted Owl said, trying to be a cheerleader. "So forget him and let's keep moving."

"Good idea," my mom agreed.

Spotted Owl, followed by John, led us down a narrow gravelly path that was only wide enough for one person to pass at a time. I was happy to go last. I followed directly behind Katelyn, and spent quite a while planting my feet right behind hers like it was some kind of mind numbing game to match her steps exactly.

Austin shattered the silence before we got too far down the trail. "Are we even close?"

"We're over halfway to Cherokee, and we're not going that far today," Spotted Owl replied. "It's only about five more miles to my camp."

"Five miles," Austin said, but quickly bit back on his whining. He turned around and looked past Katelyn. "We got this. Right, bro?"

"Yeah, bud." I said softly. "No problem."

As far as I was concerned, I could go a lifetime with no more problems.

CHAPTER 14

The gravel path switched over to dirt after the turn off to the Kanati Fork Trail.

"Keep going straight," Spotted Owl said. He stood aside and waved everyone past. "That one goes back to the highway."

I kept right behind Katelyn. I didn't bother looking down the other trail. All that mattered to me was getting to camp. Then I could hopefully pass out. Sleep couldn't come soon enough, though I knew it might not come as easily as it should.

Spotted Owl stepped behind me. "Hey, Zach," he called.

"Yeah."

I cringed, expecting some sort of words of sympathy or something; however, Spotted Owl had other things on his mind.

"I've been thinking about what you said. Tell me more about Noel."

"Like what?"

"No one ever asked you about him, did they?" Spotted Owl asked. I nodded and kept trudging down the trail. "They just took over the questioning and kinda left you out of the loop."

"Yeah, well…I've kinda gotten used to that."

"Tell me more about what he was like when you captured him. I'd only trailed him for maybe a quarter mile, you know, thinking he was probably one of your guys. That is, at least until I saw you guys at the falls watching over him like a prisoner."

"He wouldn't tell me anything." I turned around to add, "Kinda like you. It was all big secrets about whatever the enemy was up to."

"I hear you." Spotted Owl didn't quite apologize, but he said, "We need to stop that. We need to treat everyone alike. Everybody is counting on all of us, not just the older people."

I bristled at the comment. "You don't have to pretend like you're my buddy or that I'm some kind of equal. I know my place here." I choked up for a second before uttering, "Or at least I used to."

"Zach," Katelyn said, turning around.

"I'm fine."

"It's okay," Spotted Owl said. "I'll leave you alone. I was just wondering about Noel."

I relented. "I really wish I could tell you more. All I know is that he said he was a deserter when John pressed him, and everyone seemed to buy that." I paused, and went back to the edge of conspiracy theory again. "All I know is that the Feds seem to draw a bead on that guy even though y'all didn't find a tracker on him."

"We might be lucky he's gone," Spotted Owl said, and left me alone so he could hurry back up to the front.

"Too late," I muttered.

I reverted back to mindless zombie mode after that. The trail grew more rugged, and after a couple branches had brushed up against my jacket sleeve, I finally put a little more effort into watching where I was going.

Katelyn handed branches back to me as we ducked under a particularly overgrown stretch. Though not in the slightest relieved, I felt a little safer than I had out by the road. But any thought of actual safety had been irreparably shattered after that night.

We hit another cross trail, and Spotted Owl directed us off to the right. The path changed from dirt to solid rock. It didn't make me feel any better when I noticed there was a sheer drop off after about thirty paces down the trail.

At a narrow stretch, I needed to turn sideways on the pathway and pushed my back up against a cliff to keep away from the edge. As we rounded an especially tight corner, Katelyn's boot slipped in loose gravel. I shook off the lethargy and grabbed for her as pebbles showered the leaves on the trees below.

"I'm okay," she told the others. "But I sure wouldn't recommend looking down." Thinking about Jonas and the waterfall was the farthest thing from my mind, but Katelyn used it again to try to bring some levity to the situation. "Thanks for the save, babe. You should've been there before Jonas fell."

"Yeah, right. You did fine."

"I ended up at the bottom of a cliff. He was unconscious."

"Nah, he was okay…sorta. Besides, the waterfall was hardly a cliff."

"Good thing too. I'm lucky to have you with me."

"I won't let you fall," I said, keeping hold of her arm as she started inching forward again.

"I might drag you down."

"I'd let go first," I said with my first chuckle in a long time.

"Thanks, Zach." She punched me on the arm, and teetered again a little too close to the brink.

"Careful, slugger." I steadied her. "But don't worry, I'd come save you…again." I threw in a wry smile for good measure.

"I know you would."

Thankfully, the rock ledge ended soon after our exchange. The trail still wasn't wide enough to walk side by side, but just being on dirt that was lined by heavy brush felt far safer than the precipice.

We continued several hundred yards farther before Spotted Owl waved us to a halt.

"There's one more trail to cross, and probably sentries up ahead. I've called ahead to camp on the two-way, but I'd better go ahead by myself in case the guy on watch doesn't get the message."

"That's all we need to cap off this night," Austin said. He slumped back against a tree while keeping close to our mother.

She hadn't said much for quite some time. Possibly not even the whole trip since the so-called incident, at least as far as I could remember. But she seemed to be handling herself okay. Not chipper, but as well as could be expected.

I didn't feel like talking to anyone, and stayed off to the edge of the group. Katelyn stood at my side and took my hand. She seemed to understand that I wasn't in a talkative mood.

John went a little farther down the trail and hopped up onto a boulder the size of a table. His parents ambled over and stood below him as they waited for Spotted Owl to return.

I shifted my weight from one foot to the other, but resisted the urge to sit down. If I did, I thought I might pass out. As close as I assumed we were to the camp, I decided I could stay awake a while longer—if I could even sleep at all. After all the walking, I was pretty sure it would be lights out, toes up the minute I got to the camp, but the awful images wouldn't stay away.

Cold leached into me. I felt like I was shriveling up like a corpse. I could almost literally see my dad's blood pouring out of the side of his abdomen, and somehow got the idea that it was my own blood. I clamped a hand to my side to staunch the imaginary flow, but it gurgled through my fingers, babbling onto the dark ground like an unstoppable stream.

The longer I waited, the more my feet ached. But that wasn't all. There was too much free time when I really needed to keep moving. My ribcage seemingly tightened around me like a straitjacket, making my heart hurt.

I refused to cry again. I shook my head and exhaled loudly. Katelyn looked up at me, and leaned in closer. I buried my face in her shoulder, and stroked her long brown hair.

"He needs to hurry up," I muttered.

"He'll be back."

"It could be a set up," I said, though I didn't really believe it. Of the two strangers, Noel had seemed far more suspicious.

Then again, I couldn't help but notice that Spotted Owl had been around for all the same bad things as Noel.

My overactive mind spun off on a wholly unexpected tangent. I found myself deep in the woods after the rocket attack, watching Spotted Owl strangle Noel to keep him from sharing his secret with the others. I gasped, wondering if Spotted Owl was the double agent, or spy, or whatever.

"What's up?" Katelyn asked me.

"Nothing."

She looked at me disapprovingly, but didn't press the question.

I answered anyway. "Too many movies, I guess. You remember all those secret agent ones, like with the super spies that switch sides and all that."

Katelyn nodded, though it was easy for me to tell that she wasn't really following. I couldn't blame her for that. I could barely follow my own thoughts.

"Too many conspiracy theories," I explained rather vaguely. "Sometimes they're the only things that makes sense."

My parents had ingrained in me the need to question everything, whether it be the motivations of people or the government. I was fortunate that I didn't ever doubt the people closest to me, but I was never sure where to draw the line.

Thinking back, my dad should've been on high alert around the other two guys, but he'd seemingly welcomed Spotted Owl into the camp with open arms. I didn't know enough about the system of dealing with the other camps to know whether I could trust the adults' judgment. But they'd never steered me wrong. Even their rantings about the government had all proved true.

"It seems there's more truth than fiction in conspiracies these days," Katelyn said softly.

I wished she hadn't just added fuel to the Spotted Owl is a traitor fire, but she made me chuckle nonetheless. "You're not helping," I said with a grin.

We waited quietly for what was probably just a couple more minutes. It seemed to me like an hour. My eyelids grew so heavy that I could barely lift them, but they jumped wide open when John announced, "He's coming back. He's got company."

I tensed up, wondering which Spotted Owl was returning—friend or foe. My fingers tightened around the butt of my rifle, though I kept it slung over my shoulder. Spotted Owl appeared a second later with a pair of heavily-bearded, middle-aged men.

"Alright, guys. We're ready for you." He waved for us to follow them. "Just had to roll out the red carpet."

"And call off your dogs," I mumbled, though I had noticed little trace of animosity from the two new men. They'd just eyeballed our group from a distance and offered no more than guarded nods for a greeting.

We hiked down the trail another quarter of a mile, skirting along the base of a cliff of exposed rock. On the other side, a wooded slope tumbled down into a valley well below, though we were not so close to the edge of the dropoff that I was concerned about falling.

The flat, cleared knob of Newton Bald towered over us as we made an arcing turn around the base of it. When it seemed like we were halfway around, the cliff face above us transitioned into a forested slope of dirt and scattered boulders.

Not more than fifty yards ahead, a thin ribbon of a stream tumbled off the knob. It turned out to be the staircase for climbing farther down the hill. Spotted Owl guided us in that direction. About a hundred steps later, he abruptly left the stream and headed off cross country. Shortly, we arrived at the cave.

The similarities to ours were striking. There was slightly less open ground in front of the cave, but a huge field of boulders all the same. Like our camp, it seemed as though they'd rolled down the slope at some point and made themselves into a maze on the flat ground in front of the opening.

Up under a short wall of solid rock, the cave opening showed up as dark as a blackhole. We were all drawn to the safety of the nook like an old friend.

"It's late, and we've had a helluva day," Spotted Owl said once we'd negotiated the rock field and stood under a wide opening no taller than a door. He gestured to his quiet, bearded companions. "Besides these guys, everyone's still sleeping, so we'll do introductions first thing in the morning."

"That works for me," Katelyn's mom replied.

I squinted inside the cave, but couldn't make out a single feature.

"Let me get a lantern." Spotted Owl fished a small flashlight out of his pocket and turned it on long enough to enter the cave. He reemerged a few seconds later with a solar-powered lantern that he clicked on. The warm white glow didn't do much to illuminate the area, but it was enough that my group could follow without tripping over ourselves, or our hosts.

"Follow me and we'll get you guys comfortable," Spotted Owl said, and guided us to the far right side of the opening. He stepped under the ledge first, and pointed out a row of cots, each with a small camp pillow and a heavy wool blanket. "Looks like they've got you some beds set up already. Have a rest."

I stood back and let the others move in first.

Austin stuck with Mom and made sure she was next to Spotted Fawn and Katelyn's dad. Then he claimed the cot on the other side. John filled in next to his dad, leaving three empty cots at the end next to Austin, which were closest to the cave opening.

That part didn't bother me. It was the numbers. Only Katelyn and I were left.

"What the heck?" I mumbled, but kept my thoughts to myself. I assumed Spotted Owl had called ahead on the two-way and let our hosts know that Noel and my dad were coming. But there was only one extra bed.

I wracked my brain trying to solve that mystery, thinking maybe they'd been told that one of those two men weren't coming to the cave, which made even less sense. Or maybe Spotted Owl was bad at math. The more I thought about it, the more my head hurt.

Katelyn sat on a cot, leaving a gap between herself and Austin. My mind still overanalyzing, I sat on the one between the two of them and fell asleep without bothering to take off my boots or pull up the blanket.

CHAPTER 15

A faint glow filled the cave. Best as I could tell, the opening faced south. If so, that meant we wouldn't get any direct sunlight first thing in the morning, especially with the boulder field blocking the entrance. However, there would be a decent chance the place would warm up nicely by late morning.

My body, on the other hand, wasn't about to warm up. Somewhere in the early hours, I'd finally pulled up the wool blanket, but it wasn't enough to cut the chill.

My arteries seemed to circulate cold blood, which slowly drained back into my tired heart like water to a sump pump. I rolled over again, and found myself unable to get comfortable on the hard canvas of the cot.

Every time I moved, the thick fabric creaked like the bones of an old man. It was stretched so tight across the frame that I felt like I was sleeping on solid rock. The thought of my father alone in the woods under a pile of stone made me jerk upright, and I hopped up to never touch that cot again.

I crouched at the end of the bed and looked around the cave. It seemed as large as ours, though the ceiling was less uniform. A narrowing toward the middle was low enough that I would have to duck underneath, and behind that point remained all shadow.

No one seemed to be stirring in the rear. As I turned back toward the opening, I heard the soft clinking of metal. I remained crouching and watched as an older woman put a battered tin coffee pot on a small metal burner to boil.

I straightened up slowly, not wanting to draw attention to myself. She noticed me anyway and gave a friendly wave.

I waved back, but otherwise didn't move.

The lady mashed a finger over her lips, apparently letting me know that she'd keep quiet to avoid waking the others, and I nodded in response. As she turned back to tend to the burner, I slipped over to the opening of the cave closest to me and got my first look outside in the daylight.

As expected, the boulder field obscured most of my view. Above, the towering high plateau that was Newton Bald made me feel tiny. The endless trees ringing the rest of the camp should've added a degree of comfort, sort of like the warmth and security of a heavy blanket, but it made me feel more alone that I ever had before. It was far worse than watching the roadblock by myself after John had bailed on me to hunt.

I shook my head and sucked in a breath of cold autumn air. A faint orange glow radiated from beyond the boulders. I slipped farther out into the early morning light, and felt the chill descend over me even worse than it had been inside the cave.

"So much for warming up," I mumbled to myself, and decided a short hike might help get the blood pumping. But I didn't dare go too far and risk running into a sentry. That would've definitely been an awful way to start the day, and it was already bad enough.

Weaving around the boulders, I reached a spot where the flat area ended and a slope tumbled down to a valley far below. I hesitated at the edge, tempted to remain with my back resting against a boulder. But I felt too unprotected there. Anywhere that I could see the sky was too exposed, and I assumed it probably always would be.

I quickly identified a little foot trail leading away from the camp, and struck off down the path. Wanting to stay close yet get away, I didn't go more than twenty yards before I found a boulder as big as a Volkswagen protruding from the ground, holding back dirt that spilled all around it.

I sat on the low side of the boulder, putting it between myself and the camp. I hunched up my shoulders, and pulled my jacket tight. Though I'd never tried meditating or put much stock in quiet reflection, I decided it was worth a try. Something had to ease the pain besides keeping on the move. I'd wear myself out trying to run away from the pain, and knew that wasn't an option.

It would be even less possible in a few short weeks when the bitter cold settled in to stay. I watched as the vibrant, but dying, leaves fell by the hundreds. Each one was another layer of protection, falling to the ground in piles of blood red and rusty orange colors.

Somewhere early in my failed attempt at meditation, I heard a branch crack. My head shot up. My eyes scanned the somber woods. Somewhere through the brown trunks and falling leaves, I expected to see a deer. Hopefully not a bear.

Finally, I pinpointed a new sound. Soft footsteps padded down the trail from behind me. I remained curved in on myself hoping the camp sentry or whoever would pass me by.

Burying my head in my arms, I peeked out between a gap. A long, brown ponytail swished as the prettiest girl in the junior class traipsed down the trail.

"Crap." I debated letting her walk past. It took only a second for me to decide. "Psst, Katie," I whispered.

She spun around, clutching her chest. "Dude. You scared the crap outta me."

"Sorry. I didn't mean to." I patted the ground next to me. "Have a seat."

"Couldn't sleep, huh?"

"Not really. What're you doin' out here?"

"Looking for you. I heard your cot creak."

"Like a thousand times," I replied. "I thought it was gonna collapse. That thing was awful."

"Yeah, I'd take my air mattress over that rock anytime."

I grimaced at the unfortunate reference to a bed of stone, and quickly brushed off her comment. She had no way of knowing what I was thinking, not that I necessarily wanted to share any of that with her.

"So…" she said, looking at me with those warm brown eyes that made every day better than the last. I needed that warmth. "You want to, uhm, talk…you know?"

"Not really." I forced a smile. "But I want you to stay."

"I'm not going anywhere."

She leaned against me. I took her hand. With fingers linked together, I laid my other hand over them. She sighed.

I focused on the brightness in her twinkling eyes; the subtle smile that tugged at her cheeks. If she could be happy stuck out there in the middle of nowhere, I resolved to find a way.

The sun popped over the distant mountain, bathing the valley below in yellow light. It accentuated the fall colors, making the Great Smoky Mountains come alive with blazing reds and vibrant oranges of leaves clinging to their last moment of glory.

"It's beautiful," Katelyn whispered.

The sunlight did wonders for her too. Through the dirt and grime and lack of sleep, she sparkled like a diamond.

"Yes, you are," I said, once again looking at her perfect face.

"Don't be silly," she replied. "I'm a mess."

"A hot mess."

"I don't think that means what you think that means." She chuckled. "But thanks, I guess."

"I'm just joking," I said. "It's what I do, you know…to avoid."

"I get that."

Katelyn leaned her head on my shoulder. I reached over to brush stray locks of her hair away so I could still see at least part of her face.

"Seriously, though. It's really pretty out here," she whispered. "Fall has always been my favorite time of year.

Campfires and brilliant colors and just a little bit of coolness after a warm day."

"My favorite, too," I agreed, but quickly grew somber. "Or it used to be."

Katelyn stayed quiet, but looked up at me as if she was urging me to talk. Something about her persistence made it to where I couldn't hold back the grief any longer.

"All I see is death," I admitted. "One minute it's color and beauty, and the next dead leaves are raining down. I see cold winds making the trees bare, but helicopter blades too. I don't see anything but winter coming, and I can't seem to get to the other side." I sat back and groaned. "It's dying leaves and brown grass, and trees like skeletons. Skeletons. How can I go on having seen what I just saw, you know? My pops bleeding out. Every creek runs red with blood. Red like these leaves. They're frickin' everywhere."

"I'm such an idiot. I never should've said anything about fall." Katelyn never cried, but a fat tear rolled down her cheek.

I wiped it away, and cursed myself for making her feel even the slimmest fraction of the pain that haunted me. "I don't ever want to take that away from you. You love fall, and I used to. Maybe I can again…but, right now, spring is looking a whole lot better. If, uh…forget it."

Katelyn had to know I was talking about rebirth. She nudged me with her shoulder. "I wish I could help you over to the other side where it's all green, and birds singing and sunshine."

"I wish you could too, but…" I exhaled sharply again. "I just need to stop wallowing."

"It's not even been a day," she said. "I think you're entitled to grieve."

"Entitled, huh? My pops always talked about entitlement, and how that was killing our country. Everyone thought they deserved everything for free, and never taking responsibility for anything." I gave her a wry smile. "Somehow I don't think the entitlement argument will convince me."

"I can't say anything right."

"I'm just kidding," I said. "But it wouldn't hurt to change the subject."

She nodded, and we sat there in silence for a while. The sun climbed high enough to peek through the tree canopy, enveloping us in a golden spotlight.

"What's your favorite color?" I asked out of nowhere.

"Not pink," she replied.

"I didn't think so. How about purple?"

"It's okay. I like some shades." Katelyn pointed to a maple tree with leaves of such a deep purple that they might have qualified as maroon. "That one's not so bad."

"Orange is my favorite," I said, pushing aside my earlier, darker thoughts about the fall. No matter what, I knew I was stuck with another month of fall colors, and realized I'd better get over it quickly. I pointed out a different tree close to the purple one, but brighter and carroty in color. "I really like that one there."

"Oh, yeah. I love the orange leaves the most," she said with a burgeoning smile. "Everyone probably likes the reds or yellows, but the blazing oranges are my favorite. Even more than purple."

"My favorite part of a campfire is the orange," I said. "The way the coals ripple with heat as they glow. The orange is the strongest. It burns the hottest."

"We could use a little heat. I love cuddling by a campfire." She snuggled back in next to me, and rubbed her hands together in the sunlight like she was at a pretend bonfire.

"I'm on fire for you," I blurted, having been weak enough in the moment to spill my thoughts. It's not like it was a secret, though I'd never shared anything quite that intimate before. "Ever since I saw you, I knew you were the one."

"Wow," Katelyn responded, seemingly a bit lost for words before finally giving a nervous chuckle. "You're, uhm, not so bad yourself."

"Thanks, I think."

"Oh, Zach. You know better than that."

I did. Affection was painted all over her face, which made her soft features glow like sunshine.

I wanted to kiss her so badly in that moment. To pull her tight and do things we'd never done before. But I lost my nerve, and couldn't follow through. The grief was too heavy to overcome. I wouldn't allow those kinds of intimate thoughts when my heart was still in need of mending.

Katelyn pressed the issue. She pulled her hair out of the ponytail and fluffed it seductively. Then she reached to cup my cheek in her hand.

The internal battle raged. My hands moved reflexively to wrap around her waist and pull her close. All the while, I babbled nervously, almost to the point of incoherence.

"You know, uhm, when the leaves are gone, this place is gonna look totally different," I said, trying and failing at ignoring her touch. "We're kinda, uhm…we're gonna be really exposed soon."

"I'd like to expose you," she purred, and reached for my coat.

"Good God, you're talking like me," I teased.

She smiled and took hold of my sleeve, gently pulling off my jacket as I watched. Then she sat up and shrugged off her own jacket, and twisted around to where she was sitting in front of me.

Katelyn planted her hands on my chest, and pushed me back against the boulder. My breath came in rapid gasps.

Finally, my body shook off the paralysis, and I grabbed for her. I pulled her into me, mashing my lips against hers with a hunger like I'd never known before.

My hands raced for the tail of her shirt. I grabbed her around the waist with one hand, while snaking the other up her side. She tickled at the touch, and broke the contact to shake with a nervous laugh.

"You're so cold," she murmured, and pressed her lips to mine once again.

Not anymore, I thought, and swept her to the ground. We rolled until she straddled me, covering my face with a curtain of long hair. She sat up long enough to brush it to the side before gently touching her soft lips to mine again.

The connection was electric. I burned. My body ached in a way I'd never experienced, but it was pure joy.

I grabbed for her hungrily, running a hand through her hair. I refused to break the contact. We rolled again, arms and legs tangled, lips locked.

An animalistic growl built, but not only from the back of my throat. A different kind of predator prowled; this one in the skies above. I pushed myself off Katelyn, and turned an ear to the sky.

Seconds later, the growl turned to the full roar of supercharged jet engines. A trio of swept-wing fighters passed directly overhead. The trailing sonic boom shook the ground like an earthquake.

CHAPTER 16

I slumped to my side next to Katelyn. I ran a hand through her hair, and whispered, "Dang it. Guess we'd better get back."

"They're gonna be freaked out that we're gone," she said, and looked to the sky. The sun was much higher now, meaning we were well past when the meet and greet was supposed to have started.

"Wonder why they didn't come looking for us?" I stood and offered a hand to pull her up. "No way they're not awake now."

"Yeah, probably been a while." She accepted my hand, and hopped to her feet. Before I could turn away to head back to camp, she wrapped her arms around my waist. "Alone time was amazing," she whispered and gave me a quick kiss.

"Yep, that's what you've been missing," I quipped.

"Have I ever."

Katelyn quickly gathered up her hair in a ponytail and took off for the camp. We hurried up the trail to the boulders in no time. Before I could wonder if we really should've come back together, we'd already weaved through the maze and stood at the opening to the cave.

Six pairs of eyes locked on us in a matter of seconds, but no one said a word.

"Awkward," Katelyn whispered, and walked over to her parents.

"About time you got back here, young lady," her dad said.

It was Spotted Fawn who gave me the sharper look. "Just get some breakfast," she said. "There's no more time for goofing off."

"I know," Katelyn said. "Sorry."

I went over to my mom. Though I never would have under any other circumstances, I spread my arms wide and gave her a hug. "Sorry, Ma. I didn't mean to-"

"Don't worry about it," she said as softly as she'd ever spoken in her life. A pained smile greeted me as I pulled away and took my place next to Austin.

"Feeling better, are we?" my brother said with a lewd grin.

"Dude. That's not cool."

"I don't blame you," he replied. "Wish I could take my mind off things for a while."

I groaned, and definitely wished I'd come back alone. Granted, Austin probably would've assumed the same thing, and he wasn't far off from the truth. But I didn't feel the need to enlighten him any further.

"So what's up?" I asked as Mom handed me a plate with pancakes.

"These are cold now," she said, and didn't bother to answer the question.

"They've met without you," Austin said. He didn't waste time trying to sugar coat things. "We're headed out this afternoon for Cherokee."

I shrugged, and started eating. I'd already resigned myself to that fact. It wasn't like I thought we'd just turn around and go back to our camp. Even if we had, we would've had to break the awful news to Maddie. It was best for me to keep moving forward and worry about that later. There was enough to worry about as it was.

"I guess I figured as much," I said. "Now what's the real story?"

"The little, uhm, spy…" Austin paused. "What did they call her?"

I tried to remember, but could only come up with a partial answer. "Something small, like chipmunk or mousey little something."

"Oh, right, Field Mouse. It sounds like she checked in this morning while we were sleeping. She's headed back to somewhere outside Cherokee. Supposedly she's already verified everything Noel had said about temporary bridges and the soldiers massing."

"Really? That's great."

"Yeah, great…I guess." He eyed me curiously. "Anyway, she's gonna do another quick recon and then wait to meet up with us outside Smokemont."

"Weird name. Sounds familiar," I replied, already growing tired of the details. Whatever was going to happen, I just wanted it over with.

"There's something about a bridge between Smokemont and Tow String. You remember that place?"

"Weirder name, but I'm sure I've seen it."

"Of course. Tow String's the horse camp up from the Visitor Center," Austin explained. "Mom and Pops took us there to ride a few times."

"Oh, yeah. Dang." That memory hurt. I supposed they all would for quite a while, but riding horses with my parents was particularly vivid. Dad had shown up in his usual attire, a white button-up shirt and khakis. Work khakis. I had been surprised he hadn't worn a necktie, and not a string tie like the old-timer cowboy types.

Thankfully, Mom had talked him out of the tie, but he wouldn't budge on the khakis. Or the white shirt, which had needed bleach when we got home courtesy of an unplanned trip through a berry patch—all thanks to Maddie's horse getting a bit feisty.

I found a smile creeping across my face at the visual, and quickly erased it when I realized Austin was still talking.

"Mouse is thinking the soldiers are gonna try to fix the bridge below Tow String first," Austin said. "Or maybe chopper in some troops farther up the highway behind us, you know, like you saw yesterday." He paused ominously. "Or both."

"Figures." I looked around at the assembled group. Several new people had joined Spotted Owl. They were all shaking hands and introducing themselves to my mom and Katelyn's parents. It wasn't quite as many as I'd expected for a War Council unless those people were just the leaders.

"Well, we knew this was coming," John said, suddenly appearing behind me. "Come on, bud. I'll show you the gear they're letting us borrow."

I followed John to the back of the cave where I was presented with extra water bottles, a selection of dried foods to put in my backpack, and a first aid kid. I held the packet in my hand, and stared at the assortment of bandages, gauze and antibacterial. There was hardly a thing in there to patch up a bullet hole, much less a rocket.

"You have enough ammo?" John asked.

I nodded numbly.

"Good." John tried to hand me a pair of binoculars. I declined, not wanting to weigh myself down with any unnecessary gear. "These guys have some nice stuff. A lot more military than ours."

"How about body armor?" I asked.

"I wish. They're not that military…but hang on." John looked through a couple more plastic tubs and pulled out a giant hunk of green, weathered steel. "How about a helmet?"

"Yikes, that's ancient."

"Heck, yeah. But you gotta protect your brain box."

"I'm not so sure," I quipped. "It looks heavy."

"More like weighs a ton." John tossed it from one palm to the other, and held it out for me to examine.

I turned up my nose at it. "I'll only wear one if you do."

"Alright. That's a deal." John turned back around to dig in the tub. "You might be off the hook on that one," he declared.

Spotted Owl walked over to us. "Y'all geared up?"

I set the helmet on the table with a clunk. "Sorta, I guess."

"You fellas need something else?"

"More helmets," John replied. He remained stooped over. "Or body armor?"

"No can do on the second one," Spotted Owl said. "But I think there's a bunch more helmets somewhere, plus some canteens, bandoliers…"

"Band-o-what?" I said.

"The shoulder slings that hold extra mags or shotgun shells," John answered.

"You thinking we're a fife and drum corps?" Spotted Owl said with a chuckle. "Ain't no marching band here. We're all about the stealth." He looked to me and suddenly sobered up. "Speaking of which, we've got more camo if anyone in your group wants to change clothes."

I knew exactly what he'd meant without him having to say it. Though little more than dark stains, the knees of my pants were permanently stained with my father's blood. No doubt my mom's clothes were even worse.

"Yeah, I should change."

Spotted Owl scooted farther back into the cave and found replacement jackets and pants for both me and Mom. I accepted as graciously as I could muster, and took off to give my grieving mother the new clothes. The helmet remained behind on the table like the discarded relic it was.

After changing and gearing up, I gathered at the opening to the cave with at least fifteen other people. Besides the eight in my group, Spotted Owl had brought together a similarly-sized group from his camp.

The two men from the night before flanked him. Off to each side of them, there were two couples. I assumed they were married, though probably not so old that they had kids close to my age.

"It's a little under five miles to Smokemont, but we're stopping a little short of there. Mouse will rendezvous with us on this side of the highway, on the ledge overlooking the campsite."

"Another camp?" Katelyn's dad asked.

"Not like this one." Spotted Owl gestured to the group. "This is all the help we've got for this mission."

"What about the War Council?" I asked without caring whether I had the right to do so.

He brushed me off. "More on that later. It's time to head for Smokemont."

"Hold on," I said, but Katelyn's dad interrupted my follow up question with one of his own.

"So if it's not a rebel camp, what's Smokemont?"

"It's an old touristy campsite like the kind with fire grates and concrete pads," Spotted Owl answered him with details that I could've provided myself.

Thanks to Austin's earlier comments, I realized I'd seen the campsite at Smokemont a couple years before on a family trip, though my parents never stayed at a place like that. My mother always insisted that we rough it in a backwoods camp that a person would have to hike ten miles to get to. In a lot of ways, it had helped prepare me for hiding out in the park.

I watched Mom straighten up as Spotted Owl talked. Her face was eerily calm as if she'd wiped away all emotion. I had no idea if that was healthy, but wished I could do the same. Every memory was torturing me, while she had clearly woken up much stronger. Or at least less easy to read.

Talking done, Spotted Owl led us through the boulder field and to the trail that ran right past the boulder where I'd spent part of the morning with Katelyn. I was in the middle of the pack, right behind her, and reached out to tap her on the shoulder. She spun around with a giant grin, and slowed at a wide place in the trail long enough for me to step alongside.

"Want to take a break?" I whispered in her ear. She squeezed my arm and pretended to shove me away. With strangers following on our heels, I didn't smack her on the butt the way I wanted as she skipped off ahead of me.

We headed down the hill into a lush valley. It turned out to be so dense with vegetation that I felt like I couldn't see more than forty yards. Somewhere off to the side, a brook babbled over stones, but I never caught sight of it.

Spotted Owl took us up a shallow incline, encouraging us to spread out as we walked. I knew exactly why, though I couldn't think of a time that the helicopters had attacked in the woods during daylight hours. I didn't know if the thermal imaging would even work very well in the heat of the day. Still, I knew they'd have no qualms about hitting us in the wide open, and hoped we wouldn't spend a single second exposed to the clear blue sky.

"Just keep following the trail," Spotted Owl told everyone as we filed past him. "Keep close enough to see the person in front of you, but no closer than that."

I let Katelyn drift ahead of me briefly, but didn't stay that way for long. As soon as I was sure I was out of sight from Spotted Owl, I jogged ahead to catch up.

"You're a little close, bud," she said.

"Not close enough," I replied with a rogue grin.

"You're practically all over me," she said, turning around to playfully shove me back a step.

"I wish, babe."

"Is that all you think about?" she joked, but seemed to immediately regret it when she noticed my face crumble like an old brick building. Obviously, I had plenty of other things weighing on my mind. "I just meant, uhm…"

"I know," I said softly. "I'm a guy. We're all pervs."

The joking fizzled. Katelyn forced a tight smile that came out like more of a grimace. "Not you, babe," she said. "You're a real gentleman."

"My da…" I paused awkwardly. "My momma raised me right."

"Yeah, she did. She's a strong woman."

I nodded. I refused to show emotion. I couldn't bear to see Katelyn's expression every time she thought she'd said the wrong thing. It wasn't her fault I wasn't dealing with things well. I knew that was all on me.

We settled back into a rhythm. Katelyn set the pace, keeping us just within eyesight of John up ahead, and me right on her heels. The path was too narrow to hold hands, and the conversations were too much of a minefield to talk. But the proximity helped me anyway. I could be a robot, yet know that Katelyn was right there for me, literally leading the way.

Spotted Owl came running up behind us. He was too quick for me to step back and pretend like I had been following his rules.

The big man slowed as he approached, and gave the two of us a disapproving shake of the head. But he only said, "We're almost to the rendezvous," before running on ahead.

"You see that look?" I asked.

"Hard to miss," she replied. "Guess we're not spread out enough."

Before I could stop myself, I said, "I'd like to spread you out."

"Jeez, Zach. You're getting a little, uhm…"

"Okay, that was a bit much," I said, blushing. "I admit it. I'm sorry. So much for being a gentleman."

"I know you were kidding," she said, before adding on, "Sort of."

"Yeah. Definitely sort of." I shook my head. "Enough of that for now."

"For now," she joked, and took my hand. She pulled me forward faster. "I think we're supposed to catch up to the others now."

We jogged on ahead, ducking under low hanging limbs. Our boots pounded the bare dirt, and soon had us right behind John, who had already caught up to Austin and my mom.

The trail widened out to where Katelyn and I could walk side by side. Spotted Owl was up front within view, moving much slower than he had moments ago. He held up a hand for everyone to stop.

He turned, and whispered so softly I could barely hear him say, "I'll be back with Mouse."

The others stood around in a group. No one talked.

I adjusted the rifle slung over my shoulder, and twisted my back side to side to keep loose. Austin tossed his backpack to the ground with a thump that drew several sharp looks. Ignoring them, he sat down next to it. Mom also shrugged off her pack, though she kept standing. She had company a moment later when Katelyn's mom came over to whisper to her.

Footsteps on the trail caught everyone's attention. I turned to see Spotted Owl hiking back toward us, but he seemed to be alone.

"Where's Mouse?" asked the bigger of the two bearded men.

"Right here." He stepped aside to reveal a girl that looked no more than twelve years old following behind him. Though not entirely accurate, it seemed to me like she barely came up to the big man's waist.

Her face was smeared brown with mud, as was her jacket. Leaves fluttered behind her as she marched with purpose toward the center of the group. Dark eyes that seemed to be all pupils stared at us through slits.

She angled off toward Austin and tossed a backpack decorated with leafy, cut branches next to his. White teeth grinned at him as she plopped down on the ground beside him, and waved for everyone to gather around.

"I'm only going to tell you this once," she announced with an unexpected gravelly voice. "So y'all better listen the heck up."

CHAPTER 17

"I like your style," Austin told Field Mouse when she was done talking and the adults had gathered off to the side to discuss the intel she'd provided.

"Sweet piercing." She grinned as she looked at the shiny metal stud through his eyebrow. "What's your name?"

I thought he might reply with some silly, made up code name. I wouldn't have put it past my brother to volunteer something ridiculous like Snake, Cobra, or some other reptile. Turtle would've been funny, but I thought that one might've already been taken by one of the two bearded men. The shorter, slower one.

"Austin," I heard him say as I leaned in a little closer to eavesdrop.

"Cool, Big A," she said, and bumped him with her shoulder. "You can call me whatevs. I kinda like Mouse, but it's pretty much all good."

"Mouse fits," he replied.

One of her eyes narrowed. "You can talk all the crap you want, but you make fun of my height and I'll knee you in the-"

"Ha. Yeah, right," he interrupted. "You can't reach that high."

I couldn't believe she didn't knock him out. Instead, Mouse said, "Nice one, Big A." She extended a hand to him, and they bumped knuckles. "I'm glad you're here. These other guys are soooo lame."

"Does she know him?" Katelyn whispered in my ear.

I shook my head, and kept watching them with barely contained disbelief. I'd never seen my brother actually talk to a girl. He'd talked about lots of girls, mostly the black-eyed, black-fingernailed ones who liked death metal music. But he'd never brought one over to the house before. Not that I had room to talk. Katelyn was my first serious girlfriend, or really my first one ever.

Mouse hopped up and pulled Austin to his feet. "C'mon, Big A," she said. "I wanna show you something cool. Let's get outta here."

"Hold on." Austin glanced back toward our mother, who was still embroiled in a conversation with the other adults. I caught his attention.

"Go on, Big A," I said with a grin. "I'll cover for you."

"Thanks, little bro."

Mouse pulled him down the trail, saying something that sounded to me like, "That cutie's your brother?"

"Well, that was bizarre," Katelyn said as they disappeared.

"I'm a little surprised he left with her."

"I'm not, but I meant Mouse. She's a bit strange. I swear she looks like she's a seventh grader, but sounds like she has a two pack-a-day habit."

I shook my head, and pulled Katelyn over toward the adults. Spotted Owl was in the middle of splitting the group into two.

"I'll stay with these guys," he said, motioning to my mom. "Forget about Smokemont. That's all clear." He gestured to the shorter, stocky man at his side. "Box Turtle will take you guys over to the Mingus Creek Trail…cross country. We need to hit the Visitor Center tonight, at dusk. Any questions?"

"What happened to Cherokee?" I asked from the back of the group, surprising myself with the ability to speak my mind in front of the adults. I seemed to be getting a little better at that.

"I guess you missed that part," Spotted Owl answered a little snottier than I preferred. "Mouse said they've already moved units out of Cherokee. They fixed the big bridge over the Oconaluftee this morning. They're working on the Mingus Creek bridge now, right past the Visitor Center."

"Oh, sorry." The wheels turned in my head. "Then shouldn't we hit behind them, and cut 'em off? Maybe take out the new bridge?"

"You're smarter than you look," Spotted Owl said, drawing a harsh glance and a sharp intake of air from my mother. "We're headed that way while Box Turtle takes these guys to the Mingus bridge. We'll take care of our targets, and meet up at the Visitor Center to surround whoever's left."

"Speaking of that," my mom said. "Who was watching the bridges? Shouldn't they have stopped this?"

Spotted Owl turned to her. Any swagger dropped from his voice when he said, "They tried. While you were sleeping, we lost a couple guys this morning." He glanced at the sky and took a deep breath, then turned to me as if to answer my much earlier question. "That's another reason the full War Council has been delayed. We're a little short on manpower. All the other camps are freaking out and wanting to protect the bridges close to them when they should be helping us with the big push."

"I hope you don't blame that on us," Katelyn's mom said, apparently taking issue with the way he'd made it sound like we'd been sleeping in and slacking after a brutal, grueling hike to his cave. I agreed with her wholeheartedly, and nearly lost it.

Spotted Owl quickly apologized. "That's not what I meant, not at all." He wiped the back of his hand across his brow. "They were just good guys. We were pretty close."

"Then it's time for revenge," Spotted Fawn said. "We're ready to take this fight to the enemy. We've had enough sitting around."

"Right on," Spotted Owl agreed. "Grab a bite to eat and get ready to move out. We've got a ways to go yet."

More backpacks hit the ground as people gathered up in the shade to munch on granola and take swigs from water bottles. Despite all the revenge talk that kept circling around, I managed to keep my thoughts off of my own loss. Instead, I wondered how rifles were enough to take down armored vehicles and massed enemy troops. The cover of darkness clearly wasn't enough of an advantage. If anything, I wondered if it was a disadvantage.

Spotted Owl circulated among the group, offering words of encouragement to everyone as he passed.

As he walked up on me, I was compelled to ask, "How do we blow the bridges? We used propane tanks to take them out the first time."

"We've got a little surprise waiting for them." Spotted Owl flashed a sly grin. I thought it made him look more like a maniacal clown than a rogue warrior. He leaned over and added, "Let's just say we've been waiting for this moment for a while."

"Alrighty," I said, still unconvinced. And I certainly didn't like surprises. "Such as?"

"ANFO," Spotted Owl answered.

"Anpho-what?" I looked to Katelyn, who shrugged in reply.

"The world's first IED," Spotted Owl half-explained, and stood tall again. He spun around. "I need to find Mouse. Anyone seen her?"

Katelyn and I didn't answer him.

Spotted Owl turned back to me. "Where's your brother?" he asked, and quickly read the answer on my poor poker face. "Oh…"

"Is that a bad thing?" Katelyn asked innocently.

"I reckon she's got him down by the road by now, probably rollin' in the mud."

"Say what?" I said, thinking more like what I wanted to do with Katelyn.

I definitely couldn't hide my immediate reaction, and Spotted Owl saw right through it—especially when Katelyn said, "Ewww."

"I hope not that. I meant for camo." Spotted Owl wiped at his brow again. "She'll want to get him all painted up to go scouting, like commandos."

"He'll love that," I deadpanned, and had a hard time stifling a smirk. I figured my brother might as well have a little fun, and there was no doubt he'd eat up every second of getting to play real life Call of Duty, especially with the cute girl.

"I swear that girl loves to smear mud all over her face," Spotted Owl said. "I should've named her Sewer Rat."

That sounded strange to me, and I asked, "*You* should have?"

"Well, yeah. The little runt's my daughter."

CHAPTER 18

"No way. How old are you?" I asked.

"Better yet, how old is Mouse?" Katelyn asked right after me.

Spotted Owl looked from one of us to the other and said, "Thirty-eight and eighteen."

"No way," we uttered in unison.

"You didn't think I looked that old?" he asked, seemingly offended.

"No, and she definitely doesn't," Katelyn answered. "I thought she was twelve."

"Me, too."

Spotted Owl chuckled. "She gets that a lot, but I sure wouldn't tell her that. There's no telling what she'll do."

"Yeah, she seemed kinda feisty," Katelyn said.

I was the one to chuckle. "She'll get along great with Austin then."

"Not too great, I hope." Spotted Owl glanced back down the path in the direction they had disappeared. "If they're not back soon, I'm sending out a search party."

Lucky for Austin, he showed up with Mouse right when Spotted Owl had almost fully transitioned from anxious to aggravated. He scowled at Mouse, and didn't bother saying a word to Austin. With a growl, he announced to the group, "We're burning daylight."

"It's time to split up," the bearded man codenamed Box Turtle added. "My group over here." He stepped toward the trail that Austin and Mouse had just walked back up.

I scrutinized my brother as we gathered around Spotted Owl. He'd definitely spent a little time rolling in the mud. He had two big swipes of dirt below his eyes that made him look like a baseball player. His pointed nose had been similarly covered, though not quite to the extent of his cheeks. The mud did nothing to hide the grin plastered all over his face.

"Have fun?" I whispered.

"You have no idea. She's wild."

"I really didn't need to know that."

"No, dude. I just mean she's like so, uhm…free. Like not a care in the world." He swallowed slowly, and the smile slowly disappeared from his face. "I guess I needed that."

"Now you know how I feel," I mumbled under my breath and edged over closer to Katelyn.

I stood next to her, waiting for Spotted Owl to give the order to move out. For all the supposed rush, he kept standing there as the other half of the group disappeared down the trail.

"We don't have quite so far to go," Spotted Owl explained to several questioning looks. "Might as well give them a little head start."

Mouse had already sidled over next to Austin, and I hadn't even seen her move a muscle. The little girl slipped a hand through the crook of Austin's arm and looked at him like a baby bird waiting for a meal.

The stupid grin crept across Austin's face again, and I felt happy for him in a way that I never had before. Everyone needed someone to be their cheerleader, or just to be there for them. And Mom has no one, I thought, and stole a look at my stoic mother.

"Not so long that you can get comfortable," Spotted Owl clarified, having apparently seen his daughter snuggle up to Austin. He stared at them. "We've still gotta get to Tow String to grab the supplies, so we might as well get moving. Come on."

I soon learned that we wouldn't have a trail to follow all the way to the old horse camp. We took off down a slope leading away from the knob, and crossed a ravine on a path no wider than a game trail. Soon we were huffing and puffing as we headed back up a steep incline.

Spotted Owl showed no signs of stopping. I noticed that he turned around often, and scowled every time he noticed Mouse and Austin right on his heels. I was happy to be back bringing up the rear with Katelyn. Still, it irked me that Spotted Owl looked at my brother so contemptuously. As far as I was concerned, I was the only one allowed to do that.

Mouse seemed itching to get out ahead of the group. She often ran right up on her dad's heels, dragging Austin behind him. I was impressed with my brother's endurance. Certainly, showing off for Mouse had a good deal to do with it. Austin's only exercise prior to our time in the woods was flexing his thumbs on the newest video games.

After clearing the hilltop, I stiffened at the view ahead. Far below and off in the distance, I caught sight of a little ribbon of asphalt glimmering in the noonday sun.

"That's the highway," I told Katelyn, though she could have easily figured it out for herself. I stared for a moment longer before feeling too exposed on top of the ridge. The craggy slope knifed into the sky, and I had to hop over a few rocks that seemed sharp enough to slice us in two.

I helped Katelyn down, and hurried her along to the waiting woods. We hunkered under a huge bush to wait while her parents finished the climb.

"Did you see the camp?" she asked me.

It took a moment to catch my breath. "Not really. Seemed like there might have been a little clearing down by the river, but I don't remember if that's the place or not."

"You've been there…to Bow String or Two String or whatever it is."

"Tow String," I corrected her, "though it never meant anything to me. Bow sounded a lot more logical, especially with the reservation on the other side."

I thought I saw a cartoon light bulb pop on over her head. Slowly, she said, "Duh. Cherokee."

"Exactly. It's a town inside the reservation. Anyway…I've been to Tow String a few times. They used to rent horses out of there."

"I'd love to go horseback riding sometime."

I flashed back to what had become my least favorite movie, and got an image of the teens in Red Dawn riding horse like Afghan rebels as they attacked Russian helicopters. It didn't end pretty, and I shook my head to clear the image. Though not completely like the night before, it hit way too close to home.

"Zach?"

"Nothing. I just…" I paused to collect my thoughts and sort out the bad ones. It took a while, but Katelyn waited patiently. "Riding's kinda fun, I guess. It'll make your butt sore, especially on these hills. But the horses were real tame."

"I'd like that," she insisted. "It's a shame we can't do that kinda stuff anymore."

"We will someday." My countenance firmed up, and I looked at her with more determination than I'd mustered in weeks. "We definitely will."

She nodded, surely humoring me, I thought. But somewhere along the way, a tiny flame had been lit inside me. I wouldn't look at the same orange leaves and see decay. I'd see fire, or so I hoped.

As the fire smoldered, Spotted Owl walked along the edge of the rocky spine to gather up the troops. "Follow me. It's down to the creek, then out to the road."

A few groans replied, but no one offered any disagreement. In short order, we were working our way back into our usual places as we trudged down the slope toward the bottom of the canyon.

Austin skipped past me trailing behind Mouse. I called out to him.

"Bro! How's this awfo stuff like an IED?"

"Awful? What are you talking about?" He seemed anxious to follow after Mouse, but slowed to listen.

"Spotted Owl said he had a surprise for the soldiers. Something like anpho, or awfu, or something that was like an improvised explosive device." The IED word I had no trouble understanding. Too many people knew too much about those kinds of weapons.

"Oh, ANFO," Austin said. "It's an acronym."

"What for?" I wracked my brain. Words came to mind, but not a single one made any kind of logical sense. Finally, I admitted, "I don't have a clue. Enlighten me, smart guy."

"The A-N is Ammonium Nitrate. F-O is fuel oil." When I shook my head, Austin said, "A fertilizer bomb."

"How do you know about that?" I asked, looking at him incredulously.

Austin seemed more concerned about whether Mouse was going to wait for him. I saw her skipping on ahead, right behind her dad. I would let him go, but only when I got a couple more answers.

"So how do you know?"

"Grandpa used to talk about it. They used to blow up tree stumps at the farm by mixing diesel fuel with fertilizer."

"I vaguely remember that," I said, though it was about as miniscule a recollection as possible. Given all the times that the Feds had bugged our phones and confiscated our computers, I had to point out, "At least you didn't research it on your computer. That really would've set the Feds off."

"Not that it could've gotten much worse," Austin said. "But, yeah, it was mostly Grandpa. Oh, also that nut who blew up those offices in Oklahoma City. Pops told me how the guy had mixed up a big batch in a van or truck or something and parked it outside the building."

"And totally destroyed it," I said, cringing at the memory. We'd driven past there once, and my folks had wanted to stop to look at the memorial. "My God, that was sick."

"I remember hearing about that," Katelyn said. She slipped her hand into mine as we reached a wider place in the trail. "That was so awful. I can't believe anyone would do that to innocent people."

"Yeah, but it happens all the time," Austin said, his mood shifting like a storm cloud, growing darker by the second. "No different than what they're doing to us now."

"You think?" I objected at first, though he could see Austin's point in a way. Evil was evil, no matter the purpose or cause or whatever.

"Could you imagine the power?" Austin said with a maniacal grin spreading across his face. "Just think of the fireworks we can make. Forget propane bottles. If Spotted Owl has the right ingredients, we can do all kinds of damage to the Feds. This time, they'll deserve it."

I shuddered at the thought. Even though they'd killed my dad for no reason, it was a hard argument to swallow. Even though they'd killed civilians and bombed cities. Even though the fire was smoldering inside me, begging for revenge, I wasn't sure I could pull the trigger when the time came.

I tapped the rifle on my shoulder reflexively and shivered.

Austin ran on ahead to catch up to Mouse. Probably to cheerlead the plan, I thought, and found myself wracked by tremors again.

"Are you okay?" Katelyn asked.

"Not really. My stomach's killing me."

"It's a lot to process," she whispered.

I wanted to keep hold of her, but the woods thickened up again with brambles that forced us back to single file. As I let her go ahead, I thought back to the picture of the crumbled building at the memorial site, the names of the deceased, and the photographs of the families with all their tears.

I fought back my own, and mumbled, "No one deserves that."

CHAPTER 19

"How you holding up?" Mom asked me once we stopped again. Spotted Owl had just told us that the highway was a scant hundred yards away, and had wanted everyone to get another snack and a drink.

"Fine," I replied, but it couldn't have been much further from the truth.

The guilt ate at me as I realized that I'd barely even spoken to my mother the whole day. First, I'd run off to hide half the morning with Katelyn. Then I'd been distracted packing to leave, followed by a long, thought-filled hike across the mountains.

I glanced up at Mom and patted the ground next to me. Katelyn went to leave, and with my other hand I grabbed for her wrist. "Stay," I pleaded with a whisper.

She settled back down and munched on some granola as I turned to my mother. I analyzed her face and thought I caught a glimpse of anguish behind her steely eyes. But so little. The woman was a rock. I wished I'd gotten a little more of her iron constitution and perhaps a little less of my dad's sense of obligation. He had been one to please others, except for the new regime.

"And how are you holding up?" I asked. "For real."

"One day at a time," she said, and patted me on the shoulder.

"None of the platitudes, or whatever they are." I focused on her like a laser beam. "Are you okay?"

"I'm torn in half," she admitted, and it broke me. I swallowed down the tears and listened as she explained further. "It's like a piece of me is gone. The most important one…the one that kinda holds me together. When I was crazy and impractical and bouncing off the walls, your father was the glue that held me together. And I don't know how to go on."

I was too choked up to reply.

"Mrs. Walters," Katelyn said. "I don't guess I could know anything about that, but I…I just have a feeling you're gonna be fine. I mean like someday, you know? Soon, I'm sure. It's like, uhm, you're always so prepared."

"Not for this, hon," she replied. "I don't know how anyone could be."

"Oh, gosh." Katelyn stammered, "Th-that's not what I meant. I was just thinking that you're always so tough. I don't know anyone as strong as you."

"Thank you, dear," she said softly. "I'd say there's two kinds of strength. The outside is holding up alright, I guess. But that's as thin as wallpaper."

"The way I remember it, wallpaper is impossible to remove. My mom made me help her once, and it was like the hardest job ever."

"Good God, girl. You're right about that. That stuff sucks." Mom chuckled. It was a good, deep belly laugh that soon had all three of us smiling. Tears ran down Sunning Bear's face the harder she laughed. "Then maybe I just need to work on the inside a little more."

"No one cares about the outside," I offered. "You never did."

"You calling me ugly, kiddo?" she said playfully.

"No, uhm…it's just what you always taught us, right? About being better people on the inside." I cracked a smile upon seeing that she wasn't upset about my unintended insult, and tried to continue lightening the mood. "And not letting

Maddie wear too much makeup. You wanted us pretty inside and out, not covered in black eye shadow."

"At least you listened." She smiled at me. "And I think it worked. You're even nice to your sister."

"Usually," I agreed. "But if she had a code name, it would have to be Raccoon Eyes or something like that."

All three of us belly laughed again. Spotted Owl hurried over and stopped just short of calling us out for being too loud. We needed this, and a stern look from me was enough to send him back the other way.

The point was taken, nonetheless. I knew it was time to get back on our feet and finish the first part of the mission. The sun had started its descent several hours earlier. It wouldn't slip behind the mountains for a little while longer, but there were only a couple hours left until dusk. Then things would really get serious.

"We're following the creek down to the road," Spotted Owl told the group. "Stick right behind me."

"We'll go ahead," Mouse said, chattering like a squirrel. "I can run on up there to check it out." She reached back to grab Austin's hand and pulled him up next to her. "I'll take Big A with me. We'll be careful."

"Big A?" Sunning Bear said to me. "Is that your brother?"

"Yeah," I said. "It came as a bit of a surprise."

"That's a curious nickname. It's…not all that fitting."

"He is kinda tall, I guess."

"And hanging all over that girl," Mom whispered incredulously.

"I thought you'd be more upset about him running off ahead to scout."

"I don't like it, but he can take care of himself." She kneaded her hands together as she watched the two speak softly to Spotted Owl. "It's more that she looks like a child."

"She's like eighteen," I guessed, having not exactly remembered Mouse's age.

"Huh. No way." Mom smiled wryly. "Anyway, I didn't think Spotted Owl would seriously let them go."

To our surprise, a quick nod from Mouse's dad had been all it took for the new couple to hurry off down the stream. They seemed more about speed than stealth at that point. I hoped they'd at least slow down when they got close to the highway, though Mouse had seemed jacked up on adrenaline. I wondered how she made such a great scout. I'd always thought recon was better suited for the slow and silent types.

Austin and Mouse were probably halfway to the road by the time the rest of the group started moving again. Spotted Owl was in the lead, urging us to follow him down the flat creek. Unlike the mountain streams, this one seemed wider to me, and considerably slower running.

There were no rocky steps to climb on the smooth gradient. Instead, Spotted Owl kept us right along the edge of the water, stepping over rocks and ducking under branches as we hiked toward the road. Every so often, when the brush closed in on one side, Spotted Owl would meander back and forth across the stream, choosing rocks carefully to keep his feet dry.

He held up a hand. I skidded to a halt on a flat rock. Seeing Spotted Owl crouching and unslinging his rifle, I mimicked his posture in every detail, and stared ahead. A gap in the trees seemed to indicate the road, but I couldn't see around Katelyn's parents.

Wordlessly, I gestured for Katelyn to slide over a little. She made room on the boulder where she was perched, and I shuffled over next to her to get a cleaner view.

The trees ended about thirty yards ahead before picking up again on the other side of the highway. A dirt embankment holding up the roadway was severed at the creek where the long span of a bridge had once stood.

I had never been so relieved to see a missing bridge. I let loose a breath I'd been holding, and ran a hand through my hair.

"They haven't fixed this one yet," I whispered to Katelyn as I hung the rifle back over my shoulder.

"No. But I thought they said the soldiers were close?"

"Could be, I guess. But this seems like good news, so far."

Suddenly, Mouse and Austin came out of nowhere, bounding down the creek as our group sat there waiting. They moved so fast I thought they might be running from someone. Tension gripped me in its talons.

I dove for the woods, pulling Katelyn behind me. The second a big tree shielded us from the approaching scouts, I unslung the rifle from my shoulder again.

"Easy, bro," Austin's voice called out. I peeked around the tree, and he flashed me a thumbs up, nearly sliding off a slippery rock in the process. It was enough to keep him from teasing me about my mini-panic.

Regaining his footing, he hurried to catch up to Mouse. She stopped well short of the group and cupped her hands to her mouth.

"All clear," she announced loudly, only to be shushed by her dad.

Spotted Owl rose to his feet and waved the rest of us onward. We met just short of the bridge. I crept closer, with five beats of my racing heart to every footstep.

The sun rained down on the opening, making me feel like we were spotlighted. I shook my head to try to dislodge the dark thoughts, but my brain wasn't having any forgetting.

Katelyn pulled me forward, seeing how I'd frozen just short of the bridge.

"Come on," she urged, and kept her hand locked on my wrist.

I looked at the devastation numbly as we walked under where the bridge had been. Piles of old masonry littered the bottom of the creek, though much of the debris had apparently washed downstream.

A couple of older, blackened timbers had been pushed up against the side of the stream by the rolling water. Smaller, splintered pieces had been wedged in the remaining rock piles. As I looked at the devastation, the shattered bits told me a story—though it turned out to be one I hadn't expected. Obviously, the resistance had blown the bridges, not the government, but somehow the story got turned around in my head.

The charred wood and blackened stones were a home. I imagined someone sheltering inside a little building right before it had been blown apart. The splintered wood seemed more like little knives than matchsticks, and the longer pieces swords and lances discarded from a medieval battle.

The bits and pieces of total destruction all took on a life of their own. It reminded me way too much of a missile strike, and my feet froze up again like a stubborn mule.

"Keep up," Mom called, having already cleared the wreckage and taken off downstream toward the horse camp.

I looked up the slope to the road. Some stone of the old foundation was still standing at the bridge abutments, but most had been wrecked by the blast. The stones had rolled like a cave-in to the streambed and been carried on downstream. Katelyn tugged on my arm, trying to do the same.

"We need to go, Zach." she pleaded.

"I'm...trying," I said.

John came back toward the old bridge crossing. Standing at the edge of the woods, he asked, "What's up? Everything alright?"

"Yeah," Katelyn replied, and tugged on my arm again.

Embarrassment was a more powerful motivator than anything else. I put my head down and trudged toward the woods before anyone else could call me out for being slow. Still, the images of a ruined village, broken stone and wood, filled my mind.

I imagined helicopters firing missiles into groups of poorly armed, medieval peasants, and it was obvious which group I represented. Two words, suicide mission, started swirling in my head again. Though we would be armed with homemade bombs and rifles, I didn't see how our little insurgency could hold up against a trained, professional military force.

I blinked, realizing Katelyn had asked me something, but only managed a weak, "Uh huh."

"You didn't hear me, did you?"

"Not really," I replied sheepishly. "Sorry."

"I didn't mean to bother you. It was nothing important.'

"I'd rather you did." I exhaled and quickly surveyed my surroundings. We'd gone so far downstream that I couldn't see the bridge anymore. The horse camp would be up ahead a little farther. Letting myself get lost in my own head was dangerous when I should've been concentrating on my surroundings. Nevertheless, I admitted, "My head's swirling with all these crazy thoughts."

She hesitated as if unsure to ask, but finally said, "Like what?"

"Missiles and helicopters and…I dunno."

"I swear I heard a chopper a minute ago."

"But we're still walking…" I looked to the sky, and mentally kicked myself for not paying more attention. "Shouldn't we be hiding?"

"I know what I heard," she insisted. "I told John."

"And he didn't believe you?"

"No."

"I believe you." I squeezed her hand. I stopped walking and cupped my free hand to my ear to listen. "I just don't know what to believe myself," I muttered, and pointed to my head. "I'm the one hearing all kinds of crazy things in my brain."

"I don't hear it anymore. It might've gone a different way."

"I wish they'd be quiet," I said, meaning the rest of the group as they tromped down the stream toward the horse camp. Rocks tipped and clanked, and boots pounded the dirt, drowning out any faint noises.

"We should go, Zach."

"Hold on." I swore I heard something buzzing in my head, but wasn't sure if it was my imagination.

"That's the sound," she said, her face brightening.

As the volume grew to a roar, Katelyn's satisfied look quickly erased. I pulled her down into the underbrush. The whopping sound confirmed it was definitely not my imagination.

CHAPTER 20

"Get down!" I yelled ahead to the others.

Bodies crashed through the brush, getting far away from the creek. In the distance, I noticed the much more open forest of the campsite. Luckily, we hadn't made it that far. But I was no less terrified.

I debated splitting up from Katelyn, not wanting to be close to her if the bullets started flying again. Thinking of thermal imaging, I eyed the creek ready to jump in the water like Austin had the previous night, though it was so shallow that I couldn't submerge my whole body.

Before I had the chance, the trees swayed all around me. Wind rushed, stirring leaves. I shielded my eyes from the dust. A helicopter came out of nowhere to hover almost directly overhead.

I reached out blindly for Katelyn, and found her arm. My hand locked on her wrist, and pulled her close. The trees whipped violently in the downdraft.

I chanced a look, and was surprised to see the chopper had glided off a little farther to the west. It hovered over the blown out bridge.

Dust got in my eyes, and I had to look away. I blinked rapidly and stole another quick glance.

It was the longer, more bulbous profile of the type Austin had described as a Blackhawk. From open side doors, ropes tumbled down.

"They're dropping troops," I yelled to Katelyn, who had her head buried in her hands.

Despite the racket, she heard me and reacted immediately.

Remaining concealed, I pointed to the troops rappelling to the ground barely a hundred yards away. Blinking away the dust, I gestured farther down the creek toward the rest of our group. "We need to get outta here."

A second helicopter trailed in after the first. Katelyn and I hunched over and raced downstream as fast as we could go, while the second chopper hovered over the drop site and began unloading four more soldiers.

I caught up to John first, and motioned for him to follow us ahead. We got as close to the open woods of the camp as we dared.

I could make out the location of concrete pads where tourists would've parked their big campers. There was no way I was going any farther, and was relieved to see my mom and Katelyn's parents off to our right at the edge of the woods. I waved to get their attention, and they came over as soon as the second helicopter sailed off to the south.

No less stressed, I quickly asked, "Where's Spotted Owl?"

"I don't know." Katelyn's dad cupped his hands to his mouth.

Spurred with fear, I reached for the man's hands. "Don't yell," I said sharply.

He spun around to stare at me. "What?"

"There's soldiers, Dad," Katelyn interjected. "They dropped them at the bridge. Didn't you guys see them?"

"Oh, crap," John said. "I wondered what they were doing over there."

"Wow, we just missed 'em," my mom added. "Good work, kids."

"Yeah, it pays to be a slacker," I said bitterly. "We saw the whole thing go down. Two sets of four rappelled down right where we were at."

"I thought that might be the case," a deep voice said from behind me. I turned to see Spotted Owl rise up from behind a boulder.

I wondered what he was hiding for, but didn't follow up on it. Instead, I sat back as the adults talked strategy. At that point, I figured the less I knew the better. Though it didn't necessarily make sense, I had gradually come to realize that I worked best when things were spur of the moment. The more I thought about something, the more it froze me.

"Analysis paralysis," my dad had always said, though he'd meant it more with regard to the banking industry. It was something about watching the markets fluctuate and not making the right move until it was too late. Still, it seemed to apply to a lot of different situations in my life, and I couldn't afford to let the freezing happen anymore.

The time to analyze, or overanalyze, would have to come later. Until then, I resolved once again to be an emotional blank, and just react—hopefully wisely. It was a gamble, and Dad had also liked to say, "Gambling is a tax for people bad at math. The odds are never in your favor."

I could only hope they would be with me this time.

I looked up and saw something dark flash at the edge of the woods. As the adults continued talking in hushed tones, I zeroed in on the movement. It seemed to be a pair of shadows slipping between the trees like the sun coming and going from behind a cloud. Right when I was convinced my mind was playing tricks on me again, Mouse and Austin stepped out into the open and approached a small, concrete block building at the edge of the horse camp.

"There's Big A and Mouse," I interrupted the others. "We should head over there."

"Quietly," Spotted Owl added, and raised a hand. "Follow me."

We kept deep enough in the woods to remain concealed, moving at a painfully slow pace. I stared out across the camp as we crept along. I couldn't help but think about how popular the place used to be. I imagined families tossing washers and laughing. People cooking on the grill boxes, and spreading out tablecloths over the splinter factories that were the old wooden picnic tables. Kids riding their bikes around the paved areas, dodging the crush of cars and people on a busy summer weekend.

Off in the back, well behind the little block building, a large wooden barn stood. Though once majestic, it looked more decayed than the hundred year old structure on my grandpa's farm. The whole barn leaned heavily to the side as if a stiff breeze could topple it like a kid's Popsicle stick craft.

The only thing solid about the structure was the roof. It still appeared to be watertight, though the metal roofing had aged about forty years in the last five. The red metal had dulled to an unpleasant brown. Big dents and rust showed through in several places.

The neighing of the horses was long gone. As a breeze howled through the valley, the campsite seemed to moan instead. The barn creaked, setting me further on edge.

"Get it together," I mumbled under my breath as we closed on the shower house where Mouse and Austin waited.

The brick portion of that building had held up well. I was even surprised to see the windows hadn't been broken out. A few were cracked, though, and all were glazed over so thickly that they looked more solid gray than clear.

A bathroom door hung open crookedly, held to the frame only by the bottom hinge. The shingled roof was covered with so much green moss and grime that I thought it seemed more like the forest floor than a roof. I wasn't surprised when we got closer to see grass growing between the gaps in the thick wooden shingles.

More brown grass had grown up through the wide cracks in the sidewalk around the building, some reaching to knee-high. The road beyond was potholed to the point that the once black asphalt looked like weedy gravel.

"This place is wrecked," I muttered. The whole park was devastated, like an apocalypse had swept the land and left no life behind to maintain it. The crooked door hinge creaked, reminding me of the once proud barn—and pretty much the whole world as I'd known it.

Pressure built in my chest to the boiling point. The soldiers were too close. There was no civilization, and the man who was going to help lead the change lay dead by a stream. I cursed under my breath, drawing yet another concerned look from Katelyn.

So much for being an emotional rock, I thought. Having seen the decimated buildings and painfully empty park, I felt yet another piece of my humanity fall away. At that rate, it would be gone faster than sand slipping through my fingers.

CHAPTER 21

"Wait here," Spotted Owl told the group. He crept toward the bathrooms, calling out under his breath for Mouse and Austin. Oddly, he stayed away from the front side of the building with the separate entry doors for men and women. Instead, he moved toward a small, metal door at the back of the building, again saying, "Mouse?"

A dirt-smudged face peeked out the back door. Mouse hopped out and waved, saying, "It's all still here."

"Not so loud," he chided, and practically dragged her away from the building. A confused looking Austin followed her, and they headed back to the waiting group.

Spotted Owl dropped to a knee, and motioned for everyone to gather around.

"There's some good news." He spoke so softly that we had to crowd in uncomfortably close. "All the ANFO supplies are still here, so we can make a big ole boom. The only question is how to go about doing that."

"If it's just eight soldiers, then maybe we don't want to waste the big stuff now," John suggested.

I thought eight well-armed soldiers seemed like no small force, but Spotted Owl nodded approvingly. "That's what I'm wondering."

"It seems to me like bypassing the soldiers and getting down to the Visitor Center is a better plan," Katelyn's mom suggested. "We're on a schedule to get there, right? Granted that does leave us with soldiers behind us."

"It sure does," John said. "And they're here for a reason, meaning they're securing the bridge site before a convoy or whatever gets here to rebuild it."

"And that convoy is probably already on the way," my mom added. She turned to Spotted Owl. "Will the other group be able to intercept them?"

"I don't have a radio to find out," he answered. "Or to know if they even can. Without any ANFO, God knows they can't do much against APCs."

"Armored Personnel Carriers?" I asked John discreetly.

"Yeah, bud. That's what Noel said."

"We maintain radio silence on missions," Spotted Owl was saying when I tuned back in to the conversation. "No need for anyone to overhear us when we're this close. Speaking of that…we need to make a decision one way or the other. We can't hang out here all day if those soldiers decide to spread out and comb the woods."

"I doubt they would," John said. "Surely they're sitting tight, maybe digging foxholes or something, waiting for the convoy to come."

"Then that could be a plan," Katelyn's mom said. "We could forget those guys, and get down to the rendezvous point."

"But if we take them out, we'll get better weapons." Austin surprised me by arguing for the attack. I knew my brother was militaristic, but he seemed genuinely bloodthirsty in the moment. "We need their stuff, like machine guns and body armor. Maybe grenades."

"It's not Call of Duty, Big A," I retorted. "There's no easy weapons upgrades or care packages for us."

"You think I don't know that?" Austin looked more serious than I had ever seen him before. "But we've got a mission to do, and the gear those guys carry can help us."

"We could pick them off. It should be easy enough to sneak around." Mouse tapped her rifle. It hung so low on her shoulder that it seemed like it would drag the ground. The little girl straightened up to her short height. "Me and Big A can do it."

"If we do it, we all do it," Spotted Owl said, and looked over the group.

"So it's settled then." John turned to Spotted Owl. "I vote to attack."

"They'll know we're coming if we hit one little outpost," Katelyn's dad argued.

John wasn't dissuaded. "Dad, they're gonna find out soon enough."

"True story. And I'm willing to take that risk," Spotted Owl said. "I'd rather have a clear line of retreat, and we sure can't let them get any farther up the highway."

"Alright," my mom agreed. "It's sure as hell time to shoot back. God knows they started it."

I cringed but kept my thoughts to myself. I leaned back on my heels and stared at the sky as Spotted Owl sketched a quick map in the dirt. He circled the bridge, and said, "We need to hit them from all sides. They'll be sitting tight, probably dug in." He drew x-shapes all around the circle. "So we need to split up into teams and surround them. When I fire the first shot, everyone needs to open up on 'em. Got it?"

Several nodded in agreement. I felt my stomach wrinkle up into a little ball and squeeze bile into the back of my throat. I failed at swallowing the bitter taste initially, and had to resort to a couple long drinks from my dwindling water supply.

"If anyone surrenders, we take 'em alive," my mom said firmly. "We don't slaughter prisoners."

Spotted Owl twisted his head as he looked at her, but held his tongue. After an uncomfortable pause, he said, "We'll tie up prisoners here, in the shower house…if there are any."

"Alright. The sooner we get there, the sooner we can beat the convoy," John said, rising to his feet. "Let's roll."

Katelyn shared a nervous glance with me. I didn't have any words of encouragement. It had been one thing to run into Gatlinburg to save her mother, or to cower in the woods as the rockets rained down, but I'd never fired a shot at anything bigger than a deer. And I'd felt bad enough when it fell over—at least until I'd tasted fresh meat for the first time in days.

"Stay with me," I said softly, and fell in behind the others.

Spotted Owl led us back toward the road, but avoided the creek. We moved so slowly I thought a turtle could beat us in a race, but speed obviously wasn't the concern.

Not much later, Spotted Owl stopped and held up two fingers. He pointed to the right first, then held up two fingers again and pointed to the left.

Austin and Mouse were quick to jump forward and take off to the road without a look back. More timidly, Katelyn's parents went off to the right.

"You're with me, okay?" Spotted Owl whispered to my mom, and I almost objected. Before I could open my mouth, the big man pointed at me and Katelyn. "You two stay with John."

"Ma?" I said weakly.

"It's okay." She nodded firmly. "Just keep your head down, kiddos."

"We will," I mumbled, and watched as she slipped away through the forest.

"You're my problem now," John whispered with a laugh. "Stick close to me and you'll go places."

"Straight to hell," I muttered under my breath, but quickly erased the frown to concentrate on following right after John one footstep at a time. The closer we got to the enemy, the more concerned I was about shielding Katelyn.

Apparently, she didn't want to be shielded. Every time John stopped to plot his next few footsteps, she snuck up next to me to look.

My heart thrummed so loudly, I was certain the soldiers could hear it.

John stopped again, abruptly. The sound of something metal chinking on rock carried through the deathly quiet forest.

"They're digging in," he whispered. "We're close."

I watched with fascination as John dug his fingers into the ground and pulled up a wad of dirt. "Don't move, sis," he said, and smeared it all over her pretty face.

She scrunched up her nose, but bit her tongue. I thought she looked like a child having a parent wipe chocolate off her face, or more like wiped on.

"You're next," John whispered, turning to me.

"I'll do it myself," I said, waving him off.

He flapped his muddy hand in my face. "C'mon, bud."

"No, I got this."

What I got was dirt in my mouth, and had to spit to clear it out. Once John finished with his own make-up, he pulled his rifle off his shoulder and motioned for the two of us to do the same.

"It's time to get into position."

"Where?" Katelyn asked.

"We'll just crawl a little closer. We need to be ready for the signal."

The signal, I assumed, was the crack of a shot and a soldier toppling over. It wasn't far from the truth.

John got us close enough that we could see the shapes of soldiers scurrying across the roadbed on the side of the bridge closest to Cherokee. Spread out shoulder to shoulder, myself in the middle and Katelyn on the far end of the line, John raised his rifle and looked through the scope.

"There's two men up on the road. The others must be dug in on the slope."

The vagueness didn't make me feel any better.

"Looks like they dropped in some sandbags," John continued. "They've got body armor. Nice helmets too, not like the one I tried to give you." He looked to catch my reaction, but a glum face was all I could offer. John focused back in on his scope. "They're moving pretty cautious, but I don't think they have a clue we're coming. Get your rifles up and pick a target."

Target. Seemed like a good way to look at the situation, I thought. Targets weren't people. In a way, neither were the Federal agents. They were cruel creatures that harassed and killed without mercy. I wasn't like that.

My finger resisted touching the trigger guard, but I managed to ease off the safety as I looked with my naked eye at the shape of an enemy soldier. Through the leaves and branches and failing light, the figure seemed more like a shadow. Maybe a bit like those paper outlines that I'd used for target practice at my grandpa's farm years before.

Targets, I told myself again. That's all they are.

But one of them spoke. Yelling rose from the bridge, followed by the sharp crack of a rifle. As the thunder rolled down the valley toward me, the target toppled off the slope into the creek.

CHAPTER 22

John opened fire. The blast from his rifle shoved on my eardrum, instantly deafening me. I blinked for a second, expecting the world to stand still like it had when I'd fired on the deer, only to have the sound gradually come back. And it did, but with a shrill ringing that drowned out everything but thumps of more rifle fire.

John shot again before I could shoulder my weapon. In my haste, it took a while to get lined up with the scope correctly. The lens blackened around the edges as I moved my head. I finally got a clear view, but of nothing but brown. Lying on the dirt, I adjusted my body to try to find the road somewhere among the mass of never-ending forest.

Two more shots came from John before I finally located the road. A green lump was stretched out on the pavement, not moving. Another soldier, rather target, knocked down.

I searched for more targets, but still hadn't gotten my finger close to the trigger.

A fusillade of bullets whizzed over my head. The burst sounded more like the grumbling, burping sound from the helicopter's Gatling gun than a normal rifle.

"Machine gun!" John shouted over the racket. It sounded like he was underwater.

Limbs fell off the trees above us. I thought I heard a bullet whizz past my good ear. I rolled to look at Katelyn.

She was trying to peer through her scope, but seemed to be having about as much success as I'd had at finding a target.

I shouldered my weapon again, and tried to scan the bridge site. Once more, it took a moment to find the roadway. This time I came at it from below, working along the embankment, and caught sight of a helmet poking out of an earthen hole like a prairie dog.

Its owner looked no older than Austin. But Mouse was a lot older than she seemed, I reminded myself, and settled back in behind the trigger.

Before I could work up the nerve to shoot, the gunshots tapered off. From across the road, my screeching ears could barely make out Spotted Owl yelling, "Drop your weapons!"

"Screw you!" someone yelled back.

"That bridge worth dyin' for?"

Gun shots raked the hill where Spotted Owl had called from. While the machine gun blasted away, no one seemed to fire back at it.

I quit watching the boy in the foxhole, and swung my weapon around, trying to find the machine gun. I had to return fire. For all I knew, Spotted Owl might've been hit in the burst. He needed cover fire.

As I scanned the woods all around the bridge, a dark realization struck me hard as a bullet. My mom was with Spotted Owl. She might've been hit.

My heart clenched up like a rock in my chest. I couldn't lose my mother too, and only a day apart from my dad. Fueled by rage, I hunkered back behind the rifle scope again.

A single shot ripped out from well off to my left, and the machine gun fell silent. Austin whooped, "Got him!"

"Anybody out there? You better drop your weapon!" Spotted Owl called again, relieving me enough that my heart started beating again. But until I knew if my mother was okay, I couldn't be myself.

John rose, and I tugged at his jacket.

"There's a kid still up there. This side of the bridge, on the left."

"Then we go get him." John raised his voice to shout, "Stand up and show yourself! Lose the gun and step away or you won't see another day."

Katelyn and I followed behind John as he stalked toward the road. When he got close, he rushed forward with rifle trained on the embankment. I jogged behind, praying the soldier would be smart enough to give up.

When I saw him up close, I was even more certain he was a kid. Somehow I felt older, and definitely more composed, however unlikely—especially considering how I had been an ordinary high schooler a few months before. Being thrown into a firefight and hiding in the hills was a world apart from trying to avoid a bully in the hallways.

John pointed his rifle at the boy, and gestured for him to climb up onto the road.

"Don't shoot me," he whimpered. When John motioned more forcefully, the kid quieted and complied. Without another sound, he climbed up the slope unsteadily, and cowered on the pavement, close to the lifeless body of his former comrade in arms.

"He's the only prisoner," Spotted Owl announced as he emerged from the woods across the road. To my delight, Mom was right behind him looking perfectly healthy, if a bit pale.

"Everyone okay?" John called out.

Several voices replied, though the ringing in my ear prevented me from making out all their owners. I stood on the edge of the road, and watched the woods as the pairs filed back to the bridge. It was easier to do that than concentrate on the sprawled out soldier leaking dark blood onto the pavement.

"Nice work," Spotted Owl said when everyone had been accounted for. "We need to make tracks, so grab the gear and let's get the heck outta here."

Austin leapt off the roadway, and skidded down the slope toward a hastily dug pit. I didn't move, but watched as my brother tried to lift a huge machine gun from a foxhole ringed with sandbags.

"Damn this thing's heavy," he said, straining until I thought he'd give himself a hernia. Mouse scurried over to help him, and together they lifted it from the pit. They barely managed to carry it up the road, and dropped it with a metallic thunk on the asphalt.

"Thanks for the help," Austin said, looking at me.

"I thought someone with a name like Big A could handle it."

"I did, didn't I?"

"Not really," I mumbled under my breath, not wanting to start a fight.

Katelyn asked Austin, "What are you gonna do with that?"

"Duh. Take it with us."

I bristled at the way he spoke to her, but Spotted Owl came over to Austin before I could reply with something unkind.

"Good find." He bent over and easily picked it up in his meaty paws. "That's mine now."

Skinny Austin seemed to shrink before the big man, and slowly stepped away.

"Go grab ammo for my new toy," Spotted Owl told him. Then he turned to address the group. "Take their uniforms and body armor. We might as well gear up like soldiers."

I didn't want any part of touching the bodies. I mustered up enough resolve to pick up the helmet of the dead man on the road, but I wasn't going to do anything with their clothing. Seeing how many had leaked blood all over their uniforms, I had no desire to start undressing the dead, much less wearing any blood-soaked garments.

I was somewhat more willing to collect the soldiers' weapons. I picked up a black assault rifle and hefted it in my hands. It was metallic and tinny sounding, which stood in stark contrast to the finely crafted, wooden-stocked hunting rifle of mine that felt both heavier and better put together.

"Bring that over here," Spotted Owl told me.

As I went to drop the rifle in a growing pile of weapons, Katelyn left me for a moment to help her parents gather up gear.

Heeding my unspoken thoughts, the group opted to pick up the body armor and helmets only. We'd look enough like soldiers that way, except for one person. As we gathered up the gear in a pile down by the creek, I did a quick headcount. With nine in our group versus seven fallen soldiers and one prisoner, I realized one person wouldn't be getting any armor. Though I wouldn't have minded some extra protection, I was fine with that person being me.

Spotted Owl went through the gear pile, rapidly handing out helmets and heavy vests laden down with steel plates. When he got to Mouse, he paused.

She looked like a child trying on school clothes in a department store as he held up an armored vest that would drape to her knees. "That's not gonna work." He plucked a helmet off the pile, and set it on her head.

Austin laughed, drawing a sharp rebuke from Mouse.

"That's no good either," Spotted Owl said, and passed it off of to Austin. "Sorry, little Mouse."

"It's fine," she said, and kept her trademark spunk. "I don't need that stuff. I'm ten times stealthier without it, and twice as fast."

"That you are."

It came time for me and Katelyn to get gear. I hung back, but that didn't prevent Spotted Owl from shoving a heavy vest in my arms.

"Put this stuff on." Spotted Owl looked quickly to the sky. I got the impression he wasn't thinking about the waning daylight when he added, "We're wasting time."

I nodded, not willing to argue. I thought about tossing the gear aside when we took off hiking, but realized that wouldn't go over well with the group. So I walked to the side to examine my new armor.

If I'd seen even a speck of spattered blood, I might've filled the helmet with vomit. Thankfully, it was clean. Almost new looking, which surprised me. I'd assumed the soldiers' gear had deteriorated as badly as the roads, the schools, and pretty much every other aspect of society. But deep down I had known better. Those that enforced the laws would have the best gear. The bulk of the country's budget went to the military, the police, and the spies who kept tabs on the people.

The body armor was similarly clean looking. I wasn't sure why it wasn't blood spattered, and quickly realized I must've been given the scared kid's gear.

"Lucky for me," I mumbled under my breath, and returned to Katelyn.

"I look ridiculous in this," she said, pointing to the oversized helmet on her head.

"You look, uhm…fine," I said, momentarily taken aback at seeing her dressed like a solider. Like the enemy.

"You paused," she pouted.

I blinked and cursed under my breath. There was no way Katelyn was the enemy no matter how she was outfitted.

"Babe, you look gorgeous in anything," I said, and honestly believed it.

Her face was hidden in shadows, though her cheeks still shone. Her long brown hair spilled out the back of the helmet, since she'd had to undo her ponytail to get the helmet to fit properly. Still, it hung slightly crooked on her head.

"There's a chin strap to tighten it up," I said. "Let me get that."

Like a child with a bicycle helmet, I tried my hardest to adjust the strap without pinching the flesh under her chin. Mission accomplished, I stood back with a grin. "You look good, like ferocious."

"I still feel ridiculous," she said, but offered no further complaints.

I shrugged my shoulders, now weighted down with what felt like twenty pounds of steel. "It's gonna be hard to move in this stuff."

I noticed the rest of the group had geared up. They'd moved over to the pile of weapons. Austin was really looking the Call of Duty part and a little bulkier as he towered over Mouse.

"Only a few hand grenades," Austin told Spotted Owl, who had picked up a pair of baseball-sized objects from the pile of black rifles and ammunition magazines.

"You and John can hang onto those," Spotted Owl said, and handed them out first. "Just don't jack around with 'em."

"Of course not," John said, and he stooped over to choose an assault rifle and a couple magazines from the pile.

"I'm gonna miss my trusty old rifle," he told me as he came to stand next to me and Katelyn.

"What should we do with those?" I asked. "Leave 'em here?"

"Maybe. It's a lot to carry."

"Bring them with us," Spotted Owl said, having overheard the conversation. He handed a rifle to Katelyn, and then gave me a black one just like it. "We can leave them back in the horse camp when we grab the supplies."

"Oh, yeah," I mumbled. I'd forgotten we still needed to go back to get the bomb-making stuff, and then there was a whole heck of a lot more work to do after that. And it was getting darker by the second.

The sun had dipped below the mountain sometime during the shootout, and we'd since spent a fair amount of time gathering up the supplies. We'd been moving very quickly grabbing things up, but still spent arguably too much time. The longer I stood there in the edge of the woods, the more the nerves crept up again. I'd lost the aching in my gut from when the battle had started, but it came back with a vengeance.

What hadn't gone away was the ringing in my ears. They shrieked at me, and I fished a finger underneath my helmet to press on the flap of skin in front of my left ear. Other than a temporary easing of the pressure inside my head, it accomplished nothing. Still, I would repeat the motion countless times throughout that evening.

"Grab the prisoner and let's go," Spotted Owl said, waving us off into the woods. "We're pushing our luck."

I agreed with that sentiment. I started walking with Katelyn, happy to be back under thicker cover. I looked over my shoulder so many times that I nearly slipped on a couple different occasions. But I was curious about the kid, and continued to do so.

I watched John lightly take the kid by the arm, and urge him to follow. By my assessment, there was no need for guns poking the prisoner in the back. He was perfectly compliant, if terrified.

The kid kept his eyes to the ground, saying nothing as John guided him along the creek. But eventually he looked up, and caught me staring at him. Again, his eyes went back to the ground. I slackened my pace to wait for John to catch up, though I wasn't sure why I slowed. I would've much rather been done and back in Spotted Owl's camp—or back in my own.

"Now I've got my own prisoner," John said as he caught up to his sister and me. He cracked a giant, seemingly fake, smile. "You're not the only hero."

The kid looked up at me, and examined me through narrowed eyes. I felt uncomfortable under the gaze, and even more so by John's ribbing.

"I'm no hero," I said softly, thinking about how I'd performed under fire. I hadn't turned and ran, but I hadn't exactly saved the day. Nor had I wanted to. Fortunately, that hadn't been necessary.

Katelyn nudged me with her shoulder, and said, "Doing okay, Zach?"

I ignored the question at first, and let her slip ahead of me. My boots pounded on the hard ground. Each step seemed extra heavy with the steel-plated vest weighing me down.

The prisoner's armor bore a name plate sewed onto the right breast pocket. I pulled on the fabric to try to read it upside down.

"Call me, Bullinger," I told her, announcing the name aloud.

"Okay, Bull." She looked down at her own armor. "Apparently I'm Sylvester."

"Stallone. Now you're Rocky," I said with a grin.

She seemed to like the nickname. With a wink, she said, "Maybe you should be Bullwinkle instead."

"I don't even know what that means."

A deep voice rose from behind us. "Kids. No appreciation of the classics."

I turned to see Spotted Owl on our heels. With the big gun hefted in his hands like a metallic baby, he was only missing a couple of bandoliers crisscrossed over his shoulders to make him look like the ultimate action movie hero.

"It was like some kind of ancient cartoon, right?" Katelyn asked Spotted Owl.

"At least you got that right. It's kind of an old one...about the adventures of a flying squirrel and a moose."

As I stood there clueless, Katelyn asked, "And Bullwinkle's the moose?"

"That's right," he answered. "Rocky and Bullwinkle."

"So you're calling me a moose," I said with pretend annoyance.

"Maybe in that armor."

"Hey." I hefted my rifle into my left hand so I could playfully smack her with my right one.

"You forgot to mention the dim-witted part," Spotted Owl told her. "The moose was dumb. Happy, but really dumb."

"Ouch," I said. "This just keeps getting better."

"I'll leave you guys to figure all that out," Spotted Owl said, excusing himself to head closer to the front where Austin and Mouse had scampered on ahead. Those two always seemed to be in a hurry to get somewhere the fastest.

We were close to the horse camp when a shrieking roar built up from the south. Definitely not helicopters. Jets streaked in low and fast, seemingly heading right for us.

"Hit the dirt!" Spotted Owl yelled.

Katelyn and I launched ourselves to the ground, right beside the creek. As the jets roared immediately overhead, the world turned bright white.

Multiple explosions burst all around us. The booms shook so hard that I thought the earth might split apart beneath me. My ears screamed in protest.

Earth and rock rained down over us as I buried my head deeper in the dirt.

A woman screamed.

CHAPTER 23

"Sound off!" Katelyn's mom seemed to be screaming frantically, though she sounded like she was submerged in a swimming pool. "Kids, where are you?"

I couldn't respond. My ears shrieked with pain. Too disorientated, my brain swam to the point that I thought I might vomit.

"Everyone alright?" Spotted Owl asked. He rose up from in front of John and the prisoner, and dusted off his heavy vest.

Katelyn groaned next to me. I reached for her, and rolled her to her side.

"I'm okay," she mouthed, or so I guessed.

I kneeled at Katelyn's side, and helped her sit up. Leaves and dirt clods covered our clothes. I picked a leaf from underneath her helmet and helped her stand up. Her mother came running over a second later, her dad in tow.

I accepted the hug and a jumble of rushed words that I couldn't fully hear. Leaving Katelyn to continue hugging her mother, I scanned the area for the others.

The woods looked more like a jungle. Smoke hung low, and not the usual wispy clouds that twisted light as a fairy. It was not Smoky Mountain humidity hanging like a clean mist. The air stank of explosives.

From the direction we had recently vacated, the forest was wrecked. Trees had toppled, some still diagonal like the vines of a tropical rainforest. I had no idea how many bombs had fallen, but they had devastated the forest around the bridge and all the way to the horse camp.

My mother emerged from the smoke, walking with a limp. I ran to her.

"I'm okay," she said, waving me off.

I cupped a hand to my ear. "I can barely hear you."

"You're yelling," she said, and motioned with her hands for me to lower the volume. She raised her own. "I said I was fine. Just banged up my knee when I hit the dirt."

"Thank God," I said, and leaned in for a hug.

"It looks like everyone's okay," she added, and spun me around so we could march back toward the others.

"It's like they knew where we were going," I muttered, and looked ahead to the camp. It didn't appear to be as devastated, but a pair of bomb craters and the force of the blasts had leveled a number of trees.

The concrete block of the shower house seemed to have held, but the stables in the back had finally fallen over. I whistled under my breath, and found my feet pulling me away from Mom to get closer to the camp.

The horse barn had toppled over in the direction it had been leaning. Boards poked out from a giant pile.

I wondered about the supplies, and hurried on ahead to where I saw Austin and Mouse dusting each other off. Before getting too far in front of the others, I stopped to wait for Mom, and then Katelyn and her parents to catch up. Bringing up the rear, John came along with the prisoner.

It had been a miracle, I decided. Obviously, someone had heard the racket or gotten a call or something when we'd assaulted the bridge. We were just lucky that it took a little while for the jets to get there, though not so fortunate that the government forces had basically carpet bombed the woods trying to wipe us out. Things were getting serious, perhaps desperate.

"They might come back and hit us again," Spotted Owl said. "So let's hurry."

He rushed with Mouse and Austin over to the shower house, but pulled up short. I jogged with the others behind him, and soon noticed why he had stopped.

The blown out windows along the front came as no surprise. The bigger issue was the far side of the building. It had partially caved in, scattering concrete blocks across the sidewalk.

We rushed around the back to find the door to the supply room blocked shut with more blocks. The roof in the far corner sagged.

Spotted Owl dropped the machine gun to start chucking blocks from the door. The rest of us joined in and essentially set about dismantling the whole back corner of the building by kicking out loose blocks and tossing the broken scraps into the woods.

"I can climb through there," Mouse said when we'd removed a good portion of the wall to about halfway down. The rest seemed too sturdy to bust out without a sledgehammer, and the door was still tighter than a rusty bolt.

Spotted Owl looked from her small physique to the opening. Though most of the upper wall had been removed, there remained a solid four feet of wall. She could barely look inside on tiptoes. And the roof sagged even lower.

"Dad," she said, and made up her mind for herself. She dragged Austin over to the wall and motioned for him to squat. "Give me a boost, Big A."

In a rare moment of contradiction, he said, "I should go in first."

She wasn't having that. "Just follow me." To everyone's surprise, she jumped on his shoulders, trying to drag him to the ground.

I decided Rocky was the wrong nickname for Katelyn. If anyone reminded me of a flying squirrel, it was Mouse.

"Now get down here and give me a boost," she demanded, and he listened that time.

Spotted Owl came over to peer inside, but didn't turn around to where I could read his expression. Instead, he turned his attention to the sagging roof, and reached up with both hands.

"Help me hold this up," he said over his shoulder, and Katelyn's dad joined him in keeping the rafters propped up.

Austin helped Mouse inside the little building. Then John gave him a thigh to step on so he could hustle inside after her.

"It's all okay," he announced a second later. My ears had cleared up a bit, and I leaned closer to hear what sounded like heavy bags sliding on the concrete floor. Plenty of grunting and cursing followed. "But no way we can get it outta here."

"The door?" John asked.

"Not going anywhere."

"Stand back." John tried to kick it down, but to no avail.

"Told you," Austin said. "Hold on."

"We're going out the front," Mouse said, "if we can beat this other wall down."

"What wall?" John slid in front of his father to look into the room. "Alright. I'll come around from the other side."

The sound of shoulders and feet thumping against drywall rose until it sounded like a construction crew was inside the little room.

"Oww!" Austin cursed again. "Why's this stuff inside here anyway?"

Through gritted teeth, Spotted Owl said, "It needs to be kept dry."

"So it's in a shower house? That's dumb."

"Actually it's in the pump room." Spotted Owl failed at biting back all the sarcasm. "As you've probably noticed, that's separate from the showers."

"Oh I've noticed," Austin replied. The pounding started up again.

Wood cracked, and I instantly looked to the ceiling, expecting to see it come crashing down. But it was the crew inside finally having some success breaking down the interior wall. That was my cue to get back to work.

I took Katelyn around to help unload before the adults had to tell us. We jogged to the door on the women's side of the bathhouse. She yanked open the door, the one with two working hinges, and held it wide open. The floor was littered with broken glass.

I stopped in the doorway.

"You can go in," she said. "I'm sure you've always wanted to."

"It's not that," I replied cryptically. Though I was admittedly curious about what kinds of features were inside the women's room, a reflection in a tiny fragment of glass stuck in the window pane had caught my attention.

"What's up?" she said as I backed away from the door.

"Something's moving out here," I whispered. "Get down."

I crouched next to the building, pressing my back up against the cold blocks. Through the descending darkness, I scanned the open area. Beyond the first few rows of picnic table and grill boxes, the campsite grew gradually murkier until all details eventually faded out. But I knew I'd seen a shape move.

"Maybe it's a bear," Katelyn said, no doubt remembering back to our earlier trip to Gatlinburg when we'd seen a black bear in a similar campsite.

"Maybe." My eyes focused in on a big green dumpster about halfway across the camp. A bomb had fallen short of the dumpster, and the resulting blast had tilted the sturdy receptacle to one side.

I knew bears liked rummaging through trash, but they wouldn't find any handouts in the camp. It had long since been deserted. Besides, all the dumpsters had special locking mechanisms on the handle to keep out nosy varmints.

Our moms and John made all kinds of noise from inside the shower house, trying to help Austin and Mouse break free from the back room. With the two men still holding up the roof on the other side, I was left to either explore the noise or wait for more movement.

Waiting had never been my strong suit.

Something had moved, and I knew it was there.

"The best defense is a good offense," I mumbled, repeating my father's clumsy sports analogy. "Stay here, Rocky. I'll be back."

"I'm coming with you," she said, and slipped away from the door to the women's room.

"There's something behind the dumpster." I pointed across the campsite. "Just wait here and I'll be back."

"Not a chance, Bullhead."

"I thought it was Bull-twinkle."

She laughed, momentarily breaking the tension. "Bullwinkle, and you're acting all stubborn now. Let me help."

"Fine." I waved my rifle to the side for her to keep to my right. "We'll go at it from both sides. Slowly."

We hadn't gone twenty paces before I thought I saw a head peek around my side of the dumpster. Bear or not, I made the quick decision that a charge was in order. Better to take the creature by surprise, if that was even still possible.

I reached over to tap Katelyn's arm, and hoped she didn't feel the trembling in my hand. "Forget slow," I said between ragged breaths, and I hadn't even exerted myself yet. "We run, on three."

She nodded. I saw the way her slender fingers gripped the rifle until her knuckles turned white. Only then did I notice I was doing the same thing.

Katelyn looked at me questioningly, and I realized I hadn't started the count.

"One...two...three!"

We took off at a sprint. I ran straight for the corner before eventually veering out wide to the left. Katelyn's boots pounded as she kept pace with me, circling to the right.

Just short of a big tree, not twenty yards from the dumpster, a dark shadow rustled and jerked away from the corner.

I threw myself behind the tree and yelled, "Come out with your hands up!"

No one answered. Pointing the rifle toward the corner, I advanced slowly. I swung out farther to the side and called again.

"Come out or we'll shoot. We've got you surrounded." Unfortunately, my voice cracked on the last phrase, dramatically weakening the effect.

Still no answer.

I wanted to tell Katelyn that it had to be a bear, but I kept my thoughts to myself. She had advanced across from me. A few more steps and we'd both find out.

I sucked in a deep breath, and jumped ahead with rifle leveled.

At the top of my lungs, I yelled, "Freeze!"

It was no bear. A brown-jacketed figure startled and backed away, clanking into the side of the dumpster. From a dust-caked face, wide eyes stared back at me.

CHAPTER 24

"Noel!" I shouted, but didn't lower my weapon.

The cowering man straightened up when he recognized me, but immediately raised his hands when the rifle wasn't lowered.

"What the heck?" Katelyn said as she rounded the other side of the dumpster.

"Yeah, Noel." I slowly looked to her. "And, of course, we got attacked again." I pointed the rifle menacingly, and waved for him to get up.

Noel pointed to his ears, and mumbled something. His eyes, always dull, seemed even more off than normal. Perhaps because his face was dark with soot. His mouth hung partly open, leaning to one side like the broken bathroom door.

He mumbled something and gestured to his ears again.

"What's that mean?" I asked.

"I think he's trying to say he's deaf." Katelyn hurried around to join up with me. "Looks like you got yourself another prisoner."

"Yeah, the same one."

I waved with my weapon for the man to move. He struggled to get to his feet, but I had no interest in helping the man. Instead, I encouraged him to hurry up.

Noel got himself balanced and pulled up. Splotches on his canvas coat were as black as ash, though not as dirty as his pants. It seemed to me like he'd rolled around in a campfire, and sounded about the same way with how his breathing rattled in his chest.

"His lungs sound funny," Katelyn said loudly, not able to whisper and have me hear her.

Noel seemed to understand what she'd said, and bobbed his head. He rubbed his throat with his hand.

"We'll get you some water," I said. "Now move it out."

I gestured toward the shower house for Noel to walk, and the man complied. With slow, jerky steps, he hobbled toward the building. Before we got all the way back, I spotted John. He carried a five gallon bucket in each hand as he stepped through the doorway to the bathroom.

He dropped them both on the sidewalk and ran toward us.

"Are you kidding me?" He looked from Noel back to me. "Guess you had to one up me on the prisoner thing, didn't you?"

I was happy to hand over my captive to John. Though Katelyn's brother wasn't carrying a weapon, he made up for it with attitude. He roughly grabbed the man by the hood of his jacket and guided Noel back toward the shower house.

My mom was the next one out of the building, also carrying a pair of five gallon buckets. She set hers right next to John's and hollered for Spotted Fawn as soon as she saw us coming. They both met us not far from the building, and instantly peppered us with questions.

"Hold on," I said before they could finish. "I'm not telling the story five times."

"Fair enough," my mom agreed. "He looks a little worse for the wear. Dump him here and help us carry out more stuff. Katelyn can watch him." She gestured toward the young soldier. "And the other prisoner."

"Yes, ma'am," I said, and hurried inside the building—that time with no qualms about entering the ladies' room.

Broken glass crunched under my feet as I headed past a row of sinks on the left and stalls on the right. It seemed pretty much like a normal bathroom, minus the urinals. That gave me valuable insight into where I might have made the wrong assumption in the past. I'd always thought girls were just slow in the bathroom, primping for hours in the mirror, when it seemed like maybe they just needed more toilets. Urinals took up far less room than stalls, and the troughs at the ballpark even less. Not that I was a fan of the trough. I was almost willing to wait in longer lines for a little more privacy.

"Back here," Austin called, pulling me from the fascinating revelation.

In the back, a few tiled stalls for showering stood off to the left. Austin was on the right peering through a giant hole in the wall like a cross between the Kool-Aid man and a peeping Tom.

"Hey, bro. Take these."

He passed a bucket through the wall. My arm sank to the ground, and I had to grunt to pick the bucket back up off the floor.

"Feels like sand," I said through clenched teeth, and took a second bucket.

"Fertilizer isn't light," John said, "and five gallons of it makes a good forty pounds. Just wait until we add the fuel."

"That's not in here yet?" I asked as I staggered toward the door.

I added my buckets to the growing stack, and rushed back inside a couple more times. The pile grew to the point where I wasn't sure how we could possibly carry that many buckets. With nine in our group and some weaker than others, I did a quick count of the bombs. I came up with fourteen stacked outside on the sidewalk.

And that was before John brought out red plastic cans like the ones my dad had used to fill the lawnmower. That was my least favorite chore. I'd quickly grown to hate the mower, but as the youngest male I'd been assigned the job anyway. Though only a year older, Austin had paid his dues, and Maddie was supposedly too fragile to help out. Still, I would've given anything to go back to the way things had been, even if it meant wrestling with the world's toughest pull start. I'd nearly thrown out my shoulder trying to get that beast to run, but Dad hadn't the inclination or the money to replace it after he'd been fired.

"What's that?" I asked John, though I was sure I knew the answer. It was more what he was planning on doing with those cans. We didn't need anything more to carry.

"Diesel fuel," Spotted Owl explained as he rounded the corner of the building, no longer needing to hold up the roof. "Pop those lids and let's get it soaking."

I was about to question him about whether that was a good idea, but knew we obviously couldn't carry all the fuel cans and the buckets at the same time. I was even a little relieved to find out it wouldn't add much more weight to the loads.

"It's five percent diesel, ninety-five fertilizer mix," Spotted Owl explained as he handed Austin and John the fuel containers.

"And if we run out of diesel?" John asked.

"There's enough for this batch," Spotted Owl, alluding to the possibility more buckets remained behind. "Besides, kerosene works too…but we've got more use for that stuff in the camp."

"Cool," Austin said as he snapped the lid back on the first bucket. "And how do we blow them?"

"Blasting caps," Spotted Owl said. "I'll fetch those in a minute."

"What about dynamite?" John asked.

"That would work better, but that's not an option." Spotted Owl finished filling a second bucket. "You remember Wood Duck? He worked heavy road construction, so he had access to blasting caps."

"That was fortunate," Katelyn's mom said. She reached over to pick up a filled bucket and move it aside. Though she obviously strained, it wasn't more than she could handle. Nevertheless, I saw blistered hands and aching backs in our future. And we had our weapons to carry too. Fortunately, we could sling those over our backs.

That reminded me of our other weapons. "Where are we leaving our hunting rifles?"

"I was gonna say the stables," Spotted Owl replied, "but I think we'll have to drop them here."

"Along with the prisoners?" John asked.

"Prisoners? Like more than one?" Spotted Owl paused and looked up to see John pointing to Noel. "Whoa, he's back!"

Noel raised his slumped head ever so slightly, and locked eyes with Spotted Owl.

"Now that's crazy! Never thought we'd see that guy again." Spotted Owl looked to John. "Any clue what he's doing here?"

"He won't talk. Zach found him hiding behind the dumpster."

Spotted Owl patted me on the back. "Nice work. You're really wracking up big numbers on the prisoner count."

I ignored the praise. "I don't know why he won't talk. I mean he sounds really scratchy when he breathes, but he acts like he can't hear a thing."

"Too close to the bombs?" Katelyn's dad asked.

Spotted Owl shook his head. "If he'd been that close, the concussion should've killed him." He fastened the lid on the last bucket, and straightened up. "Well, we've got us a dilemma."

"You're not gonna kill me, are you?" the kid whimpered.

Everyone turned to him, seeing how he'd barely spoken other than to beg for his life back at the bridge.

"Of course not," Spotted Owl snarled. "That's something your people would do."

"We're just going to tie you up nice and tight," John said with a sneer. "Maybe find you a nifty little gag and a blindfold."

"Don't leave me here," he begged. Tears poured from below droopy eyelids.

"Why not?" John said sharply.

"I won't tell nobody," he pleaded. "Take me with you."

"No way," Spotted Owl said.

"You're a blubbering mess," Katelyn's dad said, piling on to the poor kid to the point that I almost felt sorry for him. "We sure as hell don't need you slowing us down."

The kid sniffled. He raised his head a little taller, and more firmly said, "I'll help you guys. I don't want nothing to do with my unit." He wiped his runny nose on his shirtsleeve. "I been wantin' to leave, but they'd never let me. You guys done saved me."

I traded a look with Katelyn, and noticed a similar sympathy in her eyes. Spotted Owl, ever the brute, wasn't as moved.

"We don't need two deserters. One was enough."

"Believe...the kid," a very scratchy Noel said, startling everyone. His voice was so rough he could barely get out the words. "Only the...truly evil...don't wanna desert."

"I thought you couldn't hear," John said, getting right in Noel's face. He grabbed him by the shirt and pulled him to his unsteady feet. "Why you playing us?"

"Leave me. I'll only...slow you down." He coughed until his eyes bulged, and slumped back against the building.

"You didn't answer the question," Spotted Owl said, stepping next to John. "What are you up to?"

"I didn't..." Noel began coughing again, and couldn't stop until my mom offered him her water bottle. He took a couple drinks, but his throat was no less scratchy. "I didn't sell...y'all out." His dark eyes flashed accusingly. "You left me...in the woods."

"After we were rocketed," John said, taking the words out of my mouth. "Everyone else found their way back except you."

"Did you...look?"

"We were busy," I said, stifling the emotion as well as I could.

Noel reached over to pull up his pant leg. A bloody shirt was wrapped around his lower leg. "I laid in a hole...all night." He reached up to unzip his jacket. His hands were so unsteady it took a moment, and he only lowered it far enough to expose the top of his bare chest.

"At least you're not dead," I muttered, but instantly regretted it. I looked away, ashamed at the outburst.

"You bandaged your own wounds," Mom said somberly. "And we left you."

I turned back to see Noel nod. The deserter didn't shed a tear. Instead, he looked at his lap. "You can…leave me…again. Just come back."

"He could watch the prisoner," Katelyn's dad suggested.

"Unless that kid has some use," John said, though I wasn't sure that Katelyn's brother actually believed it. "We should find out."

"Fine," Spotted Owl said. "But we've gotta hurry. We're way behind and only getting later."

"Spill it," John told the kid.

"Private James Bullinger," he replied. "First Calvary. Fort Benning, Georgia."

"Not that military crap," John said, but Spotted Owl jumped in.

"So you're from the same base as Noel." He turned to the deserter. "Those details check out?"

Noel nodded. "First Cav was posted…there too." He cleared his throat. It didn't help much with the scratchiness. "But I don't…know him."

"So what's the deal, Private?" Spotted Owl asked. "Why'd your people take the bridge?"

"They're rolling out tonight at dusk. Gunships and armored vehicles." He looked at Spotted Owl, and showed no remorse. "As long as it took to fly up here, I thought we were too far out front…but the officers didn't listen. They never listen."

"Where are they massing at?" John said, no doubt knowing full well that the answer was supposed to be Cherokee.

"Outside this little town, in some Indian reservation or something." He shrugged and didn't completely melt from the sharp, questioning glares from the group. "That's all I heard…honest. I'm not from around here, and grunts don't get to see maps."

"Anything else?" Spotted Owl asked. "Seems like you don't know much, and that's not worth a whole lot to me."

"I'm not supposed to. I'm supposed to do what I'm told." James scratched his head. "But I did overhear the guys in my squad talking to some drivers. They said something about having to cross the Ocalufty bridge…first thing tonight, at eighteen hundred hours."

"Oconaluftee River," I whispered to Katelyn. "By the Visitor Center."

"That's where we're heading. We're going right toward them."

"I think that's the idea," I said with a shiver.

Before I could follow up, a boom rumbled from off to the south. It carried over the hills like thunder, but close enough that the ground shook underneath us. A second blast followed from even closer, shaking the roof of the shower house.

"Are we too late?" Austin asked Spotted Owl. He seemed itching for a fight, which unsettled me. Spotted Owl's reply was more distressing.

"That's not our guys." He pointed to the buckets, and nervously looked back to the sky. "At least not our bombs. We have all the ANFO."

I spun to run for cover, but I was a second too late. The scream of jets broke overhead like the rush of a freight train. More blasts rumbled in the distance.

CHAPTER 25

Thankfully, we didn't need to hide.

"There's no more time," Spotted Owl said as the jets wheeled off to our right and faded away. The roar of the engines and the blasts faded too, but not the dread in my belly.

"How about we take the kid and leave Noel?" John said, though as much of a statement as a question.

"Nah. Bring 'em both," Spotted Owl said. He zeroed in on Noel. "You better keep up. We're not stopping for you."

Spotted Owl hurried off to grab the blasting caps as the rest of us started picking up the buckets. I overheard John tell his father, "I don't like this one bit."

"It might work out better than you think," the older man replied.

I wasn't sure how, but didn't want to get involved in any drama. Instead, I slung the military rifle over my shoulder and nestled it to my side next to my backpack. I considered leaving the pack, but figured it wasn't taking up too much space. How could it when there was little more than another granola packet, a half-empty water bottle and a small first aid kid inside?

I picked up a bucket in each hand and walked away from the shower house, but not far.

Katelyn saw me leaving. She grabbed a bucket and came over to stand with me while the rest of the group took their time getting ready.

I dropped the buckets and nervously bounced from one foot to the other. My eyes kept going to the sky, which was turning more of a steel gray by the second. Off to the west, a little hint of orange hugged the top of the mountain, but it wasn't my favorite shade. This color meant lights out, and nothing about the darkness reassured me anymore.

"I thought we were in a hurry," I muttered.

"They're coming." Katelyn switched her bucket from one hand the other, and ended up setting hers down too. "This thing weighs a ton."

"More like forty pounds," I deadpanned.

"Okay, smartass."

"I'm just telling you what your brother said," I protested, and felt bad for the tone I'd used.

"Like a jerk."

"You know I'm kidding," I said weakly, but it appeared she wasn't convinced.

"Yeah, right."

"I smiled when I said it," I explained. "That's the code. It's a joke when I smile."

"I must've missed that, but it's good to know." She looked at me with narrowed eyes. I felt a lie detector behind them, and hoped I passed. Apparently I did, because she said, "I guess I should be glad you're back to joking around. It's my fault for walking on eggshells around you."

"I don't even know what that means," I said. "But thanks. I know it's been hard on you too."

"My mom always says that. You ever do that thing where you just repeat these like really old sayings, you know, like a penny for your thoughts?"

"All the livelong day," I quipped, and corrected myself. "Actually, no. And a penny wouldn't go very far nowadays. My dad always said precious metals was a good place to keep your assets, but there's hardly any copper in a penny anymore."

"That's what I mean, right there," she said. "We are who we are because of our parents, right?"

"Yeah. So does that make me half the man I used to be?"

"See? You can quote. And it really is good to see you joking around." Katelyn took a slow breath, and lowered her voice. "You know, I think you'll be twice the man you were before. Even though you don't have to, I think you'll step up for all of us in so many different ways."

"I do have big shoes to fill," I joked with another common saying, but felt the weight of that one bear down on me. Combined with the other thoughts, the mental load grew heavier. Ever since that night before, my life had become like I was carrying dozens of buckets around. IED buckets. I just hoped one didn't go off and blow me apart.

"I'm hanging by a thread," I whispered, once again hiding behind jokes and platitudes.

From underneath her helmet, Katelyn's eyes sparkled in the fading light. Slipping a hand into mine, she went to nestle her head against my shoulder—and forgot about the body armor. Her helmet thunked off my shoulder. I stifled a chuckle and held still as she laid her head against me more carefully. The steel plates of my armor and the nylon webbing that served for padding inside her helmet couldn't have been comfortable. But I wasn't going to complain if she didn't.

"It's really getting dark fast," I whispered as I fished a hand under her helmet to massage her neck.

"It seems darker tonight already."

"Yeah, I reckon so," I replied. "It's kinda like there's a haze."

"You think? I thought it was getting cloudy."

"I'm not going to argue with you, but you're wrong." I punctuated the statement with a smile.

"Glad to know you're kidding," she said when she noticed my grin.

"Yeah, I'm not joking." It was definitely hazy, I thought. Probably from the bomb blasts, either there or the ones farther to the south, but I didn't mention that. Instead, I said, "It's past dusk, and I think we've got a long way to go. So much for meeting the other group, if…"

Katelyn seemed to realize that I was hinting at the more recent bombing, and wisely didn't take the conversation down that route. She looked up at me, and said, "Then what's taking so long?"

"They're probably still arguing over the prisoners. I never should've caught Noel again. Or that other kid."

She stared at me curiously. "You taking credit for capturing him too?"

"Well I did see him first," I replied with a little added swagger. When Katelyn harrumphed, I added, "I'm smiling, babe."

"I'm not," she said, but quickly broke into a laugh. "Maybe I am. I'm getting delirious."

"It's better than the alternative. Anyway, I'm gonna get really crabby if we don't get the heck outta here."

"I know."

"You do, do ya?"

She held up a hand to shush me. "Here they come."

"Finally."

Spotted Owl was back in the lead of an overloaded procession. Buckets were in both of his hands, meaning he was undoubtedly disappointed at having to leave the machine gun behind. It would have been nice to have brought the extra firepower, but the huge number of buckets was somewhat encouraging in their own scary, painfully heavy way.

He took our group past the shower house to a narrow gravel road. All the while, I wondered why he hadn't kept the whole group together rather than splitting into two groups long before the shootout at the bridge.

"I don't want to hear any complaining," Spotted Owl said, which spelled imminent bad news to me. "We've gotta stay on the roads as long as we can. We're weighted down something fierce, and it'll take forever to get there cross country with this crew."

"He means you," Austin whispered to me.

If I'd had a free hand, I would've smacked my brother. Instead, Austin skipped safely past. Of course, Mouse was right behind him.

"Wait up, Big A," she called. The poor thing seemed more like who Spotted Owl had been talking about initially. She had both hands on a bucket, but looked like she needed four more. She leaned forward as if she was fighting a stiff wind, and was turned to the side so severely that I thought she would be dragging the bucket before they made it halfway back to the highway.

Remembering there were fourteen buckets, I quickly inventoried the rest of the group as we hiked. Spotted Owl, John, and Austin each had two, just like me. Katelyn's dad also had two, but that was it for the doubles. Both of the women and Katelyn were managing with one a piece, though I suspected my mom could handle two. As Katelyn had said earlier, she was one tough lady.

That left the prisoners with none, which seemed foolish to me. I totally understood that Noel seemed to be in no condition, but James was in perfectly good shape. The military had him physically fit, and I thought that made him a flight risk. No one had a free hand to train a weapon on the kid, so he could easily slip off into the woods before someone could drop their bucket.

I slowed to settle into my spot at the end of the line. As James tromped past, I stepped out to cut him off. "You got two free hands. Go grab that bucket from little Mouse."

The kid looked up at me somberly. I didn't think he had anything to be moping about. Maybe he'd lost some buddies at the bridge, but it sure didn't sound like he was that close to any of them. If anything, he'd made it sound like he didn't even like them.

Then again, I could appreciate both sides of the situation. I certainly didn't have any love for the soldiers, but that didn't mean I couldn't feel remorse. Unlike James, I hadn't known them at all.

"Go on," I said, frustrated the kid wasn't moving to help out. "Get her bucket."

"They told me I couldn't have one."

I picked up the pace to hurry after him. "Who?"

"The guy in charge."

That seemed short-sighted on Spotted Owl's part, I thought. I gazed ahead to see Austin and Mouse faltering. They'd already been passed by the two moms, and we weren't even back to the highway yet.

No matter Spotted Owl's concerns, I knew Mouse would be far more helpful scouting than worn out from lugging around a load half her weight. "Just go take it. I said so."

I watched as the kid hurried on ahead and tried to take the bucket. She refused at first, but relented when Austin said something to her. She handed it over, but ended up sharing the handle on one of Austin's. It was almost like they were holding hands, though balancing forty pounds of highly combustible material. Much like their potential relationship, I thought with a chuckle.

The sun had fully set by then, leaving at most twenty minutes of a deep, dusky brown. Worse yet, there was nothing to like about being out along the road. Thanks to an eternity of monotonous hiking, I took the time to overanalyze the situation.

Of course, I couldn't shake the feeling that we were defenseless, but no more so than in the daylight, I supposed. Either way, whenever the jets or helicopters came boiling up out of the valley, we would have to drop our loads and sprint—again. But at least it was far easier to hike along the edge of the road than deep in the forest. Especially at night.

The winding road that led from the horse camp grew steep right before it met the main highway. I was huffing and puffing as loud as an old locomotive. I should've been chilled with the sun fully gone, but my insides were boiling like a steam engine.

The body armor wasn't helping, and I was sorely tempted to shed the vest and helmet along the way.

"Keep going," Spotted Owl encouraged between labored breaths of his own.

Based on what I'd seen before, I didn't think there was any way Noel could keep up. I looked over my shoulder expecting to find the man had already dropped out. Surprisingly, he was keeping up rather well. Though he still leaned to one side, his left leg dragging in the gravel, he was hanging in there. If anything, I thought he looked stronger than before. And that only made me more suspicious.

The explanation Noel had given to the others about hiking along the highway had seemed flimsy at best. Granted, he'd had a couple days to walk that far, so I figured it hadn't been an impossible distance, even in his current condition. Even hiding in the horse camp made some sense, though it was far enough off the road that it seemed a little too coincidental. But Noel had explained that away by saying he'd seen the helicopter troops rappel to the bridge, and he'd diverted off the highway and just accidentally run across the campsite.

My helmet couldn't hide the deep frowns creasing my forehead.

"What?" Katelyn asked.

"I just don't trust that guy," I whispered, then cringed realizing I might be shouting thanks to what sounded like the buzzing of a million mosquitos in my ears. "Was that too loud?"

"No. But which guy? Noel or James?"

I hadn't noticed James dragging behind us. I turned back around and saw him plodding along right behind Noel.

"Who's watching those guys?" I uttered.

"I thought John was." Katelyn looked ahead to find her brother way up near the front by Spotted Owl. That guy seemed to be her brother's new best friend, which I didn't completely understand either. While I didn't dislike the older man, I found Spotted Owl a bit abrasive at times. Perhaps because he seemed a little too bossy, and I had little use for authority.

I felt like my mother would have been better suited to taking the lead, but assumed it had something to do with her unfamiliarity with the terrain. My dad had been the one who could read a map backwards and forwards, and generally kept her on track. While he had provided the directions, she provided the motivation. In that moment, she seemed lost to me, but not just in the literal sense.

I stopped well short of the highway and waited for the two stragglers to stumble past.

"Get on up there." I had a feeling Katelyn was going to chide me about falling behind the rest of the group, so I added, "And hurry up. We need to stick together."

Noel nodded weakly as he filed on ahead. James remained sullen, and didn't look at me. That didn't sit well. I called out a couple more times for them to catch up to the others before realizing that I was being the authoritarian. No wonder they didn't have anything nice to say to me.

Finally, we hit the highway pavement. I'd just about closed the distance behind the rest of the group, though I was completely spent from the effort of lugging around the buckets. My shoulders burned. The ligaments had stretched out until they wouldn't possibly shrink back where they belonged.

Noel didn't look much better than I did, though he had no heavy load to complain about. His leg was clearly bothering him, yet he soldiered on. If the injured, or supposedly injured, guy could go, I wasn't about to admit defeat.

Spotted Owl barely looked over his shoulder long enough to see if we were keeping up, and kept right on going. At least the terrain had flattened out. We stuck to the shoulder of the roadway, tired feet scuffing in the gravel.

My feet ached. My back had stiffened up to the point that I could barely bend over, but the real pressure was on my hands. Blisters had most definitely formed where the thin plastic handles of the buckets threatened to cut my palms in half. I would've done anything to have padded my hands, but didn't have a scrap of fabric to borrow.

In not time, my shoulders felt like my arms were permanently pulled out of the sockets. But still I trudged on, no longer caring about the two prisoners, or whatever they were.

"Where'd Austin go?" I suddenly realized, but could answer my own question when I noticed Mouse had disappeared too.

"Scouting," Katelyn confirmed. "Spotted Owl sent them on ahead while you were kinda zoned out there."

"Me? Zoned out?"

"Like a zombie, babe."

"I know. I kinda wish I was one."

"So you could eat people?" It was hard for her to play act while carrying the bucket, but she gave it her best stagger, and repeatedly mumbled, "Brains. I need brains."

"Better to not have a brain," I said.

"Don't be so sure. I remember a couple guys like that. There was the one boy in Spanish class who totally couldn't take the hint."

"The hint?" I narrowed my eyes at her. "From you?"

"Well, it was a little more than just him. Some super cool football guy kept trying to ask me out. I don't know how many times I had to say no, but it was getting ridiculous."

I hadn't shared any classes with her, but I really wanted to know more. I certainly wasn't surprised that someone had asked her out. As far as I was concerned, every guy in the school had probably been after her. In a way that almost made me appreciate getting to spend every minute of every day with her, not that I was the jealous or overbearingly needy type.

"Oh, really," I said, failing at hiding my curiosity. "Who was that dude?"

"It doesn't matter."

"C'mon. Humor me."

"Fine." She turned to me and whispered, "Billy Dickins."

I nodded knowingly. "Yeah, the name says it all. He was a total-"

She cleared her throat to interrupt me. "Anyway, I don't want to talk about him...or school."

"I hear you. I won't miss a lot of those kids, but I can't help but wonder about some of 'em." I looked to the sky and exhaled loudly, thinking about my old friend Joe and the others. "We've been here so long now, with no real clue what's going on out in the real world. I've just gotta wonder..."

"It doesn't do much good, does it?"

"Not really, but I can't quit thinking about what it's like back home...and if we'll ever get there."

"We will," she said. "I've gotta believe it."

"I hope so," I mumbled, and focused back on the present. "Anyway, so who's carrying Austin's buckets?"

"Your mom has one. I think they took the other one with them."

"Better hope he doesn't have the blasting caps," I said. "He'll light one up just to see what happens."

"I'm pretty sure Spotty still has those."

I grinned. "Spotty?"

"Why not? Everyone needs a nickname."

"Okay, Rocky."

"Exactly, Bull-twinkle."

"Very funny."

"I know," she said. "It helps keep my mind off this bucket. Good God it's heavy."

"Can you imagine the boom this thing's gonna make," I said. "I have no idea how we're gonna use them, though. Won't we have to get super close to the building or vehicles or whatever to make it work?"

"Probably," she said. "Or maybe we just leave them along the road."

"Like a roadside bomb," I said. "That's, uhm...wow. If they didn't think we were terrorists before, they really will now."

"I guess so," she said softly. "But what choice do we have?"

"None," I admitted. "But I don't like it."

Katelyn looked at me curiously, but held back on a response.

I had a hard time putting my concerns into words, and finally said, "It's one thing to blow bridges and keep them out, but I'm a bit, uhm, worried…no, concerned about, uh…"

"You have issues about fighting back?" she asked, betraying no opinion of her own.

"I guess so. Is that weird?"

"Not really. I don't like it either, but they fired the first shot. Or shots."

"And bombs, and rockets, and pretty much everything else." I took a deep breath that had more to do with the anxiety than the exhaustion, though I was about ready to drop if Spotted Owl didn't let us rest soon. "I know I shouldn't feel this way."

"I think it's perfectly normal to worry about other people. If more people did that, maybe we wouldn't be in the mess we're in right now."

"That makes more sense than anything I've heard in a long time."

"I'm not so big into peace and love and all that stuff…at least not now," she said, which perfectly echoed my thoughts. "But I like to think I have a neighborly streak in me, as my mom would say. If we cared a lot more about our neighbors, even total strangers, then this world would be a whole lot better place."

"Hmm. You're pretty smart."

"I know. I get that a lot." Katelyn said it so seriously that I had to turn to look. She grinned back at me. "When I'm joking, I smile too."

"Good to know."

"Keep it down back there," Katelyn's mom said from somewhere in front of us. Evidently, she'd slowed a little bit, and had fallen behind the two straggling prisoners. If she was that tired, I figured it was no wonder she was a little snippy, but I didn't dare say that out loud.

"Spotted Owl says we're getting close," Spotted Fawn added between labored breaths.

"Hey, Rocky. Spotty says we're getting close," I told Katelyn just so I could use my favorite new nicknames.

"You talking about my mom?" she asked.

"I guess she's a Spotty too, huh?"

"Yeah, we might need a new nickname for her."

Katelyn's mom turned around again. "You kids need to keep it down. I'm not telling you again."

I pinched my lips shut. I wasn't usually one to go against authority, and aggravating my girlfriend's mom was really low on my list of things to do.

"That was a little rude," Katelyn whispered. "How about we call her Snotty?"

I covered up a laugh with a fake cough, which only served to have Katelyn's mom turn around one more time. Her dark eyes gleamed in the moonlight like a raven's.

"Do I have to separate you two?"

"No, ma'am," I said. "We'll be quiet."

"You think you'd take this a little more seriously…"

Her admonishment faded away. I didn't need to be reminded about the severity of the situation, but wouldn't dare talk back. Instead, I stewed inside thinking how Snotty couldn't possibly know how I was feeling.

In a way, the anger served me well. We probably hiked a half mile, and I didn't once notice the pain in my hands. We'd made it up a shallow incline and back down the other side, as well as past a couple sharp turns. We rounded a particularly sharp curve to the left, and Spotted Owl sunk to a knee with a hand raised.

Once everyone had gathered around him, he whispered, "We're really close now. Mingus Trail is up on the right."

"I haven't seen any signs of bomb craters," John said.

"Mouse is up ahead checking it out." Spotted Owl pointed off to the woods where a creek babbled alongside the road. "We should hop the creek and wait for them up by the trailhead."

"That sounds like a plan," John said. He picked up his two buckets with a grunt and gestured with his head for everyone to move out.

I was less enthusiastic, but it sounded like we'd get a quick break if we just made it a little farther.

"We can do this, Rocky," I told Katelyn.

"We have to, Bullwinkle."

"I still don't even know what that means."

"Me, either, but I like it."

I frowned, and grumbled, "That makes one of us."

My back complained as I stooped over to pick up the buckets, but I was able to stifle a groan. Following Spotted Owl, we slid down the road slope toward the creek, and somehow managed to not topple all the way into the stream. As much as I thought a break might feel heavenly, I knew any relief would be temporary. There would be no actual rest until the night was over. If we lasted that long.

I stumbled across the creek. As soon as we'd gathered up on the other side in a secluded little flat spot where we could watch the road, I dropped my buckets. I sat on one and tapped the other for Katelyn. She sat next to me without a word.

The longer I sat there, the heavier my eyelids became.

I was too tired to move. Right before I could pass out, shadows came rushing through the woods toward us.

CHAPTER 26

As soon as I knew there was nothing to be alarmed about, my eyes closed. They refused to reopen despite the voices swirling around. Seconds or minutes later, I was rudely awakened having forgotten that our scouts had returned.

"Psst, Bullwinkle!" Katelyn whispered. "Oh, forget it." She shook me. "Wake up, Zach."

"Wh-what?"

"Your name's too long."

"I'm awake, Ma," I mumbled. I rubbed the sleep from my eyes, expecting to find myself back home in my bed, probably late for school. When my eyes cleared, I saw Katelyn's face shining in the moonlight. "Wait...what?"

"I said your name's too long."

"You woke me up to tell me that?"

"Uh, no. I woke you up to tell you that Big A and Mouse are back."

"Yeah. I know."

"With news," she added with extra emphasis.

"Oh." I sat up straighter and looked around. The others were gathered around the new arrivals. Katelyn pulled me up, and we walked over to join them. Mouse had everyone's attention.

"There's a bridge right past the trail, right about where the road curves," she said. "They're working on it now."

"Our guys?" Katelyn's dad asked.

Mouse shook her head. "No, silly. There's soldiers crawling all over the dang place. Can't you hear them?"

I had assumed the lower-pitched buzzing in my ears was lingering effects from the gunshots and bombs, but came to realize it was the whining of heavy machinery. "Oh, great," I mumbled.

"The soldiers are lowering a temporary bridge into place right now," Austin said. "What do we do?"

"Stop 'em," Spotted Owl said as matter-of-factly as if he was talking about going to get groceries or taking a stroll on a city sidewalk.

"Don't we have to find the others first?" John asked.

"Oh, crap. I almost forgot," Mouse said. "I saw them taking some of our guys away, like all handcuffed."

"What?" Spotted Owl asked. "Where? How?"

"I mean they were walking, but not real well. There were two, kinda hurt looking, 'cause they were limping like really bad." She scratched her head. "It looked like Turtle for sure…maybe Duck or Eagle or whatever that bird guy is." She finished with a non-committal shrug that set her dad off.

"Mouse," he growled. "You got that close and you don't know who it was?"

"Guys with beards all look the same in the dark."

"Great. This changes everything."

"How so?" Katelyn's mom asked Spotted Owl.

"They bombed my guys, and now they have prisoners."

"Well, yeah…"

"They'll kill the prisoners if we attack," he told Katelyn's mom. "We'll have to get 'em loose first."

"We could still set our bombs, right?" John said. "Just not trigger them until it's time to make a distraction or whatever."

"That could work. But we'll have to get real close, especially to that crew working on the bridge. I want that thing blown."

"So how do we coordinate without radios?" John asked. "I don't even have a watch."

"That's why we don't carry radios on missions like this. No need to let the soldiers grab 'em when something goes wrong..."

"So how do we pull this off?" Katelyn's dad asked Spotted Owl. "John has a reasonable question, and you're stalling."

"Yeah, I am," he admitted. "We were set to launch the attack at dusk, at the Visitor Center. Now we're gonna be a couple hours behind, and the other group might be out of commission." He paused and looked to James. "Where do your people take prisoners?"

"I wouldn't know." He paused, before adding, "I don't know for sure, but I don't think we ever had any."

Noel's gravel voice rose from behind John. "They'd want to interrogate 'em," he said. "If they don't have prisoners, then they don't have intel."

"So they'll torture them," Spotted Owl said.

"Yeah," my mom said, finally entering the discussion. "I think we can pretty much guarantee that."

I waited for her to add something along the lines about how we couldn't let that happen, but she grew quiet again. Though I wasn't opposed to having someone else like John speak up for my concerns, I would've preferred that Mom took a stronger role. But I couldn't complain when I couldn't bring myself to do the same.

"Alright, so prisoners first," Spotted Owl said. "Okay?"

A few heads nodded in agreement. If anyone objected, they kept their thoughts to themselves.

"Good. That settles it." Spotted Owl fished into the cargo pocket on his pants and pulled out a couple of long, shiny metal objects no bigger than a pencil. Wires extended from each of them. From his other pocket, he rummaged around and pulled out a cell phone.

The appearance of the phone particularly surprised me seeing how Spotty had just made a big deal about keeping out of contact. Before I could ask, the big man said, "I like John's idea. We set the charges for a distraction while Mouse and Austin go locate the prisoners."

"What's that?" Katelyn's mom asked, pointing to his hands.

"Blasting caps and the trigger device. We've got to remotely detonate it, and I need to show one of you how to use it."

Austin immediately volunteered. Spotted Owl seemed okay with that, but also insisted on John joining them for some hands on instruction.

Spotty seemed hesitant to have Noel or James overhear, so the rest of the group was kept in the dark, literally and figuratively, as he whispered instructions to the two guys. It didn't take long, and soon they were back in the circle with the rest of us.

"Now about those prisoners," Spotted Owl said. "Where would they take them?"

"I'd assume they'll take 'em to the Visitor Center," John said, drawing nods from James and Noel.

"That part of the plan remains unchanged," Spotted Owl said. "We set bombs on the way to the Visitor Center, then blow 'em all up at once to make a distraction while we bust our guys loose."

"And if we run into tanks?" Katelyn's dad asked.

"There's no tanks," Spotted Owl said quickly. Once again, Noel nodded along.

"Armed vehicles, or whatever," her dad snipped back. "You know what I mean."

I wasn't entirely sure I did, but that didn't matter. So long as the more informed adults were convinced we weren't going up against tanks, I was happy—or at least I wasn't completely terrified or feeling utterly hopeless.

"Well, whatever," Katelyn's dad was saying when I focused back in again. "It's gonna be impossible either way."

The more I heard the guy talk, the more I thought he might be as pessimistic as I was. Probably more so.

"We'll worry about all that later," Spotted Owl said. He turned to his daughter. "You two run on ahead and scope out the Visitor Center. We'll be coming up behind you. We'll meet you back in the woods, along the west side of the road, just this side of the parking lot."

"Ten-four," she said. In a rare moment of softer emotions, she stepped across the circle. Spotted Owl was so stout compared to her that she couldn't even wrap her arms all the way around him. She tried anyway. "Love ya, Moose."

"That's a good nickname," Katelyn whispered to me. "That guy is large and in charge."

"Definitely better than Owl. Other than stocky, I don't get that one."

"I dunno. He is kinda wise, I guess."

"Maybe. Either way, Moose is way more fitting than Big A," I replied as I watched my brother give our mother a quick hug. Before he slipped away, he flashed a thumbs up to me.

"Good luck, bro," I called after him. I could think of nothing else to do or say as my only brother left on undoubtedly the most dangerous mission yet. So I just stood there watching the two shadows disappear very quickly into the forest.

From far down the road, a huge metallic boom echoed through the hills.

"What was that?" Katelyn's dad asked.

"I'd say that's more of the new bridge going into place," James volunteered. "It's all metal, like a prefab thing. So they just kinda drop it into place when they've got everything set up."

"Which means they could be driving this way any minute," Spotted Owl said.

Before I could freak out about that, I had a sudden realization. "So…as long as we don't care about them getting behind us, it could actually mean that they'll be leaving the bridge unguarded."

"Sort of," James confirmed. "I wouldn't quite guarantee that, but they'll probably move most of the equipment up the road. If anything, they might only leave a squad behind to guard it."

"Unless they've learned their lessons about that," John said.

"That's true, thanks to us," James agreed. "Or…they could be done working for the night, and they'll all camp out at the bridge to protect it 'til morning."

So much for being optimistic, I thought, but I was almost happy that I didn't have to be the only pessimist for a change. James seemed like a good fit for that job. Or Katelyn's dad, who continued to pace around the woods.

I had enough of the chatter. Right when I was about to complain, Spotted Owl finally got the group headed off. I felt a little stronger after the extended rest, though a couple more metallic booms did nothing for my nerves. The never-ending jolts rattled my confidence, and seemed to sap my strength like I'd used up all my adrenaline bursts and had nothing left in the tank.

Spotted Owl led us across the highway at a run, at least as fast as we could go with the homemade bombs, and then back into the woods on the other side. I stayed up by the front. There was no particular reason, but deep down I supposed it had to do with keeping closer to my mother. With Austin gone on ahead and the enemy at hand, I didn't want to be away from her if anything went wrong.

Being up by Spotted Owl helped me overhear him tell John, "It's almost a blessing to be this close. They won't use the thermal imaging if we're right next to their troops. They won't be able to tell us apart."

"So that's why you're keeping us so close to the road?"

"Exactly." He held up a hand to stop the group for a moment and leaned over to John. "I might need a volunteer to help me set the charges."

"You stay with them," John replied without delay. "I'll do it myself."

Spotted Owl looked like he wanted to object, but John wasn't having it. He quickly asked, "Is one bucket enough, or should I take two?"

"Might as well do two, if you're sure you got this."

John nodded confidently.

"Alright. Sounds like the soldiers have been working hard, and we've got the goods to spare." Spotted Owl turned back to the rest of us. "We're gonna drop off John here to set the charges. Then we're gonna get going nice and quiet like. He'll catch up."

Against my better judgment, I found myself saying, "I'll go with him."

Katelyn latched onto my arm, but didn't say anything.

"It's okay, bud," John said. "I can handle this."

"It'll be easier with two people like Spot-"

"Not really. One person moves more silently."

"I don't like this one bit," Katelyn said, but I wasn't sure if she meant me going with him, or having her brother go off by himself.

Spotted Owl broke into our conversation, and was more definite about the numbers that time. "I reckon one is good enough. John's gonna go quick, but safe, and catch back up to us."

"Will do," he said.

Spotted Owl quickly reexplained to him how to set the blasting caps. Then it was Katelyn's turn to wish her brother well. She offered him a hug, and watched as he carried a pair of buckets off into the woods toward the bridge.

I couldn't concentrate on anything other than the sound of engines whining and metal clanking out by the bridge. They couldn't have been more than fifty yards away. Everything sounded plain as day, but I couldn't see any trace of the workers.

When Spotted Owl adjusted course, the woods gradually lit up around us. Not much at first, but muted yellow beams of light eventually poked between the trunks of the trees. As far away as we remained, it was such a mild glow that it didn't help me avoid a single trip or tangle on the forest floor.

And then the beams shifted to stab deeper into the woods.

"They're moving out," Spotted Owl turned around to tell us, though I assumed everyone had figured that out already.

The metal bridge creaked as heavy vehicles drove over it. I hoped that meant the personnel carriers were all moving on ahead—preferably more than just a squad or two. With any luck, that would leave a smaller force for us to deal with back at the Visitor Center. However, I'd learned a long time before that luck was rarely on my side. Other than somehow winning the heart of the prettiest daughter of a fellow prepper mom, I wasn't having much success. That feat alone must have used up about all the luck I'd ever had, or so I often thought.

I had no clue how John could get close enough to the bridge to blow it up, but I hadn't heard everything Spotted Owl had told him about setting the charges. For all I knew, using two buckets might have had enough power to wreck the bridge from fifty feet away. I felt like John would surely be able to get that close. He was always careful. Anyone who could stalk sharp-eyed turkeys in broad daylight could certainly hide from a few soldiers in the dark.

When rifle fire blasted from around the bridge, I suddenly wasn't so confident.

Flashlights popped on along the road, bathing the woods in bright, white light. I hit the deck as the lights raked over my head.

CHAPTER 27

"Stay low, but get moving," Spotted Owl urged as we crawled deeper into the woods away from the light. The shooting had ceased about as quickly as it had begun, but beams of bright white still cut through the darkness. The one saving grace was they were diffused enough that I thought we could escape without notice if no one did anything stupid.

We stayed low like crawling under smoke in a house fire. It wasn't easy to keep the buckets from thumping on the ground, and Katelyn's dad began complaining almost immediately. First about the effort, then more understandably about John.

"We can't go check," Spotted Owl insisted.

"That's my son over there," Katelyn's dad pleaded.

"Bob, no. He's right," Spotted Fawn said, letting her husband's name slip in front of the strangers. Then again, I figured he didn't have a code name. I'd never heard him called anything other than Dad before. If he didn't have a nickname, I'd have suggested one of the Seven Dwarfs. Grumpy would've been perfect, with Dopey a close second. But I never would've shared those with Katelyn.

"It's our son, Margie," he protested. "Our only son."

"You've gotta get it together," she replied, and I was inclined to agree with that. But there was no way I was going to get involved in the family squabble. I had enough of my own, rather I used to. Losing Dad had definitely changed the dynamic, though I supposed that it might swing back to bickering with my siblings eventually. It wasn't worth considering in that moment.

After quickly checking to make sure James or Noel weren't looking like they were going to do anything traitorous, I turned to Katelyn. Her parents continued battling. Her brow was furrowed so deeply that her helmet had slipped down over her eyes. She pushed it back up, and I couldn't help but notice the way her hands trembled. There seemed to be nothing I could do about it, but I wasn't going to stop trying.

"We could go look for him," I whispered to her.

"No. Mom's right." She sat up on her knees. We seemed to be far enough out of danger, but still kept a low profile. Her lips curled downward to match her frown. "He's got body armor and stealth. He'll be fine."

"And a helmet." I tapped my own. "And he's the sneakiest guy I know."

She nodded, and crawled over toward her dad. Wrapping an arm around his, she whispered something to him that I couldn't hear. I watched as she talked him down from the ledge, and somehow convinced him to carry on without checking on John.

Spotty gave her a thumbs up when her dad wasn't looking, and seemed happy to get the group moving again. With a hand motion, he rose into the shape of a dad giving his kids pony rides and slunk off toward the south, leading us away from the lights.

"He calmed right down," I said when Katelyn returned to my side. "What did you say?"

She shrugged. "Just tried to tell him that John would be fine."

"Seemed like a little more than that." I didn't press the issue. I was just glad to be moving away from where the shooting had occurred, though my stomach was tied in more ugly knots than a kindergartner's shoelaces.

I felt like I walked half a mile in the form of a hunchback before I tried to straighten up all the way. The buckets had really worked over my back while I had been in the uncomfortable crouch, and I could only stand partway up at first. The burning tore through my hands. But as long as Katelyn wasn't complaining, especially with her brother still missing, I wasn't about to make a peep.

I noticed we were starting to lag behind the others. Again, I didn't mention it. I guessed it might have something to do with intentionally slacking as if she was waiting for John to catch up. I wasn't going to ask that either.

Finally, Katelyn spoke up. "What are you thinking?"

"Nothing," I replied quickly. Too quickly.

"You're a terrible liar."

"Says who?"

"You. The tone of your voice is a total giveaway."

I tried to change that tone, and wisecracked, "Maybe I'm just tired."

"Then you'd reply slower, not quicker."

I snorted softly. "Alright, you caught me. I was thinking."

"And now you're being a smartass...again."

"I didn't mean to be," I protested. "I'm just, uhm..."

"Worried."

"Yeah, that," I said. "I guess there's no fooling you."

"Nope. Not a chance." She smiled, though it faded faster than my endurance on a steep slope. "I'm worried too."

"I figured. And I was trying to not mention it."

"You don't have to watch what you say around me."

"Yeah, right." I laughed softly. "Girls don't say what they mean. It's like I'm supposed to do the opposite."

"That's crap," Katelyn said. "I'm not like that."

"I'm not so sure..." I quickly corrected myself lest I dig myself into a hole. "But you're definitely not like most girls."

"I suppose a lot wouldn't want to be wearing body armor and carrying buckets of high-explosive through the woods." She shook her head at the ridiculousness of the whole situation. "Not that I want to either, but..."

"But you are," I said. "How many are still back in the city? Like I was saying before, I wonder all the time what it's like back there."

"Me, too. I don't know if life's still going on, you know, the same...the same crappy day by day, or if things haven't gotten even worse."

"Surely it has. I mean I know it's fall and we should be starting back to school, but I don't even see how that's possible."

My mom had faded to the back of the line, struggling to carry her bucket. She'd overheard at least part of our conversation, and picked that moment to jump in.

"Well, kiddos, I don't think you're missing any school. The way I see it, when you start attacking your own people and locking them up in their own homes with crazy curfews, and then figure in fuel shortages and all that, I'd say that things have only gotten worse."

"What about our friends?" Katelyn asked. "Are they okay?"

Mom waved with her free arm around the inky woods. "I know this doesn't look good, but I think you're infinitely better off than they are."

The anxiety made me beg to differ. "How do you figure?"

"You're out here actually doing something about it. There are so many people willing to go along with anything, no matter how onerous. Others just complain, but still do nothing," she explained. "You're part of a much smaller fraction actually willing to do something."

Not that I had a choice initially, I thought to myself. The whole Smoky Mountain experience had started when I was forced to tag along with my parents . Way back then, I thought they were completely overreacting.

Mom continued with the peptalk, saying, "You guys are gonna change the path we're on, to take our country back. To fight for what you believe in. I couldn't be prouder of you two. How many other kids would do that?"

I felt the dreaded tears building up. I tried my hardest to push them aside, but it was no small feat. While I tried to regain my composure, Katelyn said, "I never thought of it that way."

"And I've been complaining about being stuck on guard duty and being bored." I grimaced at the thought of what I'd gotten myself into by volunteering for the current mission. "Guess I got what I wanted."

"Just be proud that you want it," Mom replied. "If you'd had different parents, you might be sitting home in the basement, cowering in fear."

"Yeah, but now there's only one of you left," I said, and immediately regretted it. "I mean, not that I wouldn't want to be here, you know…doing something."

Sunning Bear showed no sign of being negatively affected by my words. If anything, she grew stronger. "Your dad's still with us. He's probably prouder than I am to see his baby boy out here fighting for our future. He loved this country as much as he loved you guys, and that's a veritable ton. I think when this is all over, the best thing we can do is make him proud."

As much as the loss still hurt, I straightened up. I threw my aching shoulders back and stood a little taller, carried the buckets a little lighter, and the tears evaporated from my dirty face.

I knew Mom was right. Though I'd occasionally wallowed in self-pity, especially after Dad had died, it had been somewhat rare, or at least short-lived, thanks to the way I'd been raised. Maybe I hadn't been the first to fire a shot, and maybe I never would, but I wanted to be in the thick of the action. And in those shadowy hills, I knew that was where I needed to be.

"Thanks for the pep talk, Ma." I looked ahead to see the outlines of Katelyn's parents about to disappear into the woods. "We need to hurry up."

With renewed energy, the three of us closed the gap. I was breathing heavily, but done with pain. I ignored my complaining back. If anything, it felt better to walk more upright.

I was definitely done worrying about my feet too. Listening to my boots plod on the forest floor, I began counting with each footstep. I'd reached a hundred and was ready for a hundred more when Spotted Owl suddenly ducked down and dropped both of his buckets. In a smooth, quick movement, he unslung his rifle with one hand, and held up the other for the group to stop.

Buckets thumped on the ground, and handles clanked against the sides.

"Shhh," Spotted Owl said, not concealing his disgust.

I shouldered my weapon, and slid over to where I was back to back with Katelyn. I felt her trembling. No doubt I was too.

"Why'd we stop?" she whispered so softly that I could barely hear her.

"I dunno."

"Shhh." Spotted Owl stared at the two of us, reminding me that maybe I wasn't actually whispering. He turned back to the forest.

I concentrated on the woods. Though my ears rang like sirens, I thought I made out the sound of moving machinery. It wasn't as loud as the banging of steel at the temporary bridge, but easily as troubling.

I turned my gaze skyward to see what I could make of the topography. Mountains climbed to the sky behind us, but it was all downhill in the direction we were headed. Perhaps out of the park, I guessed, remembering that it seemed like the Visitor Centers on each end of the main highway were down in valleys at the foothills.

In every direction I looked, it was nothing but trees stretching to the sky—except for one. A large gap in tree cover sat below us and to the left. And it glowed. Not the bright white of headlights, though I knew the road had to be close by.

Seemingly comfortable with whatever he'd heard, Spotted Owl urged us forward again. We went slowly, which helped given the steep decline. In what became a choreographed movement from the front of our column to the back, we got to the point where we were taking one step and then resting for two to listen.

The sound of diesel engines was unmistakable. The grumbling grew in volume with every step we took. Spotted Owl was leading us right toward them. My pulse quickened. Breathing became labored, and not only from the exertion.

Spotty raised his hand and sank to the ground. Still standing for a second longer, I got a clean look over the man's back at the clearing ahead. Outdoor lights were scattered across a huge, open field. Only the field wasn't empty. It was lined with dark, bulky vehicles, most of which were running. And dangerously close.

So much for my hopes that big numbers of enemy troops had headed up the road to the bridge. There had to be hundreds of soldiers and plenty of armored vehicles to go around.

"Dang," I muttered under by breath. "Should've known it wouldn't be easy."

Katelyn turned to me. Her face said it all, but still I had to try to make her feel better. Before I could offer a weak bit of encouragement, pounding footsteps came running up behind us.

I wheeled and went for my rifle, sure we'd been spotted by a sentry.

CHAPTER 28

Relief flooded in, mitigating the terror.

"You're back," I told John. "Thank God."

Katelyn cut in front of me to wrap her arms around her brother and sob. I'd known she had been upset ever since we'd heard the shots, but hadn't quite expected that reaction.

"What about all the shooting?" she asked.

John waited until the others had gathered around. "I don't know if they'll find the bombs or not. I got as close as I could, maybe too close." He looked to Spotted Owl. "I put the caps in like you said, and hooked it up to the phone before trying to crawl in. It seemed easier."

"That's a good call."

"Ha, pun intended," I said, drawing a stern rebuke from Spotted Owl.

John grinned. "Anyway...I don't think they ever saw me. I dropped one kinda short, but it was going so good I got one almost all the way under the bridge. And that's when I scuffed my boot on a rock."

"And they heard you?" his mom asked.

"I don't know how, really. It was quite a racket going on under the bridge with all the trucks moving. Hell, I thought it might collapse. But it's solid, and they're definitely going on up to the next bridge, you know, where we got this guy." He gestured toward James.

"So they did see you?" Katelyn's dad asked. "We heard shots."

"I doubt it. I booked it outta there before the lights came on, but someone got a little trigger happy." He shrugged. "Hopefully they just thought it was a deer or something."

"No doubt they're a bit jumpy if they've heard about what we did earlier," Spotted Owl said. "But I doubt they'll check under the bridge. Who would expect us to blow it?"

"So we could blow the bridge right now?" Katelyn's dad asked.

"We could." Spotty took his time retrieving a cell phone from his pocket, and hefted it from one hand to the other. "But they'd hear it all the way down here."

"And that might make it tougher to get Turtle and the other guy back," John said.

Spotted Owl nodded and slipped the phone back into his cargo pocket. His hand came back out with several more similar phones. "But we should go ahead and get the other bombs rigged up." He looked over his shoulder toward the lights on the field. "We're plenty close now."

"Too close," I muttered, once again thinking about sentries.

"So how's this work?" my mom asked. "Looks like we still have a lot to rig up."

"Yeah, we've got a few to put together, but it's not too hard."

"Like twelve," she insisted. "We can help."

"Alright. So…you know how your phone vibrates when you get a call or a text?" Spotted Owl asked. "There's an asymmetrical wheel inside that shakes the phone."

I leaned in closer to hear the explanation. I'd assumed the electrical pulse of receiving a call was enough to set off the blasting cap, so all the wheel talk was confusing.

"What we need to do is remove the wheel motor, and connect the circuit to the blasting cap wires like a relay." Spotted Owl tapped the back of the phone. "It's not as hard as it sounds."

It sounded impossible to me.

"Yeah, it was simple," John said.

"You can set an alarm like one helluva wake-up call, or just call or text the phone to trigger the circuit you created. Like in the movies, when the guy calls the phone to watch the bomb blow."

"Wow," I whispered to Katelyn, who was equally transfixed by my side. "That's pretty cool."

I thought I heard her say, "That's sick." However, she showed no sign of being upset. Instead, she scooted closer to watch Spotted Owl disassemble the first phone.

I decided against helping out. After the extra explanation, I thought I could figure it out, but assumed it would be easier to let the pros wire everything up and not have to answer so many questions. As far as I was concerned, it was better this part got done correctly.

So I kept watch over the vehicles below as the others worked. Katelyn ended up joining me.

The big field stretched out beneath us. It was ringed on all sides by trees. The cleared part was at least a quarter mile long and seemingly half as wide, but it would be much farther across the entire valley to reach the dark mountains rising in the distance.

From our high ground west of the field, I watched as soldiers milled about among the machines. I thought I should be able to hear voices calling out from that distance, but it was nothing but motors churning and the ringing in my ears.

"They look ready to move out," Katelyn whispered.

"Might make it easier to find our guys," I said, though I preferred to get that over with rather than wait for however long it took for the soldiers to head out. I wasn't sure I could handle sitting so close to the enemy without action.

I went through my memory banks, trying to bring up an old picture of the place. I knew there were several buildings on the site, otherwise an open field wouldn't have made for much of a Visitor Center.

I slid over to the right, but kept close enough to Katelyn that I could keep a hand on her knee.

"What are you doing?" she whispered.

"Looking for the buildings."

I gazed between the trunks of trees that looked like pillars holding up a giant rooftop. At the right spot, I finally caught sight of a small parking lot, and the rest of my memories fell into place without needing to see any more.

"There's at least a couple over there," I whispered, pointing off to the left at the north side of the field. "I think three. One's a pretty big hall with the park exhibits and maps and stuff. Kinda turned sideways next to that one there's a big ole garage with giant metal doors. It's some kind of maintenance building. And then there's an old lodge next to that. It's all tucked up against the trees, back by the river."

"That's pretty good scouting. You should take Austin's job."

"You trying to get rid of me?" I joked. "Maybe I can cut in on Big A's action?"

"Yeah, Mouse might not like that. She seems pretty attached to Big A already."

"He can have her."

"Because you have me?"

"Uhm, yeah, of course."

"You paused." Her eyes narrowed, though she couldn't contain a grin. "You got a thing for chatty girls, Big Z?" She stifled a laugh with a hand over her mouth.

"Wait, what?"

"I just thought of it. You guys are like the whole *big* alphabet, A to Z."

"Ugh. Hilarious," I deadpanned, though a little grin snuck through.

"I know." She patted my hand. "So what about those chatty girls?"

"Not really my type," I said. "Maybe they should be since I don't like talking, you know, like what could be more boring than two quiet people. That's weird too…"

I was rambling, though Katelyn didn't seem to mind. But she pointed out the contradiction.

"You're plenty talkative for a quiet one."

"Now's not really the time for that, is it?" I whispered. "I'm nervous. Bad habit, I guess."

"It's not so bad." Katelyn looked at me. "It's nothing like Mouse. She's a chatterbox."

"Well, yeah. She's more like chatty *and* quirky. And that makes her a real good fit for Big A."

"And quiet ole me is a good fit for you?"

"You're not that quiet." I flashed her a smile and scooted back over to take her hand. She pretended to resist, and relented.

Though the back and forth had been a nice distraction, a chill rapidly came over me as my gaze returned to the field below. The rumbling of the engines mimicked the churning in my stomach. In a matter of seconds, we would be headed down to face the enemy with bombs the others had just finished assembling.

The sounds of clothing shuffling behind me drew my attention, but only for a moment. I quickly jerked back around as movement on the slope, right at the roadside, froze me in place. It had to be a patrol.

I tugged on Katelyn's arm to pull her lower. She followed suit, but focused on me with questioning eyes. Rather than speak, I pointed toward the shadows. Katelyn squinted, and nodded a moment later.

Someone rustled around behind me. I wanted to call out to them to keep it down. Before I could, Katelyn whispered, "I think it's Mouse and Austin."

I drew a bead on the two figures. One tall and lanky, and the other diminutive. "It sure is. But how do we get their attention?"

I left unsaid some cursing and a bunch of questions about what they were doing so close to the road with the soldiers right across the street from them.

"They're crazy," Katelyn said, echoing my thoughts.

"I'm going to get 'em," I said. "Tell the others if they ask."

Without waiting for a reply, I scooted down the slope. I had maybe thirty yards to cover, and wasn't about to race there and draw more attention. But I moved as rapidly as I dared.

"Psst." I tried to call for them, but the shadows kept creeping along the edge of the woods. "Austin," I called, slightly louder.

Still no reply.

I cursed again, and had to change course to move parallel to the road to keep up with them. Out of curiosity, I took a quick look up the slope toward Katelyn and the others. It was blacker than a coal mine. The moon shone down over the clearing along with the scattered lights, making the military vehicles practically gleam in the evening. But there wasn't even a shadow, much less any movement, from where I'd come.

"There was no reason to be worried," I muttered, knowing that no one would've found us up there unless they'd specifically come looking. But I was just a few footsteps off the road by then, and ten times more nervous. Worse yet, Mouse and Austin weren't stopping.

I debated moving quicker, and settled for calling out one more time. They were getting closer to the parking lot, and that meant the buildings.

"Austin," I said a little louder.

The thin figured turned, and reached out for the much shorter one.

"Zach," came the reply.

"Behind you," I said, overjoyed that they'd heard me. Unfortunately, the relief flooded right back out.

Searchlights popped on from across the road. I hit the dirt.

CHAPTER 29

Austin dropped to the ground, pulling Mouse with him. I morphed into a fallen statue as the lights stabbed into the forest all around me. I held my breath, lest I make the slightest movement, and willed myself to melt into the vegetation.

A poke in the back had me shooting upright, ready to fight.

"Quiet," Austin said. He pushed me back down and knelt next to me. Mouse slipped in on the other side of Austin, a grin painted on her round face like crazy clown makeup.

"What the heck?" I said. "You scared the crap outta me." I forced a breath into my aching lungs. "And what're you doing over here?"

"Finding you," Austin said.

I wanted to smack my brother—if not in anger, at least to knock some sense into him. "I mean with the searchlights on. They'll see us move."

"Don't worry," Mouse chirped. "It's all good."

I was ready to disagree vehemently, but Austin dropped the real bombshell.

"Those aren't searchlights," he said, though he remained low to the forest floor.

"What?" I rolled onto my side and immediately felt like an idiot. "Oh."

A trio of Humvees roared out onto the road. Their headlights had passed over the three of us as they'd driven from the field toward the highway. They weren't searching for rebels in the hills. Instead, several eight-wheeled armored personnel carriers also exited the field, and approached the road to line up behind the Humvees.

"They're moving out," I whispered under my breath.

Thankfully, Austin didn't rub in my paranoia. The earlier version of my big brother wouldn't have missed that opportunity.

We shielded our faces to avoid creating any kind of weird glow like the way a deer's eyes would shine on the side of the road. Between slits in our fingers, we watched the soldiers head off to the north. Back in the field, another row of big-wheeled, multi-axle vehicles revved their engines.

"Yep, they're headed up the road," Austin said. "We'd better tell the others."

"They're right behind me," I said, pointing up the slope. "Did you find the prisoners?"

"You betcha," Mouse said. "They're lookin' okay. We can bust them fellas out, no problem."

"It might be a little tougher than that," Austin cautioned.

"Shoot, Big A. We got in there so tight we coulda reached out and touched 'em."

"With a really long stick," Austin whispered to me. "But, yeah, we saw 'em, and they looked alright, I guess. Beat up, but plenty lively."

"Good." I glanced back toward the road. The small convoy had driven on, and the other vehicles out in the field hadn't shown any further signs of moving out. "Let's go tell the others."

With the hillside once again a shadowy gloom, we scampered up the slope. I felt like calling out to the others, but assumed they would have to know that it was us returning. At least I hoped Katelyn had shared that information.

Shortly after, we met up with her, who led us the rest of the way up to the group. Everyone descended on Mouse and Austin like jackals on a fresh kill.

"All right, all right," Austin pleaded, holding up his hands as questions came at him at a rapid fire pace. "We've seen, uhm-"

"Turtle," Mouse said. "And the other guy is Wood Duck, not Golden Eagle."

"Hard to believe he got captured," Spotted Owl said. "I sure thought he'd go down with a fight."

"He's been beat up," Mouse said. "But he's still walking. Just a big ole knot on his head. Heck we were so close I wanted to poke it."

"That's my girl. I knew I could trust you to get close." Spotted Owl beamed with praise. Still, he didn't get completely sidetracked from the gravity of the situation. "So where are they holding 'em at? Can we bust 'em loose?"

"Oh, yeah," Mouse announced triumphantly. "We darn need coulda done it ourselves, right Big A?"

Austin nodded, but I didn't think his heart was in it. Still, it all sounded encouraging, though I had long since known that nothing was ever as easy as it seemed. And how could it be, I reasoned, when the prisoners had to be well-guarded deep inside the solid concrete walls of the Visitor Center.

Mouse shot a gaping hole in that theory.

"They took 'em back to the cabins."

"The old log cabins?" Spotted Owl seemed genuinely surprised.

"Yeah," Mouse said. "It's the big one with two floors. It's past this little, uhm, barn that kinda doesn't have any sides. It's just like all open underneath."

"It seemed kinda like a pavilion, like where people have picnics and family reunions and whatever," Austin added.

"I think I remember that one," Spotted Owl said.

I did too. Their admittedly weak descriptions had stirred up memories of the little mock-up of a historic village behind the Visitor Center complex. I remembered how it nestled up against the river, but right next to the big open field which had been turned into a parade grounds crawling with soldiers and equipment. That fact sure didn't make the location of the captives seem any simpler to get at.

Apparently, Spotted Owl wasn't worried about that. He asked a few more questions as his scouts continued with their story.

"The house where your guys are at is right next to that barn thing," Austin offered. "I think it's the only one with an upstairs, but the guys were still downstairs when we left."

"We were hanging back in the woods, right along the river, when they came marching them along this back path," Mouse explained. "They were all tied up, but walking pretty okay, I guess."

Austin added one final detail. "We heard them stomping around inside on the floor, but they hadn't gone upstairs like I was saying."

"Okay. Great work." Spotted Owl clapped Austin on the back. The force of the blow knocked him into me. I couldn't fully hide a chuckle. As proud as I was of my brother finding out the vital information, it was comical to see the bear of a man beat him down with a simple pat on the back.

"So here's what I'm thinking," Spotted Owl told the group. "There's a little bridge just north of the first driveway to the Visitor Center. We can plant bombs there and get under the road." He paused for a second to sweep the leaves aside. "Dang it. I wish it was light enough to draw this out."

"It's fine. I think we're all following so far," my mom said. I was happy to hear it, as I feared a battle breaking out over who got to be represented by the stick or the rock or whatever.

"Fine." Spotted Owl looked to Katelyn's parents. "So there's a pretty big pipe under the road not quite at the far end of the big field. If we can blow out that one too, then all those vehicles are pretty much trapped between there and the bridge."

"And then we can get away with the prisoners," Spotted Fawn replied.

"Yep. And slow them down for a long time."

"Especially if we bomb the buildings too, right?" Austin asked, seemingly excited about creating all kinds of havoc. I liked the idea too, though not quite as enthusiastically.

"Oh, hell yeah," Spotted Owl said, his volume growing until I felt concerned that someone down on the road could hear us plotting. "I want to light that whole camp up like the Fourth of July. We gotta let them know who they're dealing with."

"So we need to get out into the field too?" Katelyn's dad said tentatively.

"If we can. I don't know that we'll be able to get close enough to disable some of the APCs, but we're gonna level every building. Imagine the effect that will have. They won't dare mess with us for a long time."

I put myself in the position of the soldiers. I figured they were sitting there confidently, waiting for the all-clear so they could drive right through the park and push the rebel scum aside. When all the bombs started going off, I expected they'd abandon the equipment and high-tail it all the way back to Cherokee. Hopefully farther.

Even if they didn't run, they were effectively trapped in their vehicles. They would need to bring in a whole bunch more bridge-building equipment to fix the damage our group would cause. And that would take ages.

A spark of confidence burned in my chest, though I had no reason to be so optimistic.

Maybe it was just the imminent taste of revenge. Better yet, I wouldn't necessarily have to hurt anyone to do it. Perhaps things might get hairy when the buildings came down, but I found it oddly reassuring that I wouldn't have to see another man fall. A person could get crushed or blown apart, of course. However, it seemed strangely tolerable as long as I didn't have to witness every gory detail.

"What's happened to me?" I mumbled. "This is crazy."

"We'll be fine, right?" Katelyn looked at me, her face etched with concern. I wanted to reach out and touch her cheek, but the helmet had become an obstacle. Not just physically, though she had turned slightly away from me. In that moment so close to life or death, her profile view seemed all wrong. I didn't want to see her all geared up, covered with armor plating and holding the rifle tightly in her gentle hands. Worse yet was the worried look plastered over her soft features.

She wouldn't hurt a spider, but she appeared to be readying herself for war. I supposed I needed to get into that frame of mind too, and tried to shove the demoralizing thoughts from my head.

"We sure will," I finally answered. "Just stick with me."

"Okay, Rambo," she said with a smile that softened the jab. "You must be ready for this?"

"Yes and no," I admitted. "I'm ready for it to be over."

"All of it," she added, and I nodded in agreement.

CHAPTER 30

Spotted Owl urged everyone to pick up their buckets again, and he went around passing out blasting caps. Each phone was connected with thin wire to two of the caps.

"Slip those in your pocket," he suggested. "We'll put 'em in the buckets when we're close."

I looked at the wiring curiously, and asked Spotted Owl, "Two caps in each bucket?"

"One might not have enough spark to blow it. We're not taking any chances."

"No, sir." I bit down on my lower lip and slipped the detonators into my backpack. I hefted the buckets. I couldn't wait to be rid of them so I could unsling the rifle from my back, not that I wanted to use it. But at least I would be able to move a lot quicker.

With John and the two scouts back, many in the group only had to carry a single bucket. I volunteered to take what should have been my mom's. Despite my concerns about being loaded down, I'd much rather suffer through that myself than have her stuck lugging a bucket around.

The adults had the attack plan worked out, and once again we divided our forces. Katelyn's parents and John were headed to the south. They would crawl through the culvert pipe and plant a couple bombs, one on each end. Then they'd follow the stream, skirting along the south side of the open field behind the soldiers' staging area until they made it to the river that ran behind the historic village.

If possible, John was to sneak out into the back part of the field and see if he could get close enough to leave a couple more buckets next to some of the parked vehicles. He hadn't been left with a back-up plan, meaning he pretty much had to get the bombs somewhere close. At the very least, he needed to dump them along the way, since they would have no idea when Spotted Owl would start calling the phones to set them off. At the most, they had an hour to get the job done, and then follow up the river to meet up with us.

Katelyn should have gone with them, I thought, seeing how that group was completely her family. However, she had been emphatic about staying with me. Had anyone argued, it would've been an easy win for her seeing how I was part of the bigger group that had many more bombs to set. Of the fourteen original IEDs, two were way up the road at the temporary bridge that John had previously set by himself. He and his parents had four more with them. That left eight for my group to set.

Like me, Spotted Owl also carried two. Katelyn had another, along with Austin and Mouse. Noel was still showing major fatigue, which left James to bring the other one. Worry settled over me about that, yet the kid had shown himself to be not much of a concern up to that point. Though he hadn't been altogether helpful, he hadn't stood in the way of any of our plans. Nor did Spotted Owl seem concerned.

I couldn't imagine who wouldn't want a chance to get away from the military. I had no doubt James had been conscripted against his will, much like Noel. Despite having gone through a rigorous indoctrination program, I didn't think there was any way the training could strip all the decency from the soldiers. Sure, some had to be bloodthirsty lunatics, but I felt confident that the vast majority were decent people doing what they had to do to avoid punishment, or to support their families, or pretty much whatever it took to get by.

That didn't make them real pillars of the community, but they were people all the same. Some flawed, some not the types to stand up to wrongdoing like Mom had talked about earlier, but many had to be genuinely good at heart. That was the thought that troubled me the most about fighting back with deadly force, no matter how many times they'd knocked me down.

As we hiked diagonally down the slope, the point/counterpoint battle played out in my head. I sincerely hoped that the setting of the bombs wouldn't actually hurt anyone, while at the same time I would've loved blasting every bit of the soldiers' equipment to smithereens.

I didn't know the two captives we were trying to rescue, but that didn't matter in the slightest. I knew I would do whatever it took to get them back. Or so I hoped.

If I froze up again, everything could go horribly wrong in a hurry. So I decided to quit thinking ahead and put my hopes on spontaneity.

Until that final moment, I decided to pretend we were just hiking through the woods. The buckets were gear that I was bringing to a campsite my family had picked out deep in the forest. It wouldn't have been the first time. We'd always stayed off the beaten path, carrying all our gear sometimes several miles to an overnight destination. Then we'd rise the next morning, tear the tents down, and head somewhere else.

That's almost exactly what we were doing, I reckoned. We'd hiked to the cave last night. Now I was going to drop some supplies, and I'd be back home by morning—excluding one key detail. Someone needed to break the news to Maddie. I wasn't sure if I could be around when she found out about Dad, much less be the one to help tell her. Still, I resolved to get the mission done. We needed to get back to her as soon as possible. She deserved as much. Besides, I was spent as physically as I was mentally. It all needed to end.

"Stay low," Spotted Owl said as we closed in on the little stream that crossed under the road.

Mouse and Austin had already set down their buckets to hurry off to check it out, and they came bounding back seconds later.

"All clear," Mouse chirped. "They don't have a clue we're here."

"Good," Spotted Owl said. "You two leave your buckets here, side by side under the bridge. Then keeping running on ahead."

"But not too far," my mom added.

Mouse turned to her dad, who nodded in reply to an unspoken question. She saluted, grabbed her bucket, and urged Austin on ahead.

"Don't dawdle by the bridge," my mom told the others. "We just keep on hiking down to the river."

I noticed that along with her voice, her eyes had firmed up. Sharp lines in her aging face drew at the corners of her eyes, but it made her look shrewd rather than old.

The stream wasn't terribly wide. It rolled and bubbled enough that it grew noisy. The darkness would've seemed even eerier if it hadn't been for the moonlight reflecting off the ripples. I felt oddly calm, though I usually did around the streams. Playing in the water was my absolute favorite thing to do in the park. Even in these dire circumstances, I took a quick moment to savor the smell of fresh, cold water.

A new metal bridge the soldiers had placed sometime earlier was suspended over the creek twenty yards downstream from us. Heeding my mother's advice, we went straight for it without stopping. I had to duck to get underneath and came face to face with the two buckets resting on the dirt right beneath the edge of the structure.

I imagined the heavy bridge flying in the air like a sail when Spotted Owl made the call. That elicited a smirk.

A little gust pushed at my back as I finished crossing under the road. It was as if the creek itself was generating the cool breeze. It swept under the lip of my helmet and through the webbing, giving me short-lived relief.

There was a mild benefit to the wind dying down, not that it helped me hear much better. Our boots made a racket. Tipping rocks clanked as we stepped along the rocky shoreline. Spotted Owl adjusted course to keep us closer to the water. It was a risky move considering how slick the flat rocks were, but it helped dampen the noise.

Granted, we could've gone slower, but Spotted Owl was in a hurry. I wasn't opposed to that, especially in the midst of the enemy. However, I had in the back of my mind that the slippery rocks could spell disaster. Against my better judgment, Spotted Owl had us wade even farther out into the stream to fully deaden our clinking footsteps.

I was suddenly no longer a big fan of cold water. It spilled over the tops of my boots, knifing through my socks and practically into my skin. Had it been the middle of summer, the water would still have been ice cold. Even with warmer temperatures, my skin would have turned blue in a matter of minutes. In the fall, the water was perilous.

We rounded a big bend in the stream and made it out close to the confluence with the river when I felt my toes go numb. In a sense, I enjoyed the way the blisters finally quit hurting, but knew I would pay for it later. Once my feet started to warm up, they'd burn like fire. But right then, there was no need to worry about that. We were almost ready to set a whole different kind of fire.

I looked ahead, and noticed how close we were to the river. It was much wider than I had anticipated. The view shocked me to the point that I forgot to watch my next step. Sliding on a flat rock, I planted a knee in the stream. The rock cut through my pants more sharply than the water, but I bit my lip and refused to cry out.

At least I'd kept the buckets from getting drenched.

Totally embarrassed, I quickly looked around to see if anyone had noticed. Luckily, everyone was busy trying to keep themselves from falling and hadn't seemed to detect my little stumble. Even Katelyn, inches away, apparently hadn't noticed.

I leaned my head over to try to wipe the sweat off my brow with my shoulder. Between carrying buckets and the helmet, it didn't work. I gave up and stopped for a quick breath. Blowing out a sigh, I was almost surprised that I hadn't expelled a cloud of steam. The world had definitely gotten colder that evening, which was even more noticeable thanks to my frozen feet.

I tried to forget about my little stumble, but the sound of rushing water up ahead was a constant reminder. If I went down again in the big river, I had a feeling I'd be washed away in the current.

It turned out to be not quite that serious. The river was impressively wide, but not a raging whitewater like the sound had indicated. Perhaps it had been the swirling hum still racing around inside my ears.

Spotted Owl led us out into the river, then stood slightly off to the side to wave and let the rest of us file past. "Be careful up there," he whispered. He gestured with his head to the top of the tree-lined bank behind us. "It's not far to the building. We'll go down a little and set the bombs."

Somehow I ended up at the front of the column with my mother and the two strangers trailing behind me and Katelyn. Now that Mom didn't have buckets, she was acting as the unofficial guard for Noel and James. They kept plodding along, none the wiser that they were being watched closely.

In addition to less current, the river didn't turn out to have quite as treacherous a footing as I'd expected. There were no flat rocks, and seemed to be fewer boulders, as well. The bottom was more of a cobble of stones of varying shapes, though most were baseball-sized or even smaller.

Spotted Owl stayed at the rear. He didn't have much to say. I turned to look at him a couple times, but couldn't read anything on his face. He mostly seemed to be alternating between watching the placement of his feet and staring at the thick vegetation at the top of the bank.

Someone else should've been watching their feet more closely. As I was looking up to see if I could catch sight of a building, I heard a splash so loud that it sounded like a whale jumping. I spun back around to find a person totally submerged in the river, and Spotted Owl soaked to the waist.

The big man waded to the edge. He dropped wet buckets before heading back into deeper water. He reached in to grab the shirt of the man, who came up blubbering. It was James, the least likely of anyone to fall. The kid had carried only one bucket and had seemed fairly fit, no doubt from grueling physical training in the military.

James coughed loudly. It was to the point that I wanted to mash a hand over his mouth if a scowling Spotted Owl didn't first.

"Shut up." Spotty dragged the man to shore. Over his shoulder, he said, "Someone find his bucket."

Katelyn and I set our buckets on the dry ground and jumped into action. We waded out until the water was past our knees, and felt around where James had gone under. Something that heavy wasn't going to float downstream in the current. It didn't take long to find.

I brought it over to the bank where Spotted Owl was still scowling at James.

"Were you trying to get the buckets wet?" he accused the shivering kid. "You should know, that's not gonna stop 'em." His eyes narrowed, and he turned to me. "Unless he cracked the lid open. Did he mess with it?"

I examined the lid. "It looks okay."

"So you're just clumsy," Spotted Owl whispered harshly at James. "Or did you think you were gonna take out my phone?"

I hadn't thought about that and was instantly concerned. I patted my own pant leg, wondering if I'd gotten my phone wet. With an exhale, I remembered that I'd put it in my backpack.

James didn't answer. I thought the kid's shivers were more like trembles as he cowered under the bulk of the big man.

Spotted Owl reached into the cargo pants of his soaked jeans and pulled out a plastic bag. Water dripped from the sack.

"I always keep the important stuff sealed in case of accidents." He spat the last word. "They're fine, but you won't be. Knock me over again and I'll leave you in the river."

Having seen the rage come on quickly, I was glad I hadn't knocked into Spotted Owl when I'd slipped earlier. Also, seeing the way the kid shivered, it was a good thing I hadn't soaked more than a pant leg. But it felt strangely helpful at the same time. Like the blisters, the cold water had eased the pain in my knee, which would no doubt bruise something fierce from my previous fall.

His tirade over, Spotted Owl glanced up at the top of the bank. Thick vegetation would hardly let me see over the side, but Spotted Owl seemed to recognize something. He stood back slightly to get a better angle, and then came back to squat next to his buckets.

"It's time to get these ready. We're close enough."

He pulled the blasting cap and cell phone conglomeration from the plastic baggie.

"Like I was saying earlier, we need some extra pop to set these off. So shove both caps down into the mixture and leave the wires hanging out." He cracked open the lid on his first bucket to show us. "Then snap the lid back on, and set the phone on top."

"Simple enough," my mom said.

"Very." Spotted Owl looked back up the slope. "Putting 'em in place...that'll be the real challenge."

CHAPTER 31

I was happy to be getting rid of the buckets, and volunteered to set the charges behind the first building. Now that the blasting caps were inserted and the phones hooked up, my tension level went from frayed to unraveled. Every footstep was a jolt that could potentially set the bombs off, at least in my mind.

Spotted Owl had assured us that the mixture wouldn't combust without a spark from the phone, but I couldn't help but wonder if we would be blown to smithereens any second.

When I'd cracked the lid to insert the blasting caps, the mixture had smelled like pure death. The pungent ammonia smell of the fertilizer mixed with diesel fuel was enough to practically melt the hair in my nose. More than anything else, that vile smell had struck home how serious it had all become.

Katelyn wasn't about to let me go alone. We didn't need three buckets at the first building, so she left hers behind with my mom.

"Be careful, kiddos," Sunning Bear said. She set down Katelyn's bucket long enough to wrap her arms around both of us.

I felt a shiver in the hug. It could've been my own for all I knew.

When I went to pull away, she kept me in the embrace until Spotted Owl cleared his throat.

"I love you," she whispered as she finally let go.

"I love you too, Ma." I smiled and tried to act confident. I hoped I pulled it off. "Don't worry. We'll be right back."

"It's a mother's job to worry," she said, and retrieved the bucket from the ground.

"We'll be headed down the river," Spotted Owl told me and Katelyn. "I'm doing the next building, then we'll meet up with Mouse and Austin behind the third, I hope."

I didn't like the addition of the last two words. I wanted to think that Spotty meant hope in terms of meeting up with our scouts instead of how setting the bombs might not work out the way he had planned.

"Good luck," Spotted Owl said. "Now get moving."

"Yes, sir."

I eyed the slope, searching for a quick way to the top. It was over head height, but not more than ten feet. By itself, that wasn't insurmountable. The bigger issue was the near-vertical aspect. Climbing would be difficult, but adding in the heavy buckets would make it that much harder.

"Let me get up there." Katelyn pointed to a rocky ledge a couple feet above the water's edge. "Then I'll hand you the buckets when you get to the top."

She moved ahead of me and scaled onto the pile of flat rocks. It was all dirt and saplings the rest of the way up the bank.

"Hand 'em over," she encouraged, and I lifted up the buckets to her before starting my climb.

I settled onto the ledge next to her, and looked downstream at the rest of the group fading into the distance. "It's just you and me now, babe." I flashed a crooked grin. "I thought they'd never leave."

"You're stalling."

"Maybe." I examined the slope and picked out seemingly decent footholds and vegetation to grab. "Just choosing out a path."

"These things are heavy," she whispered, rocking the buckets in her hands. "Get to going."

"You could set 'em down."

"And you could climb."

"Point taken." I tested my boot on the soil and found it a little softer than I preferred. I reached up to grip a sapling, and was pleasantly surprised to find it held my weight. "Here goes nothing."

"Don't talk about yourself like that," she quipped, and set the buckets down. She sidled over behind me as if she was going to push me up.

"You might not want to get behind me," I said, and lunged forward to grab at another sapling.

"You gonna fart or something?"

"You're gonna get dirt in your face."

My boot slipped at about the same time, sending rock fragments and soil tumbling toward her. She turned her head, bouncing rocks off her helmet, but evidently took some dirt in the mouth. I heard her spit and say nothing else as I reached for another branch and nearly made it to the top.

I wished I'd dropped the body armor and helmet along the river before I'd started the climb, but it was too late. With one final foothold, I reached up to wrap my hand around a thicker young tree. It held steady, and I looked back down as I teetered just short of the top.

"Ready," I said through gritted teeth. "Pass 'em up."

Katelyn picked up the first bucket and tried to lift the handle to me. She was plenty tall, but not quite enough to get it all the way to me. Her face turned bright red with the exertion as I strained to reach her.

My boot slipped again. She shook her head, and ended up having to stick out her lower lip and blow to clear the worst of the dirt away. "Thanks," she muttered, and strained once more to reach me.

It wasn't going to work.

"Maybe lift the bucket," I said.

"Duh. I'm trying."

"I mean like put your hands under the bottom," I explained.

She nodded. "Sorry. I'll try, but it's heavy." She lowered the bucket into her arms and leaned her body against the slope. "Can you even grab it that way? I was trying to get you the handle."

"We'll have to try."

With a grunt, she shoved with all her might. Pushing the bucket over her head, it wobbled on outstretched arms. I went for it, letting myself slide a little farther down until I could touch the lid.

As my top hand threatened to release from the tree, I made contact with the handle and somehow grabbed hold of it. With a yank, I pulled the bucket up and planted it on the ground at the top of the slope.

"One down," I said between ragged breaths, and leaned back over for the next one.

"Thank God."

We worked together to bring the second one up. It went easier, but then it was time for Katelyn herself.

"You want to wait?" I asked.

"No way." She eyed the slope the way I had earlier.

"You're stalling," I kidded her with her own jibe from earlier.

"Just give me a hand. I'm gonna charge it."

"I think I'd go slow," I said, but it was too late. She tried to race up the slope, but slipped on the very first step. She sank into the slope and melted back onto the rocks in a ball.

She straightened up and considered my suggestion.

"Hang on." After finding a better foothold and a stouter sapling, I was finally in a position to grab her. I wrapped my free hand around her wrist, and pulled her all the way to the top.

I scrambled up right behind her, and ran face first into a tangle of bushes.

"That was rough."

"This doesn't look much easier," she said.

Beyond a bramble of vines and other shrubs, a copse of heavy cedar trees stood in our way. They blocked our view of the building as effectively as a solid wall.

Despite the ridiculous climb, I understood why Spotted Owl had wanted us to come in that way. We could sneak within a few feet of the building and remain under heavy cover. But my face and bare hands would not appreciate the struggle to get through it.

I grabbed both the buckets, and said, "Follow me."

With shoulders bent over to lead headfirst, I stopped for a moment to pull my hands as far inside my sleeves as I could before trying to bull my way through the brambles. Thorns ripped at my backpack, pant legs, and pretty much every inch of bare flesh. One reached high enough to catch me below the helmet, leaving a long tear along the side of my neck above the body armor.

Clear of the vines, I sank down next to the cluster of cedar trees to do it all over again—minus the thorns. After a quick breath, I charged forward again. With no free hand, I had to keep my eyes closed most of the time to keep from catching a twig in the face.

My clothes made quite a racket as the branches rubbed against me, and I had to slow somewhat. Finally, with sweat pouring off my forehead, I cleared the cedars and dropped to the ground again.

My eyes popped open, and I found myself face to face with the back corner of the building. The trees stirred behind me as Katelyn burst through, both arms out in front of her face to ward off the worst of the vegetation. I grabbed her wrist, and pulled her down next to me.

"Yeah, maybe worse than the climb," I whispered.

She seemed too surprised by the view to reply.

Off to our right, around the corner, a couple light standards lit up a small parking area. It was empty other than four Humvees parked fairly close to the building.

The back side of the building was long, straight, and nondescript. I didn't notice any doors close by, though there were plenty of windows. Though none was particularly bright, they all cast a warm glow out onto the trees crowding around the building.

"We've got two buckets to set…one by each corner," I told Katelyn, though she didn't need a recap. She'd been there to hear the plan.

"And then get the heck outta here."

"Exactly." I sucked in a deep breath, and took the opportunity to wipe my brow with my shirt sleeve. "You ready?"

She shrugged. "Why not?"

I looked to the far end of the building, then back at her. "How about you set one right here?" I pointed to the closest corner. "I'll drop one at the other end, and we'll meet in the middle."

"Sounds like a plan."

I squeezed her hand, and then grabbed my bucket. "On three?"

"Just go," she said, and slid behind me to take the other one.

"Right on."

Keeping low, I hurried through the remaining brush and burst into the exposed area behind the building. It was no more than ten feet of green space from the forest to the building, but I felt like I might as well have been standing in the middle of an open field.

I rushed toward the first window and ducked down even lower to get well underneath it. As curious as I was about what was inside, I didn't dare stop to try to sneak a quick look. Instead, I stayed low and rushed past four more windows. Oddly, there were still no doors.

I passed under the fifth window and finally saw the doorway, slightly set back into the flat wall of the building. It wasn't solid metal like I'd hoped, and turned out to be much bigger than I'd expected. The floor to ceiling glass of double doors may as well have formed a barrier right in front of me.

I crept close enough to see the doors were completely dark. I quickly debated my options as I waited short of the nearest window. I should've ducked back into the woods, but didn't want to take the time to fight the brush to get around the doorway. Alternatively, I could've tried to sprint past it, but really didn't like those odds either. That left one option.

I crept a little farther forward to drop my bucket as close as I could to the rear doors. If I got it close enough to the big opening, I figured the blast should rip through the whole building like a tornado and make up for not getting all the way to the far corner.

Holding my breath, I tried to move slowly. I knew Katelyn had to be done by then and was probably waiting in the woods, but I wouldn't go faster. I cleared the window and scooted until I was barely an arm's length away from where the building stepped back to the door frame. As I reached out to drop the bucket, a floodlight popped on over the doorway. The handle clanked as I dropped the bomb like a load of hot coals.

CHAPTER 32

The cursing streamed silently from my lips. I froze for a moment like a rabbit before sprinting for the woods. I slammed headlong in the brush and ripped my way through the cedars in a matter of seconds, praying it was quick enough.

"Over here," Katelyn called softly.

I adjusted course to turn to her voice, but kept barreling through the woods. Branches smacked against my helmet, no doubt making a ton of noise. If I hadn't been scared to death, I would've appreciated not having to lug around the buckets anymore.

I made much better time, and soon found Katelyn crouching at the top of the riverbank.

"What's going on?" she asked as I slid in next to her.

"I think I triggered some kind of outside light."

"I saw that. Did anyone come out?"

I looked at her. "I was hoping you'd know that."

"Heck, no. I was hiding. You made enough noise," she joked, or at least seemed to be joking. "Let's get outta here."

"Good call."

I peered down the slope, but wasted little time trying to pick out a path. Instead, I sat on my bottom and scooted over until I plunged. My boots dug at the earth, trying to slow me down. With a little luck, I ended up not collapsing into a pile at the bottom.

I spun around and raised my arms to catch Katelyn.

"I'm not jumping," she said, though I hadn't really expected that.

"Just slide."

She followed my lead, and went feet first over the slope. I grabbed her as she landed. The force of the impact staggered me, and I swayed back toward the river. She reached out to steady me, and amazingly kept us both from falling into the frigid water.

"That sucked," I said as we followed the river's edge downstream.

"What if they find the buckets?" she asked.

"Then the whole plan is screwed." I'd tried not to think about that possibility. Having her mention it didn't help whatsoever. I went with denial. "The lights probably come on all the time, you know, like when a deer or bear or whatever walks by. They probably don't even look outside anymore."

"And if they do?"

"Looking is fine. The bucket is kinda right around the corner from the door." I tried to wink at her, but it morphed into more of a one-eyed squint. "They'd have to step outside to find it."

"Then let's hope for the best."

"Yeah, and speed up in case they check."

We quieted our voices, but couldn't quite do the same with our footsteps as we hurried along the river. We followed a big curve to the right. I assumed that would bring us up behind the second building, though I had been unable to see how close it was while creeping behind the first one.

The river remained wide and empty of activity. We continued down a short straightaway, hoping to catch up to the others no later than the third and final building.

When I wasn't watching my footsteps or scanning the river ahead, I looked up the slope. I never spotted a structure. It made me feel somewhat safer, but equally as anxious. I knew it wasn't really possible to get lost so long as we followed the river. At least I didn't think so. But I would've much preferred knowing exactly where we were at.

As the creek bent to the right, brush rustled off to the side. Carrying my rifle now that my hands were free, I wheeled on the noise. The sound grew as it approached the top of the bank, and I steadied in case a patrol appeared.

Spotted Owl burst out of the vegetation a second later. "Don't shoot."

I didn't tell him that I probably wouldn't have anyway.

Katelyn asked, "How'd it go?"

"No problem."

I decided not to tell him about the security light. Katelyn didn't mention it either. We watched as Spotted Owl stalked the top of the bank for a few paces before picking out a spot to slide down. He gracefully glided, holding the bulk of his weight back with saplings, and landed on both feet right next to us.

"I thought you'd be way ahead of me by now."

I mumbled an excuse that Spotted Owl thankfully ignored. He wasn't talkative at all, and let a quick arm motion suffice as a command to keep us moving downstream. Once we were fully around the bend, I spotted three shadows walking the edge of the creek.

I hadn't realized that we would be so exposed down there, and it took me aback for a moment. However, I quickly cast the thought aside and started to hurry on ahead to meet up with my mother and her two detainees.

"Hold up," Spotted Owl softly called, making me pause. "No need to run."

"It's too loud," Katelyn agreed.

My mom's hearing was sharp, and she came to halt. She waved, but stayed quiet as we slowly approached her. She eagerly listened to our quick recaps, minus the incident with the motion-sensing light.

"One more building," Spotted Owl said. He took the buckets from James, and eyed the slope above him. "I'll be right back."

"I can go with you," I volunteered.

"Nah, I got this. Just keep going, but not too fast."

I noticed the bank seemed flatter. I stepped backwards into the river until the water rose to around knee deep, and picked out the warm glow of lights from the final building.

"It's not real high up there," I told the others. "We're so close."

I instantly regretted sharing that in front of the other two guys, and once again wondered if we wouldn't have been better off leaving the prisoners back at the horse camp. Noel was walking surprisingly well, which fed in to what was becoming a natural suspicion of him. But I'd been particularly concerned about James ever since he'd dunked his bucket and seemingly tried to drown Spotted Owl's phone.

I hurried back over by my mom, and took one of her buckets from her. She thanked me with a smile and a nod.

That left James available to take the other bomb from her. I was naturally concerned about making him carry it given how he'd possibly tried to ruin one. But I didn't want Katelyn or my mom to have to lug around a walking IED any longer. Nor did I want a second one, so I was glad when she ordered the kid to carry it.

As soon as James took it, my mother kept a sharp eye, and a weapon, subtly pointed at him.

"You holding up okay?" I asked her as I slung my rifle back over my shoulder so it would be easier to switch hands with the load I'd just acquired.

"I'm great. Ready to get this done, and get outta here."

"And then what?" I asked before I could stop myself.

"Then I guess we go back. We'll need to get a real war council convened after that."

"Bigger than just Spotty's tribe?"

She chuckled at the nickname. "Yeah, definitely. We need to make a real effort to bring all the, uhm, *tribes* together." She smiled, seemingly at repeating my word choice for our band of bushwhackers. But her eyes quickly narrowed, and she quieted.

"You can say what happens next," I whispered. "I'm old enough to understand."

"You read me too well." She swallowed, and paused again as if choosing her words.

I slipped my hand in Katelyn's and pulled her alongside me. I gestured with my head toward my mother, essentially asking her to pay attention to my mother's words.

"I think one of two things happens here. Maybe the military gives up and leaves us alone. They'll decide it's not worth the trouble to try to take the park back. With any luck, there are fights like this breaking out all over the country."

"Or?" I clutched Katelyn's hand tighter. She squeezed back.

"They'll redouble their efforts to try to drive us out. Probably try to bomb us into submission."

"Or just flatten the park," I said.

"That's entirely possible."

I sucked in a breath and held it. Of course, I'd always known that a full out air assault was a possibility. In previous wars, the government had always favored air strikes over boots on the ground. It stood to reason that they needn't waste precious lives on needless territory. Especially if the newly recruited soldiers proved as unreliable as the deserter, Noel— presuming that was actually the case with him. He was still very hard to read, and always in the wrong place at the wrong time.

I made two assumptions at that moment. The first being that the highway was unnecessary, which I had doubted all along seeing how many resources the military had primed to throw into the fight. They seemed to want it reopened badly.

Secondarily, I pondered about the state of the real world. The rebels needed intel we could trust. Noel had provided some information about the country, as had James. If the soldiers were deserting or less willing to fight, then things were moving in the right direction. But that presented the same big question. Could Noel and James be trusted?

I skipped over that for the moment to focus back in on the government's motivation in assaulting the park. I wondered if they would be able to spare the manpower much longer for a big mission, especially if we could really bloody their nose—and then throw in more help from the other rebels.

On the other hand, if the Feds were willing to cede the highway to the rebels, what would prevent them from just blasting the road and the whole park to oblivion? My mother helped answer that one.

"Remember how big this place is," she said. "It's like eight hundred square miles."

I remembered my dad's description perfectly. "Eight hundred sixteen," I corrected. A huge size, which included one tiny little pile of rock that served as my father's final resting place.

"Right, and it would take how many planes and how many bombs to level this place? They'd be better off to leave us alone."

"True," I said, though I wasn't completely convinced. More importantly, I knew even greater missions were ahead of us. "And you're gonna want to take the fight to the enemy."

"I'm ready now. Maybe I wasn't earlier…not before your father was killed. Right then there was so much going on that I couldn't process. Maybe it's only been a day or two, but things are a lot clearer now. We have to fight back like he always wanted." She stopped walking to look at me and Katelyn. "I was always more about trying to hide out and survive, but I realize now how deeply this has changed me. We have to carry on the legacy and fight."

I knew exactly where she was going with her speech. My heart raced, pumping a little more of the healthy kind of anxious energy and a little less of the crippling fear. I was ready for things to change. In some small way, I'd been that way since we'd left home. My mom's impassioned words sealed it.

"Your dad might've used words and articles to advocate for freedom, but we need to use the weapons that best fit our skills." She looked at the bucket in my hand. "We need to fight a war like we know how to end it. Hard and fast. Aggressive as all hell."

"I like the sound of that," Spotted Owl whispered as he emerged at the top of the bank. "But you might want to keep your voices down." His eyes wild, he scrambled down the slope to rejoin the group. "I just missed getting nabbed by a patrol. They're not totally oblivious to the danger all around them."

CHAPTER 33

"Great," my mom said sarcastically, and cast a quick glance to the woods above us. "Then let's get moving."

Despite her words, she seemed to be growing in confidence. I was still squishy on the inside, but she'd rekindled the fire in me. It just needed a little more stoking to build into a raging inferno.

We had a job to do, and I was going to do whatever it took to finish it—and bring everyone home safe. Everybody except for one.

I wouldn't go so far as to say I had failed at that critical moment in the shadowy hills, but I felt the burden of my father's death all the same. No one could've stopped the helicopters. We'd all run like rats, but that fact didn't make the loss any easier to take. But I could continue my dad's legacy of fighting for freedom with actions as well as words. Mostly action, for it seemed no one could rival the written contributions he'd provided from the relative safety of our former home.

If only we had more contacts with the outside, I thought yet again. I had a feeling his words had already made some impact. At the very least, they'd called attention to the crisis back before anyone was giving it any real consideration. So much that he'd lost his job. When I coupled his writing with my mom's planning, both at home and on the prepper forums, I knew many self-reliant people had been able to put themselves in a situation where they could strike back when the time was right.

I wasn't positive that the right time had come. Perhaps we'd missed the opportunity to have made a bigger impact sooner, but our backs were against the wall. It was time to stop the soldiers; that much was clear.

We continued down the river, curving this time slightly to the left. To my disappointment, the tree cover seemed sparser along the side of the river bordering the field. There was still plenty of forest, as well as those cursed vines along the top of the riverbank, but the cedars had thinned out. Taller, spindly trees swayed in a gentle breeze that carried the aroma of wood smoke to me.

"You smell that?" I asked Katelyn. "It's like a big campout. They're roasting hot dogs and cooking s'mores up there."

"Really? I just smell smoke."

"Me, too," I replied. "I might be exaggerating a little, but it pisses me off all the same."

"Don't worry. We'll set 'em a bonfire they won't soon forget," Spotted Owl interjected. "We oughta be meeting our scouts and the other guys any second."

"I haven't seen 'em." My mom paused abruptly. "Check that. I've got movement up ahead."

Spotted Owl hurried on past Noel and James to hunker down next to her.

I had been perpetually on edge. Every time there'd been movement, my heart rate went into overdrive. I had a feeling I'd run out of adrenaline long before the real fight started, if there would be one. I still held out hope that we could free the hostages without firing a shot.

Shapes darted along the riverbank, definitely two. I had gotten so used to seeing Austin and Mouse running through the dark that I recognized the way they moved before I even thought to notice that one was much taller than the other.

Spotted Owl edged out in the river a little farther to wave, and then ducked back up against the bank once again. The scouts came straight to us. Austin panted heavily from the run, but Mouse looked as calm, yet energetic, as ever.

"They're still in the house," she proclaimed, but suddenly quieted to a whisper. "Them bad dudes are interrogating 'em."

"It sounds rough, like worse than threats," Austin said. "We've gotta hurry."

"For more reasons than one," Spotted Owl said cryptically.

As we pressed on down the river, I thought about what Spotted Owl meant. Obviously, he had to want to get there and save them from a beating or whatever was happening. I shook off images of intense torture like pulling off fingernails or breaking bones. Instead, I tried to think about what else Spotted Owl could mean.

I decided that it must be secrets he was concerned about, such as one of the prisoners revealing the camp location. Spotty would hate to lose his hideout. It was in a seemingly well-concealed place, and fully stocked.

But Spotted Owl could also have meant the attack. If the prisoners had suffered enough, the guys could be spilling their guts about how we were coming to attack.

My eyes started seeing soldiers hiding behind every tree. Shadows swirled through the thin woods. I had to stop the wild imaginings, and pulled Katelyn ahead so she'd be with me while I talked to Austin.

"Hey, bro. What did you hear?"

Austin shook his head. "It's bad. Like slaps and thumps and all kinds of yelling. The guys seemed quiet, but I don't know if they're gagged or just toughing it out."

"You didn't see?"

"I wanted to," Mouse said. She still sounded amped up, if a little disappointed about not getting a good look. "He wouldn't go."

"Oh hell no," Austin replied, surprising me. I had been convinced Austin was much braver than me and had surely looked in a window, which I hadn't dared to do when I was setting bombs behind the Visitor Center. "It was plenty loud enough to hear what was going on. They were firing questions at those guys about everything. Just yelling and beating and..." He exhaled loudly. "It sounded awful, but they kept beating them. And the guys didn't say a word. They just moaned."

"But they couldn't have answered if they were gagged."

"I reckon not. But maybe the thugs don't want 'em to scream when they get smacked or whatevs. It's loud enough that any soldiers close enough outside could hear it."

"Louder than my pops when he's really angry," Mouse said. "Them soldiers had to hear it."

Austin looked over his shoulder at Noel and James. "They can't all be bad guys, can they?"

"Some are the lowest scum on earth...but not all." I pointed a thumb at my chest to indicate the two prisoners behind me. "I'm not sold on these two, but I don't see them as the type to torture or murder."

"Me, either," Katelyn said softly. "I don't know what to think about them, but they've not done anything crazy yet."

"Other than trip Spotty and try to soak the bombs," I said. "Or always be around when we get attacked."

Katelyn looked like she might object, but Austin beat her to it. He hadn't been there when Spotted Owl had been tripped, so I had to talk him and Mouse through that episode. By the time I was finished, Spotted Owl was holding up a hand again.

"We're below the little village." He looked to Mouse. "That open-sided barn should be right up here, so we need to set the last bomb there."

"What about the house?" Austin asked.

"No bombs for it."

"Duh. I kinda figured that."

Spotted Owl shot him a look that said he best lose the attitude. "We surround it, and make our move when the bombs go off."

My mom stepped in to diffuse any tension. "Sounds like a plan."

"Now we just need to wait for John and the others," Spotted Owl said. "I can go set the bomb by the barn if y'all want to keep walking downriver to find them."

"Yeah, I kinda thought they should've been here by now," my mom said.

I had been wondering the same thing for a while. I looked to Katelyn to gauge her reaction. She remained expressionless, though her normally vibrant eyes seemed a little dull. It easily could've been a severe lack of sleep and the never-ending hiking wearing on her, but I knew better.

I squeezed her hand, and felt her weakly return the gesture. She continued looking downstream, so I slipped my hand from hers and wrapped it around her shoulder. She leaned into me.

"They'll be fine," I whispered. "Spotty said they had a longer way to go."

"I know," she said, though her reply sounded hollow.

I watched as Spotted Owl hopped up the riverbank and disappeared into the trees. I hadn't volunteered to accompany the older man that time. Katelyn seemed to need me more. As a group, we needed to get downstream.

Turning to Austin and Mouse, I said, "You guys are quick. Why don't you two run on ahead to find John's group?"

Austin looked to our mom.

"Go on," she answered. "It's fine. We're gonna follow right behind."

"Yes, ma'am," he said, yet lingered for a moment.

Mouse tugged on his wrist, which looked like a kid trying to pull over a tree. "Let's go, Big A. We're the fastest, the sneakiest, the bestest…"

Her voice faded away as they skipped off downstream.

"She's a bundle of energy," Katelyn said softly.

"Wish I had some of that."

"I kinda like you the way you are." She smiled demurely. "I'm not sure I could handle you that amped up."

"Well, I don't skip," I said," but it sure is funny watching Austin try to keep up."

We hadn't been loud, but my mom shushed us again. I nodded apologetically. With one hand on my rifle and the other locked in Katelyn's, we moved down the river. The cold water was generally right below the tops of my boots, but every now and then a deep pool would submerge them.

I curled my toes and tried to keep the blood flowing, but my feet felt numb—and heavy as concrete blocks.

We didn't make it terribly far before Mouse came skipping back the other way.

"What now?" Katelyn asked, but any further words caught in her throat.

Shadows moved behind Mouse. I wasn't imagining anything that time. The shapes gradually morphed into three distinct figures in addition to the scouts, and Katelyn took off running. I let her go.

She reunited with her family at the edge of the river below a fairly steep bank. A tree leaned hard to the side to where the leafy part draped toward the water. Katelyn disappeared from sight for a moment as she snuggled up against the bank under the shade of the tree. I redoubled my pace to reach her.

She was locked in a hug with her mom and dad. Her brother stood to the side while Mouse chattered with Austin. John seemed genuinely relieved to meet back up with us.

"Hey, bud," he said, lighting up upon seeing me.

"You made it," I replied, but held back awkwardly while waiting for Katelyn. "We, uhm, we've been waiting."

"C'mon, bud. Hug it out." John spread his arms out wide. "I've missed you guys."

"Good to have you back." I dipped in for a hug and quickly pulled back before it grew awkward. "Was it tough?"

"It got a little hairy crossing the road. Some Humvees came across right when we got there, and we were pretty much right up against the field a lot of the time." He looked to the top of the bank and marveled at all the trees. Then he patted the knees of his pants. They were totally soaked through. "There wasn't much cover. It's pretty much just a shallow ditch that runs over to the river."

"So you were crawling?"

"A lot of it, yeah." He looked at his parents and grinned. "The folks held up pretty good considering all that."

"And the bombs are set?"

"Oh, yeah. Right under the road, so they'll never know what hit them."

"This is getting close," I said. My whole body jittered with excitement. I imagined the chaos that would break loose when the bombs went off, and saw myself sliding down into the river as gunshots ripped through the trees.

Good thing there seemed to be plenty of nighttime left. I expected we'd probably have to belly crawl like John for hours just to get away from all the soldiers.

CHAPTER 34

Spotted Owl joined up with us. While John described his journey through the ditch and back to the river, the big man listened intently. But he grew visibly excited when John mentioned a new crossing over the river.

"So what's this about a temporary bridge?" he asked.

"It looked like the soldiers put in one of those quick metal bridges over the river." John pointed over his shoulder. "Maybe a hundred yards back...not too far from the end of the historic village."

"There's never been a bridge there before," Spotted Owl replied. I could practically see the steam pouring from his ears as the wheels turned. "There's an old Job Corps camp back in there, where kids used to go work for the summer. There's dormitories and a school building, but last we knew it wasn't being used for anything. It's been vacant for years."

"So how do you get there?" my mom asked.

"Used to be off Big Cove Road coming out of Cherokee. It's a dead end, but we'd blown the bridge at Cove anyway. Didn't think we needed the soldiers trying to set up a more permanent base in the old dorms." He glanced into the woods across the river from the historic village. "And I didn't think they had, but they might be thinking about it now if they just built a new bridge. It would be closer from here to back there than taking Cove Road."

"It's not a real permanent looking bridge," John said. "And it was dead quiet around there. The crossing is kinda low to the water, like a dozer had pushed around some trees and dirt to kind of ramp down from the field to the river."

"But it opens up another huge field for them to camp in…and the dorms way in the back." Spotted Owl fished a hand under his helmet to scratch at his temple. "Good thing they're not using it yet. Guess we got here just in time to put an end to that plan."

"I just wish we could've blown that new bridge," John said. "I thought about going back to get one of the buckets from the culvert pipe, but it took forever to crawl through that ditch to get to the river."

"You should've had two more," Spotted Owl said. "You were going to set them in the field, by the equipment, right?"

"That was a no go," John explained. "The ground was way too open to get close, so we just left all four by the culvert pipe. It was gonna be way too hard to crawl with the bombs."

I wanted to tell him that it was no picnic trying to carry them up a greasy, ridiculously steep riverbank, but Mouse disagreed with John's decision first.

"We can crawl, no problem," she volunteered, tugging on Austin's arm. "We can go get a couple."

"Not now," Spotted Owl replied. "We need to get our guys back before it gets any later."

She looked like she was about to object, but quickly pinched her mouth shut. I thought it obvious that the rescue should come first, though once the bombs went off we would have no chance to destroy the new crossing. Spotted Owl provided a little more detail on the road to the old Job Corps camp, setting me somewhat at ease.

"The road doesn't go anywhere, really. It runs kinda up toward Tow String, but not that close…maybe halfway. Like I was saying, the road dead ends at a fork in the river."

"So it's just a quiet, secluded camp?" John asked.

"Pretty much," he answered. "In a valley with a bunch of buildings like a little college campus, but there's nowhere else to go back there."

"Good, then we forget that and get your guys back," my mom suggested.

Mouse perked up again. "The cabin's right up there. There's a strip of trees at the top of the road, then the walking path. The cabin is right on the other side."

"The front faces the field," Austin said, "but it was easy enough to sneak across the path to the back side."

"There's this crappy old wooden fence out front. The timber type that's all like rickety and stuff," Mouse explained. "Past that we seen some Hummers lined up like there was a parking lot or something."

"But it's just grass...then all the soldiers and their bigger trucks and stuff past that, all out in the field." Austin squinted as he added, "It's kinda dark around the house, but I'd still stay away from the front."

"Is there a back door?" Mom asked.

"Two, but like on the sides," Mouse answered.

"She means one on each corner, but not on the back itself. So not like our house where our door was kinda in the middle."

Mom laughed. "To use your favorite word...duh. It's a log cabin, not in a subdivision. And there won't be sliding glass doors."

"No, definitely not," Austin said sheepishly. "They look kinda solid, but you can almost see through the cracks in the one on the left."

"Here's the deal," Spotted Owl said. "I blow the bombs and we give 'em a second to see if anyone runs outside. Hopefully they will." He cleared his throat and firmed up his words. "Either way, we rush inside from the back. Half through each of those doors." He looked over the group. "Agreed?"

"Yeah," my mom responded. "That's the best plan we've got."

"And the escape?" Katelyn's dad asked.

Spotted Owl deadpanned, "We run like hell."

Right back through where we were currently standing, I thought. Spotted Owl confirmed that a second later along with a suggestion on a rendezvous point in the woods behind us.

I looked across the river, which seemed even wider at that point. I estimated fifty feet, but the depth was an unknown. It didn't seem like it would be all that deep, but looks could be deceiving. With any luck we could just wade across at waist-height, though it would definitely be higher on Mouse.

Swimming was not my strong suit, but I was capable enough. It was more the idea of body armor, helmet, and weapon. Add in a couple battered captives from inside the building, and I figured it might be far worse than carrying buckets. No doubt slower, and that wasn't encouraging.

Spotted Owl led our group to the base of the riverbank and looked up into a thin line of trees. Without further delay, we started up the slope in single file, but began to fan out before we reached the crest. I kept ahead of Katelyn and my mother. Austin and Mouse were right beside me, starting a second line, with Spotted Owl and John in a third one a little farther to my right. Spotted Owl stayed slightly in the lead.

The big man dropped to hands and knees before he crested the slope. I followed suit. As soon as my head popped over the top of the bank, I caught sight of the roofline of the cabin and immediately slumped back down. With so few trees lining the river, we were situated even closer than I had been at the Visitor Center building.

I slowly raised my head and watched the second story as the others all filed into a long line and stretched out on the slope next to me, shoulder to shoulder.

There was one window on the back below the peak of the roof. It was black as night. I needed to slink a little farther forward to see the first floor. Now that we were close, crushing anxiety had been replaced with an anxiousness to complete the mission. It was like I was drawn to the building.

No longer would I ask for permission. I army-crawled on elbows and knees, working my way into the thin line of brush along the river. Sliding around a thick bush, I should've gotten a clearer look at the building. Instead, two Humvees were parked on the walking path behind the house. They weren't thirty feet away.

"Stay down," I whispered harshly to the others behind me, most of whom were still below the top of the riverbank. I kept my helmet tipped low to where I could barely see underneath the lip, and zeroed in on the vehicles.

The rumble of motors from out on the field made it hard to tell if the Humvees were still running. The headlights had been turned off, as well as anything in the interior. So they seemed empty, but I couldn't be sure. There was no way I was going to walk over to find out.

I leveled my weapon at the nearer of the two vehicles and peered through the scope of the military-style rifle. Unlike the hunting rifle's optics, it was a stubby thing with a single red dot that shone in the middle much brighter than I'd expected. However, it did nothing to help me see inside the Humvee. If anything, the world seemed darker.

Leaves rustled. I twisted around to find Austin crawling up next to me.

"I thought the vehicles were out front?" I said softly.

"They still are," Austin whispered back. "These two are new."

Before I could ask my brother if he thought they were unoccupied, Mouse had already squirted on past. Weaponless, she slithered like a snake, super low to the ground and just as quiet.

"What the heck is she doing?"

Austin shrugged. "Scouting, I guess."

"No sh-"

My outburst was cut short by the sound of a door creaking. Mouse was dangerously visible if someone came outside. Even at the edge of the woods, I was fairly exposed too. I crawled farther back into the tree line while keeping my eyes forward.

Mouse rushed on ahead. She cowered behind the giant wheel of the rugged vehicle, and slipped a knife from the belt on her pants. The blade shone in the moonlight.

The door slammed shut. Heavy footsteps closed on the Humvee.

CHAPTER 35

The door creaked again.

"Hold on," called a man's voice from the cabin.

I eased to the side to get a cleaner view around the tire Mouse had hidden behind. The high clearance of the vehicle allowed me to see a pair of legs from the knees down. The soldier had nearly reached the back of the Humvee, but spun around to head back to the cabin.

"These guys won't break," the man at the door said. "We're gonna need to call in an *expert*." The enunciation sent a chill down my spine.

"Yes, sir. I'll grab the radio."

As I watched, the man hurried back toward the Humvee. I trained my rifle on the rear of the vehicle, ready to protect Mouse if he rounded the corner.

The soldier stopped on the opposite side. He opened the passenger door and took something out of the front seat before rushing back over to the building. In the moment the interior lit up, I was finally able to see that the vehicle was indeed empty.

The cabin door clattered shut again. I breathed a sigh of relief, and looked to Austin. His weapon was still pointed at the Humvee. Mouse's rifle rested in the weeds beside him.

"Let's go," Spotted Owl whispered from right behind me. I wheeled around to see the man crouched on his feet ready to spring like a tiger. "It's now or never."

Spotted Owl urged us to line up behind the two Humvees and get ready to rush the building. My mom went to the left behind me, along with Katelyn and Austin. John and his parents slid to the right. Mouse slinked over to Austin and took her rifle back.

"You two stay out here and keep watch," Spotted Owl told James and Noel. Neither had a weapon, and that was fine with me. Even though they hadn't called out while the soldier had been outside by the Humvee, I still didn't fully trust them and was glad that Spotted Owl apparently didn't either.

I sat up, and turned to watch Spotted Owl fish a cell phone out of his pocket. He thumbed a button to light it up, and quickly scrolled through a menu to a list of speed dial numbers. With a grin creepily illuminated by the blue glow of the screen, he announced, "Cover your ears. Here goes nothing."

"Better hope it's not nothing," I said, and wasn't disappointed.

From way to our north, a flash like lightning split the darkness—coupled with a shaking of the earth. The boom carried to my ears seconds later.

"The bridge," John said, but anything after was completely drowned out.

Off closer to our right, the world came alive with blast after blast of white fire. I hid my eyes as the buildings of the Visitor Center erupted.

Massive booms rocked the Humvee, shoving it against me. Though I had palms pressed to my ears, they immediately rang again. When the bomb at the barn went off last, I thought I'd been deafened once more.

The final shockwave shoved against my body. I teetered in my crouch, and held onto the shaking Humvee as wind whipped past like a tidal wave.

I wondered if the cabin still stood. When the glare cleared from my eyes, I found it framed by a fiery orange glow in this distance.

No one had come outside.

Spotted Owl was already on his feet, urging us to the doors. John slammed into the one on the right and burst it open. Spotted Owl went in behind him with weapon leveled. Austin and Mouse raced for the door closest to me, and I couldn't let them go alone. I rushed after.

Shots fired from somewhere inside, mixed with yells. I surged through the opening right on Mouse's heels, and saw nothing but close-quarters chaos. Two men tied to chairs had fallen over onto the floor. Four uniformed men wheeled around, shooting wildly at the intruders.

The cabin was even tinier on the inside, adding to the confusion.

Austin and Mouse fired, but blocked me from getting a shot off. I could only watch the action as I rushed forward. A soldier slumped over. Then another one, as John and Spotted Owl came in from the right with guns blazing too.

John wrestled a man for his pistol, and recoiled when a shot echoed through the open room. To my horror, John slumped to the ground.

Austin had moved far enough ahead that I had a clean shot. I raised and fired before the man could draw a bead on my fallen friend.

I froze. Everything went slow motion. I could only watch as the soldier toppled over backwards.

To my side, Spotted Owl riddled a table with bullets as the final man tried to hide behind it. The soldier slumped, leaking blood from all over.

"Clear!" Spotted Owl yelled.

The gunshots ceased, and my companions went straight to the prisoners. I still stood, staring at the fallen soldier. The man I'd shot.

Katelyn bumped into me from behind as she rushed around me to get to John. I shook my head to clear it and chased after her.

"I'm okay," John said through gritted teeth as he sat up.

"The hell you are," Katelyn said, surprising me with her intensity.

I couldn't get close enough to see him. Katelyn blocked me on the right, and I couldn't bring myself to circle around to her left. The corpse of the man I'd cut down stretched out there. A pool of blood gathered, and leaked through the cracks in the floorboards.

"We need to move, people!" my mom yelled.

I knew the soldiers out on the field had to have heard the shots. It might take a moment for them to check out the cabin, but someone would definitely come. Possibly everyone.

"How is he?" I asked Katelyn.

John answered for her. "Just winged in the leg. I'm good."

"He needs to put something on it besides his hand," Katelyn said frantically. "We need a bandage."

Forgetting about the first aid kit in my backpack, I spun around to try to locate anything useful. At an old metal sink in the back corner, I noticed a dish towel and rushed to grab it. It would work as well as any little gauze pad in my kit.

As I hurried back, I took a quick glance at the captives. Spotted Owl was already on the floor with Austin and Mouse trying to rouse them.

"They're beat to hell!" the big man shouted. "Carry 'em!"

"I've gotta go help them," I told Katelyn as I handed her the towel. Over her shoulder, I asked John, "Can you walk?"

"Got to, bud." He ground his teeth together as he tried to get to a kneeling position. "It's more in the fleshy part."

I nodded and hurried off to assist with the others.

Austin was right behind me, next to Mouse. I slid in beside him. Mouse had cut the first captive loose with her knife and was starting on the second.

I helped Austin roll the man over. It took a moment to recognize him as Box Turtle. If not for the bushy beard and short, but large, frame, I might not have known who it was. His bloodied face was almost unrecognizable.

"He's gonna be a load." Austin leaned in. "Turtle? You hear me?"

A groan was all we got in return. There was no time for further questions.

"Help me get him up," Austin said, but I'd already moved into position. It took Katelyn's dad joining us to get the stocky man to his feet, but Turtle didn't have the strength to walk.

"I'll get his legs," Katelyn's dad said. Austin and I each got behind an arm and somehow managed to keep Turtle from immediately hitting the floor.

"We're screwed," Austin said.

"Not yet," I replied. Knowing the mountain of a man couldn't walk, I'd already formulated a plan. "Take him to the Humvee. If the keys are in there, we're driving."

"Huh?" Austin asked. "Where?"

"The new bridge John found."

"Good call," Mom said. "I'll check for keys." She rushed past us.

I looked over my shoulder to see John standing. Katelyn had him supported on her shoulder. Spotted Owl and Katelyn's mom were helping the other prisoner, a battered Wood Duck, to his feet. He seemed barely capable of walking, but that was better than nothing.

Mom ran back inside as I struggled to get Turtle carried out the back door.

"They're gone."

"The keys?" I asked, immediately panicked.

"No, it doesn't need any," she replied.

"Seriously?"

"There's a switch to turn it on. Anyway, I meant the other guys are gone."

"Who?" Austin asked, but I figured it out immediately.

"Traitors," I muttered. "I knew it."

"There's soldiers coming," she said frantically. "I'll cover you."

She rushed back outside with rifle in hand.

The three of us staggered and stumbled, but got Turtle out the side door without dropping him. It didn't look good for getting him much farther than that.

Shots rang out from the side of the cabin, each blast hammering at my ear drums. Mom emptied a magazine, and slammed home another one.

"Go get the door," Austin said to Mouse. She ran to the closest Humvee and opened the back door. Then the one for the front passenger. "You get in," he said.

"Heck no. I'm covering you." She ran off by my mom and opened fire.

Austin and I spun around and got Turtle lined up headfirst. We laid his shoulders onto the back seat and stepped away so Katelyn's dad could shove him the rest of the way in. Other than a deep moan, Turtle didn't protest.

I rushed over to the side of the cabin with the intent of checking on the two women. I ran into Spotted Owl coming outside, and yelled, "We're taking the Humvees!"

The big man said something that sounded like, "Good plan." He guided his injured captive to the Humvee parked behind the first one.

I wanted to go help my mom, but decided I'd better check on the other side of the building. No one was providing cover fire that direction, and passengers still needed to be loaded.

I gripped my rifle with white knuckle intensity, and crouched next to the foundation. Leaning forward to peer around the corner, a shadow stood up right in front of me. The figure lurched forward like a zombie.

My finger found the trigger guard but couldn't squeeze off the shot as the body collapsed on top of me. I shoved the man to the side. Hopping to a crouch, I leveled the weapon at Noel.

"Dude! What the heck?" I bellowed. A very woozy Noel tried to sit up, but tipped back over. "You hit?"

"Yeah, by that weasel James." He blinked with both eyes, but one lagged slightly behind the other.

I made sure no soldiers were right up on us, and then helped him sit up. "Where's he at?"

"He was gonna…rat us out. I tried to stop him." He paused his speech awkwardly, and rocked again. He mumbled to the point I could only hear him say, "…beat me in the head…with a rock."

Bullets smacked against the side of the log cabin. Soldiers were definitely converging on the building, but I had no idea exactly how close. Rather than take the time to find out, I pulled a hobbling Noel toward the Humvees, and pushed him off to Spotted Owl.

I explained the situation in staccato bursts.

"James turned on us. He knocked out Noel. We've gotta go."

Spotted Owl nodded, and helped Noel into the back seat. Then he ran around to drive, leaving both of Katelyn's parents to cram into the front passenger seat.

I saw Katelyn getting into the back of the first Humvee, and ran for her. John was already inside, sitting next to Turtle. The dishtowel was tied around his upper leg. He winced as he scooted into the cargo area in the back to make room for me.

Austin revved the engine. "Get in!" he hollered to our mom and Mouse, who were both on the way. The second they piled into the front seat, he jammed his foot on the accelerator.

The door swung closed. I fell back against Katelyn, knocking her onto Turtle. He groaned a little louder and mumbled something, but I couldn't hear it over the whining of the engine. Soon after, that racket was joined by the pinging of bullets off the metal sides of the Humvee.

"Go to that bridge John was talkin' about," I said.

"I am." Austin whipped the wheel to the side to avoid taking out a length of the fence.

I wished John was up front to help navigate, but he'd been forced into the back to make more room. All he could do to help was say, "The turn off is past the last barn."

"I'll find it." Austin took a hand from the wheel, and the Humvee jerked toward the trees.

"Dude!"

"Sorry, bro." He squirmed in his seat, reaching for something, but had to put both hands back on when bullets pelted the side again. I grabbed for Katelyn to cover her, imagining the windows shattering. Thankfully, they held tight.

"I wish this thing had a machine gun mounted on it," Austin complained, and stood on the accelerator again.

"Spotty's does," I replied. "We picked the wrong one."

"I reckon that's okay. I've got something for ya." He kept rummaging in his pockets, and ended up handing four baseball-sized objects one at a time to Mouse, who passed a couple back to me.

The grenades. I hadn't seen them since the assault on the bridge, which seemed like days before.

"Don't know if it'll blow the bridge, but we've gotta try."

"True that," I agreed.

The Humvee swerved hard to the left. "Found it!" Austin yelled.

I caught sight of the gap in the woods right before the vehicle shot down a sharp slope. It slammed hard at the bottom with a metallic thunk. I swore we'd lost an axle.

The indestructible Humvee kept churning. After another hard bump, it hit a steep incline that threw me against the back seat. The Humvee quickly leveled out, and skidded to a halt.

"Get out and blow the bridge," Austin said.

No one argued. The two doors popped open as Mouse and I stepped out into a hornet's nest of fire. Bullets buzzed in my ear like deadly mosquitos. I thought I heard one ricochet off Mouse's helmet as we waited for Spotted Owl to cross.

Spotty's vehicle raced down the slope like ours had, and slammed into the metal bridge. The structure groaned and partially sank, sending off a huge wave. But the big vehicle powered through and climbed up the other side.

As soon as it hit the high ground, whoever was manning the machine gun opened up with a tremendous burst. Gunfire swept the open field that we'd left behind.

I couldn't hear, and nudged Mouse to throw the grenades. She bobbed her head excitedly and watched for me to pull the pin, practically twitching with energy.

I went to cradle the two grenades in one hand when a stray bullet slammed into my body armor. The force shoved me backwards. Grenades dropped onto the ground as I sank to a knee. A blood-curdling scream came from inside the Humvee.

Quickly, I ran a hand under my armor. It was dented but seemed intact. My skin was wet, but I hoped from sweat. There'd be time to worry about that later.

I ignored the screaming to hunt around for the grenades, but it was hard to move. My chest ached. It felt like someone had punched the air out of my lungs and then sat on me for good measure.

Finally locating the grenades, I cradled them in my arm again. I looked to Mouse, who had slid in next to me. She copied my movements.

I fished a finger into each pin to pull them both at the same time. Something as simple as lighting fireworks and watching the fuse burn made my insanely nervous, so I didn't wait a second to chuck the primed grenades onto the bridge below.

I had no interest in watching the blast. With bullets still whipping past me and Spotted Owl's Humvee returning fire, I ran for my own with Mouse on my heels. Bright flashes lit up the world behind us. The concussion threw me forward. I face planted in the dirt.

My chest ached even worse. It felt like every rib had been flattened by a steamroller. I couldn't move at first. It took a moment to crawl back to my feet, and I was none too quick heading for the vehicle.

Mouse jumped into the front seat with my mom. Katelyn reached an arm out to pull me inside.

"Holy crap, that was awesome!" Austin yelled as the Humvee roared away from the river. "Did it sink?"

I didn't have a clue.

CHAPTER 36

"Yeah, it's toast," Mouse answered.

"Then let's outrun those bullets," John said as he stared out the back window.

"I wish." I ran a hand over my chest.

Katelyn threw questions at me, but I had no air with which to speak—and no energy.

Austin followed something that looked like a road, though it was incredibly rough. Each bump sent a shot of pain through my chest. The heavy armor pressing on me wasn't helping either.

Though it had probably saved my life, I was ready to be done with it. I wriggled within the hard gray interior of the Humvee, trying to shed the bulky vest.

"Need help?" Katelyn asked.

"Yeah. I want this off."

"We're not safe yet." Katelyn's words were punctuated by a dip in the road.

Turtle went airborne for a second and crashed back onto the hard seat. I clearly heard him curse aloud that time. It was a relief, but still not a great sign that he would be able to move when the road ran out.

"Sorry, fellas," Austin said. "I can't see the holes, and no way I'm turning on the headlights."

"That's fine," I said with a grimace. "You can drive faster if you want."

"I'm not sure it'll go much faster...or if this beast will fall apart."

"It'll be fine," John said. "I don't see anyone but our guys behind us, but you might as well push it."

"Yeah, we've gotta make tracks," I agreed. "We've gotta cross the creek, with, uhm...." I looked down at Turtle but let the words remain unspoken.

The man groaned again, and made an effort like he wanted to sit up.

"Take it easy," John said. "Rest while you have the chance."

"The hell I can." Turtle inhaled sharply and moaned again. "Not in this tin can."

I went back to trying to take off my body armor. Katelyn gave me a hand, and I pulled one arm out. My chest felt caved in like I'd been beaned with a fastball. My breathing came in quick little sips to keep from puffing up my lungs more than a fraction.

"Turn for me," Katelyn said, but it hurt too badly for me to do much.

I spun partway and locked up, the pain radiating from the front through to my back like a hole had been punched in me. Reflexively, my hand went back inside my jacket to check. The slightest pressure made me wince, and I immediately pulled my hand away.

With concern heavy on her face, Katelyn helped me finally shed the vest. She dropped the armor to the floorboard with a thunk.

"I don't see blood on your shirt, but are you sure you're okay?"

"Say what?" my mom said, whipping around. "What happened?"

"I got shot." The Humvee bounced again, the worst one yet. I slammed the top of my head against the window frame. "Dang. That didn't help."

"What do you mean shot?" She stared at Katelyn since I was right behind her seat. "You said no blood?"

"The armor stopped it," I paused to take a breath, "but it feels like I got hit by a freight train."

"Lemme see the armor," Mouse chirped. She was closer to the middle, and leaned back between the front seats to grab for it. "Ooh, wicked!"

"What?" I said softly. I had felt an indention when I'd checked earlier.

"It's frickin' huge, dude." Mouse held it up for me. "Like someone pounded out a hole with a hammer."

"Hole?" I said, and looked back down at my jacket again.

"Not all the way through," she said. "Still…dang, that had to hurt."

"You're telling me."

"We're all beat to hell," John said. "But we're gonna make it."

"Says you," Austin replied. "I'm trying, but I'm surprised the choppers haven't shown up yet. We're runnin' outta time."

"There's something up there." My mom pointed through the dark windshield. "I see shadows."

"Shadows? Shoot, they're everywhere," I said, but quickly squelched down on the negativity.

"It looks like buildings."

Mouse dropped the armor to whirl back around. She leaned over next to Austin and put her hand on top of his.

"That's the Job Corps complex," she said. "Stay to the right."

"Whatever you say." Austin jerked the wheel, throwing me up against Katelyn. She knocked into Turtle, who had finally managed to sit all the way up. He seemed pretty defenseless, but thankfully didn't collapse.

As we drew closer to the darkened buildings, I examined the man's face as well as I could in the dark vehicle.

One eye looked almost completely closed from puffiness. The other was badly swollen, and a dark crust of what had to be dried blood covered what little I could see of his cheeks above his thick, matted beard. His lower lip was split open, and his breathing ragged. Worse yet, he would have to get out and hike in a matter of seconds.

I looked past Turtle out the side window as we rolled by the shuttered compound. Low buildings of one and two stories crouched among the shadows of the trees. Each looked about as dilapidated as the road, but clearly had the classic, blocky 1960's institutional look.

It seemed obvious that it could make for a military base. I wished we had a dozen more buckets of ANFO to keep the Feds from claiming it. Then again, they would have to build another new bridge to get there.

"We did great today," my mom told us as we flew past the buildings. "The bridges are all wrecked again, and we struck a real strong blow against those guys. They'll think twice about coming up into our hills."

"And we'll definitely be ready to come out of these hills after them," John pronounced. "Tonight was huge, especially when the other tribes hear about this."

"That's the key," my mom agreed. "We've got major momentum now, and another big victory."

"We still have to get away," Austin cautioned as he slowed the vehicle, "or nobody's gonna find out."

"We have one helluva head start," John replied. "That was like a four mile sprint at max speed. We're way ahead of anyone, if they dare come after us."

"And the choppers?" Austin asked.

"Just ram this thing right into the woods. No need to let 'em see where we parked," my mom said, seemingly dodging the subject. "Drive as deep as you can get until you can't get any farther."

"Then hold on." Austin drove straight into the woods, but much more slowly than on the dark, potholed roadway. He weaved around dozens of bigger trees, flattening smaller ones, and pushed on ahead over relatively flat, yet bumpy terrain. And then he jammed on the brakes. "Crap!"

"What?" I asked, holding onto the seat in front of me.

"It's the end of the road." He laughed like a lunatic. "We almost found out if this thing can swim."

"Sweet, the river," Mom said, flinging open the door.

"Yep. That could've been ugly." Austin killed the engine and hopped out. He opened the passenger door behind him and was quick to help get Turtle to his feet.

"Thanks," the stocky man said as he braced himself against the Humvee.

The other Humvee parked behind Austin, and the whole group filed out to the top of the riverbank. Other than Turtle, Noel was the most unsteady of the rebels, but he seemed a little more coherent since I'd found him nursing the headwound. Wood Duck, the other former prisoner, was moving much better than Turtle, though his battered face and pained expressions told a slightly different tale.

"Nice parking job," Spotted Owl told Austin. "I could barely keep up."

"He's a maniac alright," I said, remembering why I had refused to ride to school with my older brother. But after that wild ride and the earlier escape from Gatlinburg, Austin's driving skills had grown quite a bit in my estimation.

Spotted Owl gestured to the river below. It looked no different than what we had hiked along behind the Visitor Center, other than a few giant boulders as big as Volkswagens out in the middle.

Rather than dawdle, we slid right down the slope, and marched off into the water. The cold assaulted me again.

"We're going straight across," Spotted Owl said. "You're gonna get really wet this time."

"More like you might get hypothermia," I told Katelyn, and I wasn't joking.

"Too late," Mouse said, and skipped on ahead. She sunk in to her shoulders before the rest of us were up to their knees.

The frigid water was a major wake up call for the weaker members of the group. Rather than sapping their strength, I was pleased to see that they almost woke up a little. However, it did no favors for my aching chest.

Though only waist deep, the cold still took what little breath I had away. I struggled to push air into my lungs, which didn't help as I tried to hurry to get across. With great effort, I made it to the boulders, and rested for the briefest of moments in the freezing, torturous river.

And then I heard the helicopters.

CHAPTER 37

The others started to bolt, but I had a different idea. Mustering all the air I could, I screamed, "Stay in the river! Get under the water!"

"Are you crazy?" Mouse yelled back. "We've gotta split. I'm runnin'."

"Then do it," I said. "We're staying here." I looked to Katelyn, who agreed with me. She encouraged her parents to do the same. I turned to find Austin.

"Sorry, kid," he told Mouse. "I'm not running anymore."

I put the line of boulders between the helicopters and us, and crouched down in the water until I was nearly flat. Once submerged to the neck, it took only milliseconds for the cold to clamp around my chest. It sapped my ability to speak. My heart seized up like the motor on my dad's favorite old Buick.

The roaring sound of helicopters built from the way we had come. The choppers would be on us any second, possibly scanning with the thermal imaging. I had no idea if the water was deep enough to mask our heat signatures, but thought we might have a chance coupled with the boulders. Besides, I'd tried running before. Austin had been correct. We'd had our big battle and won. It was time to hide and live to fight another day.

"We'll need to dunk under before they pass," I told the others, finding my voice.

"Awesome," John said with chattering teeth. He didn't have to wait for long.

The others cowered behind the other boulders and cursed as they sank themselves lower, though I still wasn't sure if Mouse was among them. Fortunately, the rocks were perched on a drop off, right at the deepest part of the river. With a shiver, everyone bobbed until only our heads were showing.

Out of the long valley, helicopters streaked to the north. "Now!" I yelled.

I sucked in the biggest breath I could, gave a thumbs up to Katelyn, and sank under the water surface.

My chest burned even worse than before. I tried to ignore it, but the pressure built up until I could take it no more. The choppers roared overhead, beating waves on the surface.

Rockets flew and impacted somewhere up on land. The muffled blasts shook the river, making it hum with angry energy.

I forced myself to stay underwater. Stars danced behind my eyelids, almost as bright as the rocket blasts.

Finally, right when I thought I might pass out, the helicopters flew on.

I popped to the surface, gasping for air with lungs that thoroughly resisted the effort. It took a moment, but I eventually managed to suck in a decent breath. It reeked of high-explosives and acrid smoke, and drew my attention to the bank we'd left behind.

The Humvees spewed dark clouds of smoke as their rubber tires burned.

"Thank God for the river. Guess the engines were throwing off a heat signature," I mumbled. Looking around, I raised my voice. "Everyone okay?"

"Fine," Katelyn answered. "Even Mouse."

I smiled to see the shivering girl climbing out on the far bank. I wouldn't be smiling for long when the cool night air hit my wet skin, but I would soon be hiking a little heat back into my tired body.

"I think we're in the clear." A soaking Spotted Owl clapped me on the shoulder with a meaty paw. "Good work…again."

Once I regained my strength, I said, "We make a good team when we stick together."

"Except for that punk James." Austin scowled. "Think he can rat us out?"

"We'll be okay," Spotted Owl said quickly. "He doesn't have a clue where our camp is at. But we'll need to steer clear of Tow String. He knows about that." Spotted Owl pointed off to the far bank. "We'll cut over to the highway real quick, and get back to my camp up the Mingus Trail. He won't have a clue about any of that."

John growled, "And if I ever see that punk again…"

I tuned him out to reflect on the night. With John talking about revenge, I immediately thought about my own situation. I'd killed a man.

"Zach, you okay?" Katelyn whispered.

I erased the frown. "Just thinking about tonight and everything that went down."

"It went pretty darn well, I think." She paused as if collecting her thoughts, but rambled anyway. "I mean a lot of you guys got hurt, some really bad. But it was kind of a successful mission…and at least we got Spotty's people back. We're in the clear now."

"Yeah, I guess so."

"It sounds like we're home free," she said. "Did I hear something wrong?"

"Not that, babe." I sighed. "I just can't get that guy outta my head. One second he's wrestling with John, and the next I blow a hole the size of Texas through him."

"Oh." She quieted, but for only a couple seconds. "You know you did the right thing."

"It doesn't quite seem that way. I mean I didn't want John to get hurt, but there's no pride or joy or whatever in killing a man."

"There's not supposed to be," she said. "He was a thug anyway, you know? Someone who sat there and beat the heck outta Spotty's guys…and tried to kill my brother."

"I totally get that." I looked to the sky and noticed a faint glow over the eastern mountains far behind us. Daybreak. The smoking remains of the Visitor Center were farther south in the valley of death. "I just can't look at it as revenge. I won't…ever. I pretty much wanted to puke right after I saw the dude fall."

Katelyn squeezed my hand as we stood at the edge of the river waiting for the others to catch up. "It's okay, babe. Let it out."

"Seeing his blood pooling on the floor was the worst." I took a deep breath and focused in on the hint of sunrise. "You're right, though. If getting involved in this rebellion or whatever meant I had to kill someone, then I guess it's best that it was some useless piece of crap like that guy."

"It's necessary sometimes. And it won't change you. Not in a bad way." She smiled at me. "Not the guy I love. It won't change you at all."

"I wouldn't change you either."

"Well, thanks." She hopped up on the bank and offered me a hand to pull me up.

"And thank you, you know…for everything."

I looked down the river and picked out the smoke rising into the lightening sky. Thinking back to all I'd been through, I decided Mom's devotion to prepping hadn't done much to get me prepared to free hostages, much less lose my father. Nor had it helped me deal with the aftermath of killing another human being. But on second thought, there may have been an unexpected benefit.

The prepper lifestyle had laid the foundation for self-reliance. I hadn't seen that back in my cozy suburban house, but it had all been some kind of strengthening, spiritual journey of self-deprivation. Whatever fortitude that had grown inside me seemed to make the burden the slightest bit easier to bear, particularly whenever coupled with my mom's well-timed words. And Katelyn's.

Those two women continued to play giant-sized roles in my life. We still needed to go back and deliver the dreadful news to the third. Maddie. She'd need to lean on all of us, the same way we had leaned on each other.

Katelyn bumped me with her shoulder. "Let's go home. We've got some healing to do."

"Home, huh? Yeah." I bobbed my head, realizing the mountains were going to be our home for a while longer. But maybe not as long as it had seemed a few days before. "The whole world has some healing to do."

Katelyn nodded. "Yeah, it does."

With everyone regrouped and Spotted Owl ready to lead, we set off in a slow, steady hike toward the waiting, shadowy hills. The darkness welcomed me like it hadn't before. My feet fell into a tired rhythm, and before I knew it we'd reached the highway.

Spotted Owl didn't waste any time. After a quick look both ways, we hurried across and into the dense vegetation. In no time, we worked our way out of the valley and kept on climbing.

The early morning sun grew in brightness and warmth as we hiked, painting the purple clouds with a soft, pinkish underbelly.

"It's a new dawn," I whispered to Katelyn, feeling more than just relief at the daylight. Despite the horrific loss of my father, something inside me had definitely changed over the last couple days. A mission had clarified, and a fire had been lit.

"Yep. Take it as a sign," she said. "It's daybreak for a whole new world."

ACKNOWLEDGEMENTS

A huge Thank You for taking the time to read *Shadow Warriors*, which happens to be part of my favorite series. I hope you enjoyed it as much as I enjoyed playing in this world.

If you are looking for something with a deeper dive into SciFi, but also with dystopian underpinnings, then I certainly encourage you to take a look at *The Savage Horde Series*. If Scifi isn't so much your thing, then you can't go wrong with another nation collapse series set in an entirely different, thousand lakes, dark atmosphere. That one is *The Northwoods Trilogy*.

Should dystopian oddly not be your favorite genre, then I can offer up a trio of standalone adventure novels. While not a big departure from my other books, wilderness survival stories such as *Game Changer, Murder Cove,* and *Creeper Falls* offer up teenage outdoor suspense adventure with new characters, exciting storylines, and unique settings.

But first, before you cast this book aside, I would be grateful if you would take just a quick minute out of your busy life to leave a review. Good or bad, I greatly appreciate any reviews left on Amazon, Goodreads, and anywhere else you please. Reviews help other readers decide whether or not to check out a story, so they can really help get this book noticed by others. I hope you agree with me that this book deserves all the notice it can get. In an oversaturated market, I hope you found its redeeming qualities.

Lastly, a big Thank You to all my returning readers! This book is my eleventh published novel. I'm past ten and pushing into double digits! I finally made it, only six years after starting this writing adventure. Huge thanks to everyone for all your support and kind words!

To connect with Chris Bostic

Add 'Author Chris Bostic' as a friend on Facebook

Follow on Twitter at @CBostic_Author

Website: http://ChrisBostic.weebly.com

Other books by Chris Bostic

<u>The Bushwhackers Series:</u>
Book 1, Prepper Mountain

<u>The Savage Horde Series:</u>
Book 1, Savage Hills
Book 2, Cold Valley
Book 3, Complex Three

<u>The Northwoods Trilogy:</u>
Book 1, Fugitives from Northwoods
Book 2, Rebellion in Northwoods
Book 3, Return to Northwoods

<u>Standalone Novels:</u>
Game Changer
Murder Cove
Creeper Falls